Faraway Love

Nancy Arey Cohen (signature)

Nancy Arey Cohen

ISBN: 978-1-63381-274-1

Designed and produced by:
Maine Authors Publishing
12 High Street, Thomaston, Maine
www.maineauthorspublishing.com

Printed in the United States of America

To my sons, Robert and Andrew,
who inspire me every day.

The Start

Charlie strode into the World History classroom surrounded by his buddies, his green letter jacket emblazoned with emblems announcing his many athletic accomplishments. As he laughed at a joke made by one of his pals, his eyes sparkled with mischief, and every female head in the room turned at the infectiousness of his laughter. Amy was no exception. She looked at him, trying to size him up, as she always did with new people who intrigued her. He turned toward her and smiled.

Charlie greeted her with interest. "Hey, you're new here, right? I would have remembered those green eyes of yours. They're mesmerizing." And with that, he chose the seat next to Amy, the new girl, amid howls from his friends and comments about Charlie having set his sights on his "girl of the month."

Amy, after a lifetime of moving around the world with her brigadier general father, her June Cleaver mother, and her older sister, was not one to be intimidated by anyone or anything. Her green eyes looked directly into his blue ones as he sat down next to her, and she said, tossing her mane of auburn hair over her shoulder, "Yeah, I'm the new girl. My name's Amy. Who are you? Big man on campus?"

The disdain dripped from her voice. She had seen his type before: jock, ladies' man, man's man. He was the guy who had it all. He probably had his pick of all of these girls leering at him through their mascara...but there was something about him, something else going on that made her think, *I could really like this guy.*

Amy's estimation was interrupted by the young, amiable teacher entering the room and simultaneously removing his sport coat and tossing it over the desk chair at the front of the room. Mr. Bruner gave a patented glare to the class that quieted them, then turned to her and, looking over his tortoise shells, said with a smiling voice, "Well, Miss Sweetser. I know these other clowns. But I don't know you. I see that you just moved to Duxbury." As he spoke, he read from a file given to him by the principal. "It says here that you have attended five other schools in three countries and two states over the years. Wow! You have your own little world history, don't you?" He chuckled at his own joke. "Well, then," he continued as he realized that no one else had laughed, "I'm sure you'll have lots to share with us. Why don't you tell us all a little about yourself so that we can get to know you?"

Amy wasn't expecting him to be so friendly. Most teachers she had encountered simply told the class that she was the new girl, gave them her name, gave her a book, and explained what they were studying at the time. This guy was really nice. And his world history joke was kind of funny since he was a world history teacher. Maybe this was going to be the great move her father had promised it would be. While most teenagers would be embarrassed by being put on the spot, Amy was not most teenagers.

She glanced around briefly, lingering a second on the guy next to her and, keeping her seat, smiled and confidently said, "Sure. I'm Amy Sweetser, and I've lived in different places because I'm an Army brat." Most of the class snickered at that term. "What I mean is, wherever my dad was stationed, we went. We've been in the States, Germany, Japan… It was pretty cool, though. I got to meet lots of kids and, thanks to social media, stay in touch with friends all over the world." She was surprised to see Charlie looking at her with interest—real interest, not feigned "I'm gonna get her" interest.

She continued, thinking, despite herself, that this guy was intriguing. "So far, everyone here has been really nice, and I'm hoping that it won't take long to feel at home." As she spoke those last words, she decided to look directly at Charlie. To her surprise, he turned red and looked away. *Hmm, so he's not as sure of himself as he pretends to be, huh?* she thought. *That's kind of sweet.*

After class, Charlie jumped up and asked her if she would like him to show her around school, introduce her to everyone. Since his offer seemed genuine, she said that she'd like that, and they agreed to meet in the cafeteria for lunch. Going from class to class during the morning, she found herself excited at the prospect of seeing him at lunch, but thought it was silly to feel that way. After all, he was obviously a player. But when she saw him standing by the door to the cafeteria waiting for her, her heart skipped a little. And when he saw her and his face lit up showing matching dimples, those Paul Newman eyes sparkling in her direction, longish, devil-may-care blond hair framing the tanned face perfectly, she couldn't help feeling pleased. But she kept her cool and simply said, "Hi, Charlie. I wasn't sure if you were serious or not."

Oddly, Charlie looked hurt. "Of course I was serious. I don't say things I don't mean. But you don't know that yet, do you?" And with that afterthought, he brightened and began introducing her to his friends as they made their way through the cafeteria. They found Charlie's usual table, and for the first time in weeks, Amy was genuinely happy. All her concerns about the move were gone. Charlie went out of his way to make her feel welcome, and if someone talked about something she didn't know, he took the time to quietly explain it to her. If someone referred to another person, he leaned over and whispered enough to her that she understood the comments, and before long she felt like she had always known these people.

After lunch, Charlie asked Amy if he could drive her home after school. He remembered where she said she lived and said that it would be no trouble to drive her home so she wouldn't have to take the bus. "No one likes taking the bus," he told her. "Besides, we can take the scenic route, and I can show you around town a little—if you have time and if you'd like that," he added cautiously. "Coach canceled practice today because he has a staff meeting. I've got more time than I know what to do with."

Amy didn't hesitate. "Sure. That would be great!" She realized after she spoke that she was, perhaps, a little too exuberant in her response, but who cared? This guy seemed nice. She decided she'd like to get to know him better.

The afternoon took forever to end, a blur of new teachers, collecting books and homework, and meeting more new kids. She was asked to introduce herself in every class, and by the time the afternoon bell rang, she was tired but exhilarated by the friendly reception she had received. She had offers for everything from hanging out on the weekend to going to a party to working on a biology project with a group of students. Finally, though, it was time to meet Charlie. He saw her first this time, and as she approached the front door, carrying a pile of new books, he came bounding toward her and grabbed them from her arms. This chivalry took her by surprise, and she almost grabbed them back. Looking up into his face, though, and seeing the smile that headed her way, she decided to let him play the gallant knight.

"Hi! Hey, how do you have this much homework on the first day?" he asked, disappointment flavoring his question after seeing how many books she was taking home and pretending not to be able to carry such weight. "I don't have much tonight and I was thinking that if you didn't have much either maybe we could go to the beach. It's still pretty nice out, and I bet you haven't walked on a beach in a while. Didn't you say your last school was in Germany?"

Amy was blown away. This guy had actually listened to what she'd said at lunch.

"I'd really like that. No, I don't have much homework. I just wanted to look over the books so that I'd have an idea what to expect this semester. I guess that's kind of nerdy, but I really want to keep my GPA up. And, no, I haven't been to the beach yet. We just got here a couple of weeks ago, and we've been unpacking and shopping, and then school started. I've been dying to see the ocean and maybe walk on the beach. My dad drove us by it, but we didn't even get out of the car. We lived for a while in Florida, and I loved walking on the beach there." Amy felt that she was doing all of the talking, telling this new guy way more than he wanted to know, but he did seem to be interested in what she said.

The rest of the day was idyllic. While they were driving from school to the beach, she got lost in her reverie of the day. Here she was, the new girl in town, and already she had met someone who was kind and considerate and popular and who listened to her and was fun to be with and smart and....

"Amy, are you okay? You look kind of funny."

Her thoughts interrupted, she looked at Charlie and laughed. "I was just thinking that it's been a pretty good first day at good ole Duxbury High. I think I'm going to like it here." And she sat back and listened as Charlie drove his beat-up old Jeep Wrangler and told her about the history of the town. It was hard to live in this town for long and not know the history of the early settlers. With Miles Standish buried down the street and John Alden's house by the high school, with Plymouth Rock a stone's throw away in the next town and every other house proudly wearing a plaque telling the world what famous early Americans had lived there, it was hard not to find this gorgeous, Norman Rockwell town interesting. As they drove past Old Town Hall, he told her how he used to go to Mommy and Me classes there when he was a kid and how his mom had even rented it out one time for a birthday party for him and his friends.

"It's just one great big room inside now and it's really cool for a party—no matter how old you are," he told her. "You look around and think of the early settlers creating the laws of a new country in the very room where you're eating birthday cake and it's pretty humbling. Only in New England…."

The comment's insightfulness was not lost on Amy. This guy really seemed to be the whole package. She told him how she had always felt the way he described. In fact, she remembered being a ten-year-old history buff who loved the gory stories of England's ruling class when her parents took her to the Tower of London. She had stood in a tower room and was in total awe of the history there. She had just stood still and "seen" Anne Boleyn's beheading, Lady Jane Grey's imprisonment by Mary Tudor who wanted to be queen, and the ghosts of Edward IV's two young sons who were killed in the tower and stuffed under a staircase, presumably so that their uncle could be king. Yes, this boy was the first she had encountered who shared her tendency to put herself in the history of a place.

They drove past the Milepost, a local tavern that, he told her, had the best fried chicken on the South Shore. When she asked him how it could be on a shore when it wasn't even near the water, he laughed and explained that "South Shore" referred to the towns on the ocean south of Boston. "North Shore" was the towns on the ocean north of Boston. It was a distinction he took for granted and found it kind of fun to explain to someone new.

They drove up the big hill to the Miles Standish monument and got out of the car. Looking up at the 116-foot granite shaft topped by a fourteen-foot statue of Miles Standish, Amy was in awe. Charlie, amused by her fascination, asked if she wanted to climb up to the top.

"We can climb up there?" Amy asked excitedly.

"Sure can," replied Charlie and, grabbing Amy's hand, he led her to the tiny door in the base of the monument. They climbed up the narrow, circular metal stairway inside to the top of the monument and, as they looked out over the Atlantic from their perch, he told her how the Pilgrims had sailed into Plymouth Bay in these very waters to begin their lives in the New World. When he pointed out Plymouth Rock, Amy was surprised that it was on the main street of the town. Even so, she thought that the view was breathtaking. She felt like a bird in flight as she stood looking out to sea. She pictured the *Mayflower* sailing into the harbor and could see miles of sandy beaches. She asked him if they were available to the public.

"Sure are," he answered, with a little chuckle. "They're our home away from home around here." Suddenly he really wanted to kiss Amy. She was beautiful, smart, interesting, and inquisitive. He knew it was too soon, though, so he turned and led her back down the circular stairs to the car, where they took off on their tour again.

Amy made a mental note to give her father a huge hug and kiss when she got home. He could have chosen to live closer to his new post as commander of the US Army Soldier Systems Center (SSC) in Natick, but he had decided to deal with the commute so that his wife and daughter could live in a normal house in a normal place, far away from the base housing they usually had. He wanted Amy to be able to finish high school in a nice little town and have normal experiences. He hadn't been in a position to offer that to his older daughter who was in her last year of college. Amy could have those experiences, though. After all, he was the one who had chosen a military life, and his family had dutifully followed him all over the world.

When he had told her a few weeks ago that he and her mother had bought an old farmhouse in a little town in Massachusetts, and that she was going to be a civilian for a change, she wasn't sure how to react because all she had ever known was bases and base schools or international schools. All of her friends had been Army brats just like her, and she didn't know if she would fit in with "regular" kids. *Well, I'm certainly getting my answer quickly*, she thought, as she rode along through the town next to Charlie. *This is going to be great!*

Charlie decided to take Amy out to the beach next since she had mentioned it. He knew that the road to the beach was special. No matter how many times he drove it, he still marveled at the beautiful houses that once were the summer homes of the Boston aristocracy but now were winterized and a year-round community. He pointed out the views of the bay and the quaint wooden bridge that went from this Powder Point neighborhood out to the miles-long beach. He drove slowly so Amy could enjoy it, pointing out where he had taken sailing lessons when he was younger, where different friends lived, and even where he had capsized his first boat in a bad storm.

He explained to Amy what a Lightning was and how much he loved racing the old wooden boat. He told her how most of the Lightnings now were made of fiberglass but that he had found an old mahogany beauty and totally restored her to her former glory. It had taken him and his friends a whole summer to do that but, in the end, it had been worth it. The boat sat low and glistened in the sunlight as it sped through the water. He had named the boat *Galadriel* after the Lady of the Wood in Tolkien's *The Lord of the Rings*, one of his favorite books. As he spoke, Amy could see the pride in his eyes and could hardly wait to see the boat. Of course, it didn't hurt that he referred to *The Lord of the Rings* as a book and not a movie, or that it was one of her favorite books too.

Charlie told her that he might teach her how to sail and have her work the jib for him next summer and then wondered why he was having long-term thoughts about a girl he just met! He decided not to point out his own house as they drove down King Caesar Lane. *Not yet*, he thought. *Let her like me for myself and not because I have a big, fancy house on Powder Point.*

After they crossed the little bridge, he confused Amy by turning right. The parking lot was to the left. Off they went down the road behind the dunes, jostling along the sand in his Jeep.

"What are you doing?" she exclaimed. "Are we supposed to be driving here?"

"Yeah," he yelled over the sound of the bumping Jeep. "Now you know why I drive this old thing," he said, laughing. "It's great for getting to parts of the beach that would take forever to walk to. The Jeep is the unofficial official Duxbury car." As he spoke, he looked at Amy and laughed at her puzzled expression. "Bet you've never ridden on the dunes before, Army girl."

Amy laughed and yelled over the noise of the ride that she wasn't sure yet if that was a good thing or a bad thing, but secretly she was having the time of her life. After a little while, Charlie took a sharp left, scooted over the dune, and parked on the beach. *Wow!* Amy thought. *Add a fire, some guitars, and kids dancing, and I could star in my own* Beach Blanket Bingo *right here.* She chuckled at the image the thought created. Her mom loved those old Frankie Avalon and Annette Funicello movies, and Amy had to admit that she liked them too. She had always wondered if that was what life was really like for teenagers who lived by beaches.

"Come on, slowpoke," Charlie called as he hopped out of the Jeep. They took off their shoes and headed closer to the water where the sand was cold and hard. It was funny the way Labor Day seemed to change everything around here from summer to fall, Charlie thought. Just last week, he and his friends had been swimming out here and body surfing in the cold waves. Now, though, there was a chill in the air, and the sand was cool. To their surprise, the only person in sight was a lady in a navy-blue jogging suit running with her faithful golden retriever a little way down the beach. They both instinctively stopped and watched for a minute as the lady stopped running, threw a stick into the small waves, and laughed as the dog happily bounded after it again and again. Quietly, Amy said, more to herself than to Charlie, "Someday I'd like a dog like that. I've never been able to have a dog."

For some reason, that seemed really sad to Charlie, who astonished himself as much as Amy when he replied with fervor, "I'll get you one someday. And we'll name him Spinnaker. He'll sail with us and go for runs on the beach with us and...." At this point he realized what he was saying and stopped mid-sentence. To his relief, Amy laughed. And as she laughed into the wind, her auburn hair blowing back from her freckled cheeks and those gorgeous emerald eyes reflecting the late afternoon September sun, he had the strangest thought: *I know I'm only seventeen years old, but I am never going to let this girl get away. We'll grow old together and walk on this beach with our canes and our dog, laughing like this. And no matter how many wrinkles come to that face, it will always look like it does to me today.* And at that strange thought, Charlie laughed too.

"You really make me feel like I'm someone different, Amy," he said quietly. "I know it's crazy, and I don't want to scare you away. After all, I've known you, what, eight hours? But I feel like I've known you forever and," he added even more quietly, "I want to keep on knowing you forever."

Amy looked up at Charlie and in an instant saw her future. It was rolling waves and sailboats and golden retrievers and laughing children. It was this gorgeous man looking at her with adoration and her returning his look. But what she said was, "I think the sea air addles the brain, goofball. We just met!" And she took off running down the beach, laughing and listening for his footsteps behind her. He easily caught up with her, and they slowed to a barefoot jog for a while and then began walking. Before they could blink, the sun was setting, and with it they turned around and headed back to the Jeep. Bracing against the car to put her shoes back on, Amy found Charlie leaning against her.

"Amy, I won't if you don't want me to, and I know we just met, but you have got to let me kiss you or I'll explode." But she didn't answer. She kissed him. In fact, they stood there against his Jeep for quite a while in an embrace that felt natural and old and right.

The Real Charlie

After a couple of months of drives around town, hanging out with friends, homework sessions on Amy's front porch, and dinners with her family, Amy asked Charlie if he was ashamed of her.

Sitting on a blanket on the bay side of the beach one late October afternoon, sheltered from the wind by the dunes, books scattered around, and her sweatshirt-hooded head in his lap, Amy turned abruptly to Charlie and complained, her voice rising with each word, "You still haven't introduced me to your parents. I have no idea where you even live! Why is that? We always go to my house or to the beach or to friends' houses. Are you ashamed of me?"

"Let's take a walk," Charlie interrupted. There is something you should know about me." Although Amy was scared and couldn't quite figure out what Charlie could possibly mean by that ominous statement, she slowly rose and, placing her hand in his, took off down the beach with him, worried by the concerned look in his eyes.

As they walked, they talked. He told her that he had wanted her to like him for himself. Everyone in town knew him and his family, and he never was sure if girls liked him or liked the idea of him. He explained that when he met her, he knew that she was different, and he wanted her to get to like him without knowing. As a grin began to sneak onto her face, and the crease of worry began to smooth, he explained that he was rich.

"You know that big white house with the dark green shutters that you always comment on when we drive out to the beach? The one that looks out over the bay? Well, I'm glad you like it so much because it's mine. Well, it's my parents'. That's where I live."

Amy just laughed. Her face exploded in laughter, and she grabbed him and pulled him toward her, wrapping her arms around his neck and smiling up into his worried face. Before he knew what was happening, she was kissing him and then tripping him so that he would fall on the sand where she jumped on top of him, pinned his arms, and playfully chastised him.

"How could you possibly think that would matter to me? I wouldn't care if you lived at the dump or in that magnificent house. I love you, you big jerk." And, with that, she planted a kiss square on his mouth, quieting any further comments from him. Breathless from her kisses, what she had said sunk in. When he realized that she had told him that she loved him, he felt free to tell her the same. He broke free, holding her at arm's length, and quietly said to her, "Amy, I've loved you since the first day I met you. I just didn't want to scare you away by telling you."

After another very long kiss, they got up and continued their walk. He told her about life as the son of a prominent Boston attorney. They compared notes on their stay-at-home moms. He already knew that hers was a June Cleaver type, baking cookies and bread, sewing curtains that made their Army houses homes, helping with homework, cheering her on at debates and softball games. She now discovered that his was a Junior League mom, organizer of charity auctions and cookbook sales, planner of Make-A-Wish galas. Amy had heard of mothers like that, had read about them in novels, but had never actually met one. All of the moms she had known were military moms, mostly stay-at-home mothers who made sure the children were okay as they were moved from place to place around the world.

"Maybe it's time you met my mom," he said, and they trotted back to the jeep, packed up their books and snacks, and headed the short distance to his house.

Pulling into the driveway, Amy could see the relief on Charlie's face. *What silliness*, she thought. *But I guess I can understand. If your whole life everyone likes you, you have to start wondering if they like you for who you are or for who your parents are. Well, Charlie Donnelly, I like you for who you are, and you should know that. In fact, I like you despite who your parents are.* As they walked up the sidewalk to the big double doors, Amy found it all a little intimidating. Her thoughts aside, she was suddenly embarrassed to be standing there in jeans and sneakers, a Duxbury High sweatshirt tied around her waist over a green T-shirt. She suddenly grabbed Charlie's arm and asked him if they could do this some other time when she was dressed more appropriately.

Charlie merely looked appraisingly at her, starting at the tips of her Nikes and stopping at her windblown auburn hair. "Nope. You're perfect just like you are," he declared. "We're going to make an entrance through the front door and surprise my mom." Once inside the house, Charlie called out, "Mom, Amy and I are here. Where are you?"

Amy gasped for a second. She had never been in a home that was decorated so beautifully. Stepping into the foyer of this home was like stepping onto a movie set. A large octagonal table stood sentry in the middle of the space with an enormous bouquet of brightly colored cut flowers perfuming the air. On glistening hardwood floors, peaceful Persian rugs rested. The furniture she could see straight ahead was all casually elegant—shiny mahogany and pale blues, yellows, and creams set against a backdrop of the bay visible through the wall of windows on the rear of the house. She could see through an open French door to the right what must be his father's study—walls of books, dark woods and leathers. It was definitely a dad's room, in her estimation. As she took it all in, she glimpsed another room through yet another set of French doors on the left side of the foyer that she guessed was his mother's study—more walls of books, but pastels dominated the room with a gorgeous walnut writing table, floral upholstered chairs, and striped accents.

On one wall of the foyer was a painting of a black lab which she figured must have been Charlie's dog. He saw her gazing at the painting and told her that it was his childhood friend Jib. His parents had given him the pup on his fifth Christmas, and they had been best friends for twelve years. Amy was moved by the emotion in his voice and the tears gathering in his eyes as he told her about Jib.

"I just lost her a few months ago. She was old and hurting, and we had to have her put down. It was the worst day of my life."

Amy wanted to hug and comfort him, but just then she heard a noise upstairs. Charlie's mom suddenly appeared on the circular staircase, gliding down the steps as one with wings. Her grace was immediately apparent, but also her charm. With a smile that mirrored Charlie's, she approached them, gave Charlie a peck on his cheek, and then admonished, "Charles, you have been keeping this beautiful girl from me, why? Are you ashamed of your old mother?" Her shimmering blue eyes could not hold the scolding tone of her voice as she winked at Amy. "Welcome to our home, young lady…finally," she said, sending one last barb in her son's direction. Holding out her right hand, she introduced herself and then wrapped a soft blue cashmere arm around Amy and led her through the living room and out into the enclosed sunroom where she gently sat Amy next to herself on a floral-slipcovered sofa.

"Charles, go and get us some lemonade, would you? This girl and I have a lot of catching up to do." And, with that, she turned her attention to a self-conscious Amy.

"Mrs. Donnelly, I apologize for how I'm dressed. My folks would kill me if they knew I wore jeans and sneakers the first time I met you, but I didn't know we were coming here." The words tumbled out, but as she spoke, Charlie's mother smiled and reassured her that she couldn't care less what Amy was wearing. She was just glad to have met her because Charlie had talked about no one and nothing else for the past two months. Charlie overheard this comment as he reentered carrying a tray of glasses and a pitcher of lemonade, some cookies, and a small bowl of fruit.

"Mom!" he exclaimed. "Why'd you tell Amy that? Stop!" But his mother looked innocently at him, and Amy just smiled.

The Junior Year

All fall, everyone said "CharlieandAmy" as if it were a single word, which made sense because together they were better than either of them was alone. All the other girls at Duxbury High gave up on snagging Charlie because, while he was still friendly to everyone, it was obvious that there was no one for him but Amy. She attended every football game and cheered for Charlie as he completed pass after pass. He sat in the front row at the fall musical and smiled from ear to ear with pride as she took the stage and sang and danced her way even further into his heart. Amy easily made the debating team, and Charlie loved watching her debate, her Irish eyes blazing at her opponents and her fiery mane swinging from side to side emphatically. For someone who stood only five foot five, she was an imposing figure when she began to argue her points. Charlie hoped they never had any serious disagreements because she would beat him every time in a war of words.

Soon the holidays arrived, and Amy witnessed the true difference between her family and his. She was, of course, invited to the Donnellys' Christmas party, a lavish, formal affair. She and her mother went in to Boston to shop for just the right dress for her to wear, and then to the Burlington Mall. It was at Lord & Taylor that she found a dress both she and her mother thought was perfect. It was a simple sleeveless dark green jersey gown by Ralph Lauren. The neckline was not low in front, a demure bateau, but dipped to a conservative vee in the back. With glamorous rhinestone accents on the shoulders, ruching around the middle, and a slit along the left side seam, the dress was "elegantly appropriate," as her mother said. Combined with a pair of strappy silver heels and silver bangle bracelets, her hair long and loose with rhinestone earrings peeking out, she felt all grown up. When the night of the party arrived and she walked down the stairs to parade for her father, she couldn't miss the moist eyes that looked back at her smiling ones.

"You look lovely, Amy—just like your mother the first time I met her."

Before he had time to tell her about that night, the doorbell rang and he harrumphed, cleared his throat, and went to answer the door. From the living room, Amy heard him exclaim, "Well, Charlie, you clean up pretty well. I like the tux. Is that a clip-on or did you tie the danged thing? Wait until you see Amy. She cleaned up pretty well too."

"Daddy!" Amy exclaimed, walking through the door into the front hall. She didn't have a chance to admonish him further, though, because when she saw Charlie and he saw her, the rest of the world disappeared for both of them. They were lost in each other's eyes.

"Well, you two go have a good time," Amy's mother interrupted. "I don't think your plan for the night was to stand in our hall." Having brought them back to earth, she insisted that they pose for a few pictures before heading off for the party. As Amy reached into the closet for her coat, her mother called to her from the living room, "Amy, why don't you wear this tonight? It goes so nicely with your dress." She walked out holding a mink stole her husband had given to her for their twenty-fifth wedding anniversary not too long ago. Amy gasped, thanked her mother, and stood while Charlie draped the soft fur around her shoulders. "One more picture!" her mother called out as she snapped three photos in quick succession.

"Mary, let these two leave now," her father said. And off they went in Charlie's dad's Lexus.

New Year's Eve came, and instead of attending another formal party at the Donnelly home, Charlie and Amy opted for a party with their friends. The Sweetsers offered to make themselves scarce and to let the kids use their home. Amy's mom baked goodies, made sandwiches, bought the fixings for homemade pizzas, and stocked the fridge with sodas. Then she and George headed upstairs where they stayed for their own little private New Year's Eve party of champagne, chocolate-covered strawberries, and the Times Square ball drop on television. They smiled at each other every time the young people erupted in laughter.

"This is why we're living here," George said.

"I know, and we appreciate it, honey," Mary purred. "I will hear that teenaged laughter until the day I die. Amy is so happy here."

As spring arrived, Amy and Charlie drove to colleges in the Boston area together and toured campuses, imagining themselves there. And they went to the junior prom together, looking as beautiful as any two teenagers have ever looked. Once again, Charlie opted for a traditional black tuxedo, but Amy made her entrance in a stunning white chiffon gown from Jill Stuart. When Charlie came to pick her up, one look at her in that white dress and he was picturing her as his bride.

Someday, he thought. *Someday.*

They had to pose for pictures at the Sweetser home, and Charlie was surprised to see his folks there as well. His father was snapping pictures alongside Amy's mom while her dad and his mom stood off to the side pretending not to be affected by the sight of their beautiful children looking so grown up. Soon, George gruffly stepped forward and said, "Off you go, you two. We'll follow you to school. We wouldn't miss the red carpet for anything." Everyone hustled out the front door and headed the one and a half miles to the high school.

In keeping with Duxbury tradition, all prom attendees strode down the red carpet from their limousines and cars to the school gym with everyone in town lining the path, taking pictures, and telling them how wonderful they looked. It was quite an experience. Amy's long, flowing dress swished when she walked, her now tanned and freckled shoulders bare and wrapped in Charlie's black tuxedoed arm. A corsage of tiny white roses encircled her wrist, and a matching boutonniere donned Charlie's lapel.

It was the perfect end to a magical year for Amy.

The Maid of Honor

Summer came and, with only a year left of high school, it was time for some serious decisions to be made. Amid the sunny days of sailing, picnicking on the beach with friends, playing tennis at one of their friends' Powder Point houses, or swimming in Charlie's pool, a thought was niggling Amy's brain. Something she had always secretly wanted was coming into conflict with her love for Charlie, and she had to make a decision.

At the same time, she was preoccupied with being her sister's maid of honor. Her big sister Susan had followed the traditional route—college at a small, liberal arts, New England school where she met the man she knew she would marry. They graduated in May, and now, in August, Amy's mother, Amy, and Susan were frantically pulling together the final details of a fairytale wedding. Since Susan had no place she could identify as her hometown after moving around so much, she had decided to be married in her college chapel. She joked that her four years in college constituted residency since she had never lived anywhere longer than four years in her life. Agreeing to go along with the idea, her mother planned a wonderful wedding, and Amy found herself commuting often from Massachusetts to Maine to attend to her sister's needs.

It was on one of these excursions that she and her mother discovered a gem in Kittery, Maine—Bob's Clam Hut. Right on Route 1 where it had stood since 1956, a little hole-in-the-wall, take-out restaurant, painted bright blue and white, became their "must stop" detour. Amy and her mom discovered tastes they had never known—clam cakes, fried haddock, and bright red Maine lobsters caught the morning they were cooked. Susan knew that if her mother and sister were late arriving for a wedding planning session, it was because they had lingered

at Bob's. Charlie often accompanied Amy on these trips when the purpose was something that her mother was not involved in, and they too would stop at Bob's.

Sometimes, if wedding plans took longer than expected or were in the late afternoon or evening, Charlie and Amy stayed at his folks' summer place in Ocean Point, which Amy thought was magical. If it was a weeknight, Charlie's mom would be there to greet them, since she moved from Duxbury to their summer house every year on June 15th and stayed until August 15th. If it was a weekend, the house would be filled with overnight guests, soirées on the lawns or by the pool, or family dinners with Charlie's parents. They would always have to assure Amy's folks that there would be no "hanky-panky" (her mother's words) if Amy spent the night away from home, although neither Amy nor Charlie ever intended to take their fooling around to that level—yet. Somehow two old-fashioned teenagers in the twenty-first century had found each other.

A short drive north of Portland, Amy thought that Charlie's summer house was the most beautiful spot on the Maine coast, sitting, as it did, high on a cliff overlooking a large bay with views out to sea. The approach to the house always took Amy's breath away. In fact, the first time she had visited the home, she had discovered tears trickling down her cheeks as she gazed from the high perch of land out over the ocean, dotted with islands, sails, and lobster boats. The sheer beauty that presented itself as she stepped up over a little knoll from the drive-way onto the lawn always had that effect on her. Driving down a narrow, paved drive from the main road, leaves tickling the sides of Charlie's Jeep, then suddenly rounding a turn, she would find herself thrust into the sunlight and smell the wisteria and rhododendrons, azaleas and roses that welcomed visitors. As they drove down the narrow drive, she would hear the crashing waves before the drive opened up into a stone circle and she could then see the bright blue ocean past the side of the house. Sailboats bobbed in the sparkling water below, and sails dotted the bay on nice days. Broad, green lawns circled the white shingled colonial, and the view never failed to enchant her. They would jump out of the Jeep and sprint around the house instead of through it,

taking time to soak in the view before announcing their arrival. Sitting proudly in the side yard was one of Amy's favorite features of the house, a heated saltwater pool. Unless lightning bolts were stabbing the earth, Amy would make time to swim in this amazing stone pool during their visits.

July passed, and soon it was early August and time for Susan's wedding. Charlie and Amy decided to stay at his folks' house to lessen the confusion for Susan. Riding with his parents down the drive from the house, on their way to the campus wedding in a white limousine, Amy felt like Daisy Buchanan as she looked at Charlie and his father, handsome in their tuxedos, Charlie's mother in an elegant powder-blue silk gown, and herself in her burgundy one. Her gaze settled on her burgundy-tipped toes peeking through matching silk-heeled sandals as she thought about how much her life had changed since her father's decision to move to a small town. She thought about the first time she met Charlie. She thought about how quickly their junior year had passed. She thought about the fun they'd had on college tours. And she thought about her future, a tiny frown appearing on her forehead in stark contrast to the smile on her lips.

When they arrived on campus, white signs with white bells and black lettering everywhere proclaimed that it was her sister's big day. Arrows pointed the way to the valet parking and the chapel, although the campus was so small that Amy couldn't imagine that anyone would get lost. Susan, though, had insisted because she didn't want anything to go wrong. The groomsmen had been in charge of putting up signs all over campus, and they had done a great job. The chapel was bedecked in white roses and carnations, baby's breath and greens, with burgundy, white, and black ribbons floating from each pew. Amy went immediately to the dressing room at the rear of the chapel where she saw her sister looking gorgeous with her auburn hair piled atop her head in loose curls and white silk floating around her, making her appear as a fairy princess. Amy stood next to her sister, and they both looked at the reflection in the full-length mirror before them. Where had the years gone? Wherever they had moved, they had known that they had each other. And now, here was Susan moving on with her life, getting married, and living in a different state. And as Amy looked at their reflections, she caught a glimpse of a decision that was forming in her own mind, seeing her reflection not in the burgundy silk gown, shoulders grinning at the sun as tendrils of her unruly hair teased them, but in something much more conservative.

Their mother returned to the room and, seeing her two girls standing there as young women and looking so beautiful, she began to tear up.

"Okay, you two. Stop being so beautiful and help me to not ruin my makeup." With that, both Susan and Amy stuck their tongues out and crossed their eyes, a face that always made their mother laugh. The sentimental moment was gone, and everyone was back in the present.

As Amy walked slowly down the aisle, carrying a small bouquet of white roses with burgundy and black ribbons, her hair sprinkled with tiny bits of baby's breath, she found Charlie in the crowd. They shared a tender moment as she passed him, and he couldn't help thinking of what she would look like as a bride—and hoped someday to find out.

After the ceremony, as the wedding party gathered on the veranda of Susan's new husband's country club near Portland for photos and to form a receiving line, Charlie stood back and watched as Amy smoothed her sister's dress, tucked a piece of wayward hair into her mother's chignon, straightened her father's bowtie, and then stood at perfect attention, angelic smile on her face, looking straight at him with those eyes of hers. She amazed him. She was in control of the day, although it had been her mother who had planned the entire wedding. Amy was determined to let her mother and sister simply enjoy themselves with no worries about details. She had decided to take it upon herself to make sure that everything went perfectly. And it did. Charlie was mesmerized.

As they whirled around the dance floor, Charlie wanted Amy in his arms forever. When she laughed that throaty, "I'm happy, and I want to shout it from the rooftops" laugh of hers, he laughed along. He whispered to her, "Amy, just think. Next year at this time, we'll be getting ready to head off to college together and start a life of our own."

And Amy smiled, but the smile didn't make it to her eyes.

The Decision

Shortly after her sister's wedding, Amy became more restless. With only a couple of weeks to go before the school year began, and her boyfriend talking a lot about which colleges they should apply to, she took more long, solitary walks and sat on the porch swing by herself, idly letting the toe that rested on the porch push her back and forth. After several days of this behavior, she could see that everyone was worrying about her. She decided to have a long talk with her father and then with her mother. She needed their honest input. Traveling from place to place over the years, always being the "new kid," she had learned to trust her instincts—and also to rely on her parents' good judgment and life experiences—probably more than other teens did. She needed to know what they thought, but she had to make this decision on her own before she told Charlie. She agonized over the pros and cons, her trained debating mind kicking in. She made lists on her laptop almost daily, but always came up with the same lists: many items in the "pro" column and "Charlie" in the "con" column.

One cloudy Sunday afternoon, the last before September, Amy found her father sitting on the front porch reading *The Wall Street Journal*. She joined him, settling into the other Adirondack chair and setting her Diet Coke down on the table between them.

"Daddy," she began. "I need to talk with you."

Putting his newspaper down immediately, her father saw the concern in his little girl's face, and his mind raced to possible causes. Outwardly calm, though, he said, "Sure, honey. What would you like to talk about?"

For the next two hours, Amy and her father discussed the pros and cons of her college options, her mother joining them for the last half hour or so of the discussion. Once their opinions were provided, Amy considered them, thought about her own feelings, and made a decision. She knew that Charlie wanted them to go to the same school, but she had to make her own choice.

A couple of days before school started, as she was devouring her second hot dog at the Donnelly Annual Labor Day Blowout, surrounded by dozens of Charlie's father's partners and their families, his mother's socialite friends, and a few of their own friends, Amy made up her mind. She stood up from the white Adirondack chair, pulled Charlie out of his, and called over her shoulder to their friends, "Be right back! We have something we need to discuss."

With their friends' comments fading in the background ("Sure, 'discuss' is code for what?" "There they go again!" and "Gee, could it be serious?"), Amy and Charlie ran down onto the dock. Amy suddenly looked somber, which scared Charlie. His irrational thought was that she was breaking up with him, and he didn't think he could take that. He had plans of his own for them. But she looked so serious, frowning at the water, a tiny furrow forming on her brow, a dot of yellow mustard in the corner of her mouth. Charlie leaned forward and kissed the mustard away, hoping he might pull her out of her serious mood. Amy usually was so carefree and happy. Yet, if he thought about it, she had been acting strangely for the past couple of weeks. He wasn't sure what could be going on.

Without preamble, Amy turned and ran a few steps down the dock, stopped at the edge, turned to Charlie, and said, almost in a single breath, "Charlie, you know I love you. I will always love you. And because I love you, I need to do something for myself that is really important to me. And because you love me, I know you'll understand." Suddenly seeing the pain and confusion on his face, she quickly added, "No, silly. I'm not breaking up with you. But we're going to have to do the long-distance thing next year. I'm going to West Point—if I can get a commission."

Charlie was dumbfounded. He didn't know if he was relieved or angry, hurt, or happy for Amy. All he knew was that he was confused. Amy had kept this thought to herself, and he'd had no idea she was considering West Point.

"But Amy, I thought we said we were going to be together forever. How could you do this to us? West Point is a million miles away, and you would hardly ever have free time, and I couldn't even see you on weekends!" As the reality of what she had said sunk in, Charlie became angry. He felt betrayed. He bellowed, "Amy, how could you?" adding sarcastically, "Thanks for telling me." And with that, he ran from her, off the dock and down the beach, running faster than she could, making it futile for her to chase him.

She stopped and thought, as she gazed after him, *Well, what did I think he would do—say, "Gee, that's great, Amy. How wonderful that you have made a major decision that affects both of us without so much as a hint to me that you were thinking about it"*? Amy resigned herself to giving Charlie time to cool off, to decide how he wanted to react. Maybe she could convince him that the notion of faraway love was actually romantic. She slowly climbed the rocks up from the beach to the Donnellys' lawn where the music was cheerful and the guests were all smiling and carefree, worried that her life might be crumbling around her. She pasted a smile on her face and told her friends she was going to call it a day and go spend some time with her own family. Her parents had come to the barbecue and stayed for a while to be polite, but it wasn't really their crowd. Then she found Charlie's parents, thanked them for inviting her, and walked home—all of two miles—to her house on the other side of town.

The Acceptance

Not really sure when or even if Charlie would call, Amy spent two lonely days thinking about her decision. The more she thought, the more she knew it was the right one. Her entire life had been leading up to the moment when she would proudly announce to her father that she had earned a commission to West Point. A lifetime spent listening to his conversations about giving back to one's country, doing something meaningful with one's life, of being the best and the brightest had informed her decision. She could recite the Army's seven core values by heart: Loyalty, Duty, Respect, Selfless Service, Honor, Integrity, and Personal Courage (arranged to form the acronym LDRSHIP). She knew that it was something she had to do, not only for her father, but for her country and for herself as well. And, if she were honest with herself, for Charlie too, even though he would never see it that way.

West Point had been a dream for so long that if she gave it up for him, she would always resent him in a corner of her soul. Their love didn't deserve resentment. She had to be true to herself just as much as he had to be true to himself. If she wasn't, then it wasn't really her he professed to love, was it? If he couldn't understand that she was becoming a woman who knew her own mind, spoke her own mind, and expected him to appreciate her thoughts and dreams, then he wasn't the guy she thought he was.

This senior year might not be as perfect as she had hoped it would be.

Waking early the next morning, as she always did on the first day of school, Amy chose to wear one of Charlie's favorite outfits instead of one of the new ones her mother and she had bought on their shopping trip to Boston last week. Her mother would understand. Amy looked at the pink-and-white sundress as a peace offering to Charlie. As she was putting the finishing touches on her lip gloss, a horn beeped out front and she heard a familiar, "Do I have to drag you out of bed, sleepy-head?" sung up to her through her open window. She pulled back the curtain and saw a smiling Charlie jumping out of his Jeep and walking to her front door as though nothing had changed.

With unfamiliar butterflies fluttering where her breakfast should be, Amy grabbed a white sweater and bounded down the stairs, the tomboy in her winning out over the pretty sundress. There at the bottom by the front door were her mother and Charlie. She could see that Charlie was being his usual charming self because her mother was blushing slightly and tee-heeing like a schoolgirl. Charlie had a power over her that could make her feel young again. *Okay,* thought Amy. *This is how we're going to play this. We're going to make believe I never said anything at the barbecue.*

Amy's smile could have outshone a lighthouse. She ran to Charlie who gathered her up in his arms and kissed her. "Sorry, ma'am," he said to her mother through his laughter. "I've missed this girl of yours. It's been two whole days!" And he kissed her again—right in front of her mother. Then, more serious, he said, "But I guess missing her is something I'm going to have to get used to, isn't it? That's okay as long as I get welcomed back like this!" And with that, he kissed her again, much to her mother's embarrassment and secret pleasure.

"Have a nice day at school, children," she called as she turned discreetly and headed to the kitchen.

Amy slipped into a pair of flip-flops, and she and Charlie walked hand in hand to the Jeep in silence. But as Charlie gallantly held the door open for her, Amy said quietly, "I have to try for this, Charlie."

To this Charlie replied even more quietly, "I know. We'll just have to make it work." And he kissed her hair gently, closed her door, and ran around to get in. To his surprise, Amy was sobbing as he put his seat belt on.

"Amy, what's wrong?" he asked, confused. "I said, 'We'll make it work.'"

"I know you did. That's why I'm crying. I'm just a silly girl sometimes."

"Well, you'd better toughen up fast or they'll eat you for breakfast at West Point," Charlie joked as he shifted gears and they headed off to their senior year.

The Promise

Senior year was a blur of laughter, games, parties, walks, and long make-out sessions; holidays, friends, and school. Before they knew it, spring had arrived and, with it, acceptances to colleges. As everyone buzzed around the school jumping for joy as they found out they had been accepted by their first-choice school or sadly bemoaning the fact that they hadn't, Amy and Charlie had agreed to open their first-choice letters together. Both of them were receiving their acceptances or refusals by mail rather than checking online and had promised not to open them until both came.

After a long morning, Amy found Charlie sitting under a glorious maple tree on the edge of campus, holding his letter in both hands. Coincidentally, she had received hers the day before. She walked up to him and sat down.

"Well, this is it!" he said dramatically.

"Yup," Amy replied simply.

And they each opened a thick envelope. A smile crossed first Charlie's face and then Amy's as they each read that they had been accepted—Charlie to Colgate University in Hamilton, New York, and Amy to the Military Academy at West Point across the Hudson. At least they were both in New York, each of them thought, only three and a half hours apart. They had sat in Amy's room one night and looked at MapQuest to see just how far they would be from each other if they both were accepted by their first choices, and how long it would take to travel the distance. Charlie could have his car on campus as a freshman, and he planned to drive to West Point whenever he could. Thrilled for each other's happiness, but also a little sad, they sat under the tree quietly for a long time in a silent embrace, lost in their own private thoughts.

After a while, they heard the school bell ring.

"Well, let the party begin," cried Charlie triumphantly, hopping up and pulling Amy up with him. They ran together back into the school where they announced their good news to friends and faculty who were all excited for them.

Senior prom and graduation came and went. Amy and Charlie made the rounds of graduation parties and invited all of their friends to a party they had together at Charlie's house. Although Amy and Charlie's parents had little in common, they did share a love for their children and cared deeply for each other's child. Amy's folks supplied the food and beverages for the party and Charlie's provided the location. Actually, Amy was amazed at how well the two families worked together for this celebration. As she was standing on the lawn thinking this, Charlie crept up behind her and whispered in her ear, "Gee, the outlaws get along great, don't you think?"

As usual, he voiced what she was thinking, although she had to laugh at his choice of words.

"Outlaws?" she laughed.

"Yeah, outlaws. It's kind of like in-laws except it has a more fun ring to it, a more realistic description of the relationship they'll have one day."

As Charlie said that, he wrapped his arms around Amy from behind and slipped a tiny ring on the fourth finger of her left hand.

"It's small because it's just a promise of something bigger to come later," he whispered in her ear, and she turned in his arms to face him. "Someday, Amy Sweetser, I am going to ask you to marry me, and you are going to say yes."

"Charlie, it's beautiful. It's perfect. And I promise too. Just because we're at different schools doesn't mean we'll care any less about each other. And," she added quietly, "I will say yes." With that, she stood on tiptoes and kissed him softly.

"Okay, you lovebirds," her father called in his big bass voice from across the lawn. "If you're not too busy, would you mind coming over here and cutting your graduation cake so I can have a piece? Your mother said I can't cut it because it's yours."

Laughing, and hand in hand, Amy and Charlie ran across the lawn and, taking the knife her father handed her, together they cut the cake, giggling because of the promise they had just made to each other.

Their short summer was just a month long. Amy had to report for Cadet Basic Training on June 30th. Charlie had to leave for preseason football practices a few weeks later. The month flashed by in a series of Lightning class sailboat races, swimming, tennis, walks on the beach, quiet nights, and happy, sun-filled days. Before they knew it, it was time to pack up and head in different directions.

The New Adventures

Amy, excited to see what new adventures West Point had to offer, but sad about not being able to share them with Charlie, had to leave first. The last Monday in June came far too soon. After packing up her dad's Lincoln with everything she thought she might need, she and Charlie held each other tightly, tears in their eyes. Her parents had gone into the house, ostensibly to retrieve something she had forgotten, but she knew it was to give her a few minutes alone with Charlie before she had to go.

"You made sure you have a Skype account, right? And WhatsApp is installed on your phone?"

"You know it is, Charlie. You did it for me, remember?" Amy tried to joke. "You did it at the same time you put your picture on my desktop and our pictures as my screensaver. My laptop is totally Charlieized." At that, he couldn't help laughing.

"Well, you're a fine one to talk, Army girl," he sassed. "You Amyized mine too!" I can't wait to see the grief I'm going to get from guys at school about that!"

Hearing laughter outside, Amy's folks figured it was safe to emerge and they approached the car. Amy's mother gave Charlie a big hug and a kiss on the cheek and said, "Now, Charles, you behave yourself. No partying or drinking or doing drugs, okay? You pay attention to your schoolwork and get good grades and you'll have no problem getting into Harvard Law." Then she softened a bit and added, "It's going to be awfully quiet around here without you. You make sure you stop by if you're in town, okay?" She gave him another quick hug and climbed into the passenger seat of the car, leaving Amy and George standing with him.

Much to their surprise, a car pulled in as they were getting ready to leave and Charlie's parents emerged from their black Lexus.

"We just wanted to stop by to wish Amy well," Charlie's father called as he and his wife quickly got out of their car. "I can see you're ready to leave, so we won't hold you up," he added, and everyone hugged in many combinations.

"Well, sweetie, if you forgot anything, anything at all, you just call," Mr. Donnelly asserted. "West Point's not all that far, and I could drive it over to you if your folks can't." With that, he slugged Charlie in the arm, hugged Amy, shook her father's hand, kissed Amy's mother on the cheek, and walked back to his car.

After Charlie's mom made the rounds of polite hugs and kisses, told Amy that she could have anything delivered at any time Amy needed something, she too walked back to their car and stood talking with her husband, backs turned to give Amy and Charlie a little privacy.

Amy and Charlie hugged one last time, kissed each other long enough to last a few weeks, and Amy reluctantly got into the backseat, hoping that she was making the right choice. As she turned to blow a kiss to Charlie, her dad put the car into gear, and they slowly drove down the driveway, turned the corner, and were on their way.

Off they went, leaving Duxbury, the nicest home she had ever had, for the unknown world of West Point and the promise of an uncertain military career.

As the miles grew between Duxbury and herself, Amy found herself thinking less about her time there and more about her exciting future. Even though she had grown up Army, now it was going to be her experience, not her dad's.

Left standing in the Sweetsers' driveway, Charlie smiled and waved as Amy disappeared around the bend. His lips silently said, *I love you* as his father slowly walked back toward him. Putting his strong arm around his son's shoulder, he began talking to Charlie's unhearing ears. Suddenly, Charlie turned to face his dad, who was saying reassuringly, "Charlie, young love is a wonderful thing. Its resilience is astounding. You'll see. It will hurt for a while to be so far apart, but before long, you'll be so busy you'll hardly think of Amy. And before you know it, you'll see each other again, and it will be as if you were never apart. Sure, it hurts now, but you keep your eye on the prize, Son."

The next few weeks went slowly as Charlie hung out with friends, sailed with his parents, and sat on the veranda reading. Soon it was his turn to leave for college. He packed up his Jeep and turned to say good-bye to his parents. His mother said, "I still can't believe you don't want me to go with you now. Are you sure you have directions? Your cell is charged? Did you remember your phone charger?"

At that point, Charlie's dad cleared his throat and said, "Well, good luck, Son. You'll do great, I'm sure. Make your old man proud." He then gave Charlie the tightest bear hug of his life, making Charlie feel like a little boy in his daddy's arms for a moment. Breaking away, his father added gruffly, "Well, you'd better get on your way. You want to arrive with plenty of time to unload your stuff and get settled. Do you need any money?" Without waiting for an answer, he pulled a handful of twenties out of his wallet and stuffed them in Charlie's fist. "Well, Grace, we'd better let this college man hit the road." He wrapped a protective arm around his wife's shoulders and banged his other hand on the door of Charlie's Jeep. "Get going before I change my mind!" he called out.

And Charlie drove away.

The Long Gray Line

As George and Mary drove Amy the four hours to West Point, they talked quietly with each other until they were well into New York. They knew that Amy needed time to process the changes that were taking place in her life. As West Point got closer, though, her father had a few things that he needed to say to her. He began slowly.

"How are you doing, Amy?" he asked gently. "Are you excited about starting this new chapter in your life?" He could see his daughter's tentative smile in the rearview mirror so he continued. "Amy, you know that your mother and I could not be prouder of you than we are right now. You have made a decision that was difficult but that you thought was right. Every parent feels pride when a child follows in their footsteps, and I am no exception. It makes me feel that I couldn't have hurt you too badly moving you all over the place if you have chosen to join the Long Gray Line yourself. It proves that your mother did a wonderful job in making every house a home and making you feel loved and protected."

Amy smiled and thought about how she had never heard her father express sentiment in such a way before. She only wished that she could be as sure of her decision as he thought she was. She missed Charlie already. She had been texting with him the whole way, and he had said all the right things, but she didn't know anyone who had been high school sweethearts, gone off to different colleges, and stayed together. She couldn't bear to think about losing him. Out loud, though, she said, "Daddy, I'm happy that I'm making you proud. This is something I guess I've always known I'd do. Now that I'm doing it, though, it's harder than I thought it would be."

"Amy," her father replied, "you are about to join a unique group of people, people who have chosen to stand together with pride and dignity, to defend their country. You will find that you'll be linked to these fellow cadets for the rest of your life. To graduate as a second lieutenant in the United States Army from the Military Academy at West Point is an honor unlike any other. You will be tested in ways you can't even imagine—both body and mind—and you'll become stronger for it. If you give the Army your all, it will reward you in countless ways. You have always had integrity, and that will hold you in good stead. As my friend Bill Cohen always said, 'Choose the harder right over the easier wrong.' Amy, you'll be fine. In fact, you'll be more than fine. You will flourish." Her mom just turned in her seat and smiled in agreement.

"Amy," her dad continued, "don't be alarmed when you get there. You'll be called Animal." He smiled in memory of his own early days at the academy. "All new Cadets are called Animal or Beast or Reptile when they arrive." He chuckled then, reliving his early days. He continued, "Just be careful not to be a fast animal," at which Amy gasped.

"Dad! Why would you say that? You know I would never cheat on Charlie!"

Her father laughed. "Amy girl, a fast animal is a plebe who puts on airs. You just be yourself and you'll be fine."

Amy sank back into the seat to text Charlie about all this new information. He thought it was pretty funny, even making a dumb joke about sometimes wishing she were a fast animal.

As George drove onto the campus, memories flooded over him, and pride welled up that his daughter would soon be living and studying here. In his day there had been no female cadets. He knew it would be tough for her, but she was capable of anything. He pulled up to Clinton Field next to the Cadet Parade Field and parked. He watched her get out of the car, give him and her mom big hugs, and take off for Ike Hall. From there, Amy would be taken, along with the other cadets, to Thayer Hall for in-processing and to receive their initial issue items—their uniforms and other basic things they'd need for at least the first few days.

Amy spent a lot of time that day pouring over the Cadet Handbook, or "smart book," which contains all the knowledge cadets are required

to know verbatim any time they are asked by a ranking cadet. She also learned how to report to a superior officer, how to salute, march, and maintain her uniform and room the West Point way. Of course, in reality, she already knew much of this, having learned it over the years from her father. It was a little intimidating, though, being surrounded by so many strangers who all were trying to impress.

Later that day, Amy joined her new company and advanced proudly onto the Plain for the first time to march in parade to the Oath Ceremony. She surreptitiously scanned the stands to find her parents and soon located them, beaming with pride. After Amy took the oath, she was released to say good-bye to her family, and then the West Point experience began in earnest.

The College Years

Charlie's first day at Colgate was much more informal than Amy's first day. He drove into tiny Hamilton, New York, past the big yellow Wendt Inn, and was greeted everywhere with banners and signs welcoming the new students. He proceeded through town, past Parry's Hardware Store (really more of a modern-day general store), the Colgate Bookstore (which is located in the center of town instead of on campus), and the grande dame of the town, the Colgate Inn (the shining white Dutch colonial inn that has sat proudly at the end of the park in the center of the historic village of Hamilton for almost a hundred years). He passed watering holes and restaurants, and soon found himself passing Fraternity Row to his right and Taylor Lake on his left. Charlie began to wish that he had allowed his parents to come with him. It would have been nice to have them to talk with about the town and campus. Within seconds, though, he was at the Reid Athletic Center. He parked and walked over to Crown Field at Andy Kerr Stadium. Finding a gate unlocked, he strolled in and looked at the field, imagining himself playing there.

"Oh, Amy," he said, "I wish you could be here too." Realizing that it didn't do any good to bemoan the fact that he was here alone, he shook it off, turned, and found his way to the coach's office to report in for training camp.

During the college years, Charlie and Amy saw each other whenever they could. They spent every vacation, leave, weekend, formal, birthday, and holiday together. They often shared their time with family, but they would always carve out time just for themselves. Their summers of sailing, playing tennis, and just hanging out with friends flew by since Amy was required to attend mandatory cadet training during more than half of her summer break. Charlie missed Amy's proud cheers as he threw touchdown passes in Division I games, and Amy missed his proud face and fists pumping the air as she pitched her first no-hitter game.

But they made it through.

Neither ever even thought of cheating on the other, something that vexed the Colgate sorority girls who saw Charlie as a real catch. They soon realized that he was not merely a challenge; he was off-limits. At that point, they became his friends, something that made Amy jealous even though Charlie kept telling her she had no reason to be. Charlie, in his own right, was jealous of Amy spending her time with so many guys at West Point. They studied together, did projects together, ran together, and had meals together. At times, Charlie really had to sit himself down and reprimand himself to trust Amy. After all, he knew he was trustworthy and had no reason to suspect that she was not.

Finally, though, graduation time arrived for both of them. Charlie stood proudly waiting as Amy marched as a cadet across the Lusk Reservoir and into Michie Stadium (named after Dennis Mahan Michie, who was instrumental in starting the game of football at the US Military Academy) with her platoon for graduation. The pomp, pageantry, and tradition of the ceremony moved him and helped him to understand why this was so important to her. Once inside the stadium, she received her commission certificate and graduation diploma, becoming a member of the Long Gray Line as a second lieutenant in the United States Army.

After the ceremony, Amy found her family, Charlie, and his folks in the crowd.

"Well, Dad, I wasn't the goat," she said, laughing.

"You're damned right you weren't," her father proudly replied. I would say second in your class certainly is not being the goat.

Charlie and his parents looked confused as Amy and hers laughed. When Amy noticed, she turned to them and explained, "Each West Point class has a goat, the last-ranking cadet who makes it through to graduation. Each other cadet gives the goat one dollar, and everyone applauds him when the diplomas are awarded."

"In this case, when *she* receives *her* diploma," her father interjected. For the first time in West Point history, a female cadet earned the dubious distinction of being the goat, collecting approximately a thousand dollars and the biggest applause of the graduation ceremony.

As is Army tradition, Amy handed her bars to her father, and he and her mom proudly pinned them to her uniform, with Charlie, her sister Susan's family, and Charlie's parents looking on. They then all headed to the Thayer Hotel, where they were staying, and their celebration reservation at MacArthur's Riverview Restaurant. Amy's dad had made a reservation for a table with a view, and they were not disappointed. Steeped in history, they all settled in to celebrate Amy's graduation. They were surrounded by other families similarly celebrating, which made for a festive atmosphere.

"I'd like to propose a toast," began Amy's dad, who had not worn his uniform on this day, even though it seemed odd for him to be at West Point without it. He had wanted this day to be all about Amy. He stood tall in his navy suit, crisp white shirt, and red power tie, and Amy was proud to call him her father.

"To my daughter, who not only followed in her old man's footsteps, but cleared a path of her own, graduating number two in her class." To Amy, he added, as an aside, "You beat me there, little girl, and look at me now. Just think how far you can go." He turned and faced the others at the table and concluded, "To Second Lieutenant Amy Sweetser!" Everyone at their table replied with a hearty "Cheers" and the champagne began flowing.

After meals were ordered, Charlie's dad stood and asked if anyone would mind if he offered a toast as well. Since no one did, he continued, "Amy, you have become the daughter we never had, and we have come to love you. Please know that we, too, are very proud of you on this day." He raised his champagne glass and said, "To Amy!" and another glass of champagne was downed.

Charlie, who was sitting next to Amy, leaned over and told her quietly how proud of her he was and how much he was looking forward to his own graduation the following week. He winked at her as he said it and grinned in a way that led her to believe he was keeping something from her, but when she asked him what was going on, he just smiled and said, "Nothing, Ames. I'm just happy for you and for me and for us. We did it. We beat the odds. We managed to stay together despite being apart so much. I have to say, though, I'm not much of a fan of faraway love. I'm really looking forward to being together now, finally!" Amy smiled as he hugged her, but once he couldn't see her face, a frown replaced her smile.

The following week, after having spent a relaxing few days in Duxbury, Amy drove back to New York, this time to Hamilton, with her parents to attend Charlie's graduation. Not five minutes after checking into the quaint Colgate Inn, a knock on the door interrupted her unpacking, and when she opened the door, expecting it to be her mother who was in the next room, she gasped to see Charlie's face smiling at her from behind a dozen red roses.

"How did you know I just checked in, you stalker?" she asked, laughing, knowing full well that because they had been texting for the past hour, he knew exactly when she arrived.

"I have been lurking on the town green all day," he admitted. "You don't think I'd miss a minute of being with you, do you?" And he whisked her into his arms, moved into the room, shut the door, and kissed her in a single move.

Breathless and laughing, Amy was exhilarated to be with him. They would actually have some time together now—for a little while, anyway.

"Shhhh. My parents are in the next room," Amy cautioned.

"Well, I don't plan on ravaging you at the sacred Colgate Inn, missy," he replied. "What do you take me for anyway? I know better than to attack an Army second lieutenant on home ground. I plan to take you to foreign soil to do that," he added, pulling two airline tickets from his pocket. "My dad decided that we had been apart for far too long, and since you have leave for a couple of weeks, and since I don't report to his firm for my summer internship for a couple of weeks, he bought us tickets as a surprise. We're going to Paris, baby! Dad said we can stay at the firm's apartment—separate bedrooms of course," he added with a wink. "An all-expense paid trip to Paris for you and me for ten days courtesy of ma mère et mon père!"

Speechless, Amy just stood there staring at the tickets.

"Well, I've never known you not to have something to say. I guess you like the idea?" Charlie asked impishly.

"Charlie, this is the best gift anyone has ever given me—us—oh you know what I mean!" she gushed. "Ten days in Paris with you? Wow! My father will kill me, but at least I'll die happy." She collapsed onto the bed in a pile of laughter, pulling Charlie down with her.

"Excuse me, miss, but I will not ravage you here. I told you. Paris. Foreign soil. Military protocol and all." Charlie stood abruptly and saluted Amy as her laughter erupted into hiccups.

Just then there was a rap on the door.

"Amy, are you okay?" It was her father.

Charlie opened the door in a split second, not giving Amy time to recover. As the door opened, Charlie saluted her father, which sent Amy into another fit of laughter. Her father just stood in the doorway looking first at Charlie, an exaggerated "Attention!" in his bearing and a salute sustained, then at Amy lying on the bed covered with a disheveled bouquet of roses, laughing hysterically, and finally at two airline tickets lying on the floor next to the bed.

"Okay, I am totally confused," her father stammered. "I don't mean to interrupt, but what in the world is going on here?"

"Sir, your daughter wanted me to ravage her right here in the good ole US of A. Being a military man yourself, you understand that I cannot do that. So, being a true American, I am planning to take her to foreign soil and ravage her there."

"Charlie!" Amy exclaimed, sobering immediately. "That isn't funny. That's my father you're talking to."

Charlie ignored her and continued, "Sir, I love your daughter with all my heart. I have been loyal and true to her for six years. I have patiently waited to defile her because that's the way she wanted it. I plan to spend the rest of my life with her. As a gentleman, if I want to take her away on a wonderful trip and love her; do you have a problem with that?"

General Sweetser immediately replied, much to Amy's surprise, "Young man, if you have the integrity to be honest and forthright with me, the fortitude to remain loyal to my daughter, and the patriotism to remove her from American soil before the attack, you have my blessing. Carry on." And with that, he saluted Charlie, turned on his heel, and returned to his own room.

"What the hell just happened?" Amy asked Charlie, confused.

"Your father understood my predicament and just gave us his blessing to go away together. Now let's prove that we are worthy of his trust. Pull yourself together, Second Lieutenant, and let's go visit your folks and thank them and explain where we're going and where we'll be staying."

After saying hello to Amy's mom and giving Amy a chance to excitedly tell her folks about Mr. and Mrs. Donnelly's graduation gift, Amy and Charlie excused themselves and went to find his parents to thank them properly. Mr. Donnelly's response was an eye twinkling, "Someone has to give you two a little romance after all you've been through. Now get out of the old people's room and find yourselves someplace to make out." And he pushed them out the door.

After they had left, his wife, Grace, turned to him and kindly said, "You old softie. People think you're so tough, but you're just an old romantic."

"Use the word *old* one more time and you, my dear, will not be the recipient of my romantic notions for the weekend," he said, taking her in his arms and kissing her.

Amy truly enjoyed the ceremony that took place the night before graduation, a traditional procession down the hill by candlelight. The entire graduating class started at the top of the hill where classes are held and marched to the bottom of the hill where they had begun their journey four years before, arriving on campus for the first time. They circled the pond, each holding a lit candle, and at the signal, threw their candles into the pond, extinguishing their college careers and moving on to the next phase of their lives. Four years earlier, they had lit their candles there and marched up the hill to the academic quad, signifying the beginning of their college education.

Hmmm, Amy thought, *the Army isn't the only place steeped in tradition.*

The following day, they all attended Charlie's graduation, proud that he had graduated from Colgate, pleased to watch him collect his diploma. Following the graduation, they gathered at The Brewster Inn. As everyone chatted, Amy realized something she hadn't thought of when Charlie first showed her the tickets to Paris. Their flight actually left the next day—from Syracuse.

She leaned toward Charlie and whispered, "I don't have clothes with me, Charlie. I'm not ready to go to Paris."

"Well, dear," said her mother, who never missed a trick, her eyes twinkling conspiratorially, "actually you are. You see, Charlie's father and mother asked us what we thought about the idea before giving the tickets to you two. I packed you a suitcase and brought it with us. You will find an envelope tucked into the bag with enough cash to buy a few new duds, and to treat yourselves to fine dining and entertainment while you're there. That is our gift to you both. So you see, you two aren't the only ones who can keep secrets."

Everyone erupted into laughter as confused expressions flashed from Charlie to Amy's dad, from Amy to Charlie, from Amy to her mom, and between Amy and Charlie.

"Sometimes we parents need to have a little fun too, Son," Mr. Donnelly said. "Now I would like to propose a toast to Charlie. He stood and raised his glass. "Congratulations, Son. You have made your mother and me very proud. You have taken the best Colgate had to offer you and now will, I am sure, do the same at Harvard Law. As you follow in your old dad's footsteps (he grinned at his wife as he said *old*), I only hope that you enjoy the law as much as I have." With that, he tipped his glass, first in Charlie's and then in Amy's direction, and emptied the flute.

"I, too, have a toast I would like to make, if no one minds," began Amy's dad, standing at the other end of the table. "First to Charlie: congratulations on a great achievement. Not only have you done your family proud, but you have achieved what few do. By studying hard and earning high marks here at Colgate, you have earned acceptance to Harvard Law. In just three short years, you will be a graduate of Harvard Law School and will take your place forever as one of its illustrious alumni."

After a tip of his glass to Charlie, he turned to Amy. "And to my baby girl, you have made me the proudest father in the country. I often wondered if I was doing a disservice to you dragging you all around the world from base to base as I was reassigned. I now know in my heart that not only was I not making your life impossible, but I was providing an example you would choose to follow. I salute you, my daughter, with pride and humility. Go with God." He saluted Amy as she stood to return the salute, and everyone in the restaurant applauded although they knew not why. It was simply a sight to behold, and they were sure that something wonderful had transpired.

"Amy, her father continued, "as you begin your first post at Bethesda in a few weeks, remember that you are first a citizen of the United States, but always a beloved and respected daughter of two very proud parents."

In all of the confusion, somehow Amy's first post had not been mentioned before, and Charlie looked dumbfounded.

Maryland? he mouthed silently, to which Amy barely perceptibly nodded. Out loud, he said, "Well, it looks like here we go again," a smile on his face, but irritation just below the surface.

Charlie stood. "Well, even though this assignment has just come as a big surprise to me," Charlie began, "I have a little surprise of my own tonight." Charlie reached into his pocket, slipped out of his chair, and bent down on one knee next to Amy. Taking a diamond solitaire out of a blue Tiffany box, he looked deeply into Amy's eyes and said, "Amy Sweetser, I have loved you since the moment I first saw you at Duxbury High School when you were the new kid junior year. I have loved your emerald eyes flashing at me in happiness and anger. I have loved your auburn hair blowing in the breeze as we sailed. I have loved your competitive spirit, your sense of humor, your kindness, and your loyalty. I have loved your devotion to country and steadfast knowledge that whatever obstacles life puts in our way we will be fine because we love each other. Amy Sweetser, in the presence of our families, will you please honor me by agreeing to be my wife, wherever that agreement may take us and through whatever obstacles lie ahead?"

By this time, the entire restaurant was listening—even the waitstaff, who had stopped serving so that the only sound anyone could hear was the Strauss waltz emanating softly from overhead speakers.

Without more than a second's hesitation, Amy smiled at Charlie, and said, "You big goof. Of course, I will. I can't imagine a life without you." Charlie slipped the ring on her finger and everyone erupted in applause. Several of Charlie's fraternity brothers were dining in the restaurant with their families because they knew what was about to happen, and they came over to congratulate him and to kiss Amy. Her parents were on their feet hugging her and slapping Charlie on the back, as were Charlie's parents. Her sister, Susan, held Amy's ring hand aloft and declared her ring to be the prettiest one she had ever seen. Bethesda had been forgotten. Love was in the air. The only hesitation was in Amy's mother's eyes. Did Charlie realize what he was getting himself into marrying career Army? He was not the June Cleaver type. But to Charlie, she merely said, "Congratulations, Son. Welcome to the family."

The Paris Trip

During the flight to Paris, Charlie slept but Amy sat fully awake and lost in her reverie. The Paris trip now made total sense. She was the only one who hadn't understood exactly what it was—an engagement present. No wonder her father had not objected more. She had wondered about that. Now that she was engaged to be Lieutenant Mrs. Charles Henry Donnelly, II, it was okay with him for her to travel to Paris with Charlie. No wonder Charlie had dared to "tell" her father that they were going away. No wonder her father had taken the news so well. She looked down at her hand. What a beautiful ring. Several tiny diamonds formed a square around a perfect one-carat solitaire, all resting in a platinum setting. It was perfect. Amy thought about all of the years she had known Charlie and wondered about the years to come. How would they reconcile her postings with his legal career? As she began thinking about the logistics of a life together, though, she finally dozed off and awoke to see Charlie gazing lovingly at her from his first-class seat next to her.

Although Amy had lived in many places, she had never been to Paris and was excited to be there for the first time with her true love. After all, Paris is for lovers. As the car his father had arranged sped them through the streets to their apartment, she mentally recorded everything she saw through the tinted windows. Hand in hand they sat, amazed at their good fortune and excited about the days ahead.

Having been deposited at their apartment, their luggage set on racks in the master bedroom, Charlie and Amy stood in the living room and looked first out the windows at the spectacular view and then at each other. Not knowing whether to laugh or jump her right there, Charlie chose a more romantic route. He strolled across the room to the bar, popped the cork of a bottle of champagne he found there, poured two glasses of the bubbly, and returned to her side where he handed one to her and raised his in a toast. "Amy Sweetser, you are about to make me the happiest man in the world. We have waited a long time for this, and I can hardly wait another second." With that, he took a long drink of champagne, turned to her, and wrapped his arms around her, still holding his glass. He began swaying back and forth, dancing to unheard music and moving them slowly toward the bedroom all the while.

"Hold on there, buddy," Amy replied as they crossed into the bedroom. "I have been waiting a long time for this, too, and I have something special planned. With that, she slipped out of his arms and crossed to her suitcase, opened it with her back to him, took something out, tucking it into her sweater, and crossed to the bathroom. "I'll be right out. In the meantime, lover boy, why don't you get comfortable?"

Five minutes later, as Charlie eagerly sat on the side of the four-poster bed in his boxers, Amy opened the door just a crack and stuck out a high-heeled foot, followed by a bare leg. Charlie stared at a side of her he had never seen. She opened the door ever so slowly, emerging one body part at a time until she was standing before him in black lacy lingerie, her long hair hanging loose around her bare shoulders, holding out her arms to him. On the way to the airport, Amy had insisted that Charlie stop at a local mall where she dashed in and returned with a Cheshire Cat smile on her face but explained nothing. Now he knew what she had purchased.

Excited by this sexy entrance, Charlie jumped up from the bed and crossed to her in three long strides, picking her up in his strong arms and carrying her to the bed where he gently deposited her on mounds of pillows.

"Oh, Amy," he moaned. "You are so beautiful. You're sure you want to do this?" Amy nodded silently, smiling seductively up at him. Wrapping her arms around his shoulders, she pulled him close and released herself into the moment.

The following morning, Amy awoke early and lay watching Charlie sleep. Would she have her happily ever after? How could she bear to be away from this man as she moved from post to post? How could they create a life when he was in Boston and she was not? She couldn't imagine being away from him for a moment, let alone weeks at a time. The past four years had been difficult, but she'd been so busy with so little free time to think that she had convinced herself that as soon as college was over, they would be together. Now she wondered if she had been kidding herself. She forced those thoughts out of her head, though, because she was in Paris with the man she loved, and she was not going to spoil a minute of their vacation.

She quietly slipped out of bed, showered, washed her hair, and dressed. Then she went out to grab cups of coffee, small baguettes, a wedge of cheese, and bunches of grapes, and returned before Charlie was even stirring for the day. Being at West Point had instilled a get-up-and-go attitude toward life, and she hated to waste a single minute of the day—especially here in Paris. As she was sipping her coffee at the bistro table on their balcony, the sun making its appearance and teasing her bare shoulders and toes, Charlie joined her, sleep still in his eyes.

"Good morning, beautiful," he crooned, kissing her neck and pulling her close. "How did you sleep?" Not belying her growing trepidation, she smiled and told him that she'd slept like a baby in his arms. It was true. She just didn't mention her fears about their future.

"You already got my breakfast? Thank you, little lady. It's nice to see that you plan to take care of your man." He grinned as he drawled this, and continued, "And I'm glad to see that you're barefoot. We're halfway there."

Amy tossed a baguette at him as he sat down across from her. "I hope that doesn't mean that you expect me to be barefoot and pregnant," she said.

"But of course I do, Charlie replied, grinning from ear to ear. "I think we'll start with a boy and then a girl and then another boy and then a...."

"Whoa, stud," Amy exclaimed in mock horror. "You just go get ready for the day," she ordered Charlie. "I have lots of plans."

Standing at attention and saluting her, Charlie practically shouted, "Ma'am, yes, ma'am" and turned on his heel, heading for the shower, chomping on his baguette, a smile growing as he went, thinking of the family they would have.

Twenty minutes later, an impatient Amy opened the door a crack and called, "Hey you slowpoke, are you ever coming out of there? We have places to go, people to see, things to do." She had barely finished her last syllable when the door opened and out came the man she loved with all her heart. Dressed in a white polo shirt and khakis, Cole Hahn loafers leading the way, Charlie strode out, popping on his aviators. As though she were seeing him for the first time, Amy realized that their four years apart had turned Charlie into a man—a gorgeous, muscular, blond Adonis. Could he really be in love with her?

Seeing her slipping into her thoughts again, Charlie joked, "Hey, gorgeous. Are you coming or what? Do I have to wait all day for you?"

Amy flew at him, arms flailing. She kissed him, tossed her bag over her shoulder, knocking down the strap of her sundress, slid her sunglasses from her hair onto her nose, slipped into a pair of flats, and led the way out of the apartment into warm, sunny, romantic Paris.

For the next ten days, Amy and Charlie were totally carefree and answered to no one but themselves for the first time in their young lives. They strolled and shopped, toured museums, sipped wine in small neighborhood cafes, and floated on the Seine on tour boats as though they were the only ones aboard. They ate when they were hungry, slept when they were tired, and drank when they were thirsty. They walked for miles each day and loved being in love in a city for lovers, falling into each other's arms each night. Several times a day someone noticed Amy's engagement ring, and their comments needed no translation. Strangers hugged her and shook Charlie's hand, and the young couple reveled in their happiness.

Soon, though, their ten days in heaven were up, and they had to return to face the realities of their life. On the airplane back to the States, Charlie leaned toward Amy and asked, "So, Ames, how are we going to work this? I'll be in Boston and you'll be in Maryland. You'll presumably have a busy work schedule, especially since this is your first assignment and all, and I'll have a killer course load and tons of work to do. Dad says that they really try, in his words, 'to separate the wheat from the chaff' during the first year. Although I'm luckier than most because I know I have a spot in his firm, I can't embarrass him by not doing well. That means that I can't count on being able to visit every weekend. Are you up for this?"

After thinking for only a minute, Amy said with assurance, "Charlie, we've proved during the past four years that we can endure anything. We will always be *we*, even if we're not in the same place at the same time. You concentrate on doing well, and I'll concentrate on doing well, and with any luck we'll be able to work it out after this. I'm sure your dad would assign you to the Washington office after you pass the bar, or maybe I'll be able to finagle an assignment in Boston or Newport. Let's just work hard during the next three years and make it work."

Yawning, Amy rested her head on Charlie's shoulder and slept soundly for the remainder of the trip across the Atlantic while Charlie, not usually one to worry about anything, sat thinking about everything that could go wrong and missing her already.

The Summer in DC

When they returned to Logan, all four parents were waiting for them. Charlie's father was the first to speak. "Son, I have a big surprise for you. There is no reason why you can't complete your internship at the DC office. It's all arranged." Everyone erupted in conversation at once. Amy and Charlie just thought how lucky they were to have parents who would help them to make things work. At least they would have one more summer before beginning the long-distance thing again.

Amy and Charlie spent a couple of days in Duxbury and then headed for Maryland. Even though she was single and would be working as well as studying online for her master's degree in psychology, she decided not to live in bachelor's quarters. The housing office had found her a nice one-bedroom apartment not too far from the hospital. The housing allowance she received covered it, and it would give her a quiet place to study. Charlie, on the other hand, would live in a beautiful one-bedroom in Georgetown, one of his father's firm's corporate apartments.

The drive to Maryland was filled with excitement as both Charlie and Amy were eager to start their adult lives. Amy would be working as a research assistant, focusing on identifying protein markers of brain injury. She looked forward to the work, knowing it would help in promoting psychological resilience in the troops. She would be working alongside some of the finest minds in medicine. One day she hoped to put this time to use as a psychologist specializing in post-traumatic stress disorder. Charlie, on the other hand, was going to be working long hours as an intern, researching, drafting, gaining a better understanding of what it meant to be a lawyer.

Their summer flew by with work during the weeks and weekends spent exploring DC. They often spent long, leisurely mornings at

Charlie's apartment. Amy and Charlie fell into a pattern of living in their own places during the week to be close to where they worked, but every Friday night, Charlie would be parked at the gates waiting for Amy. She would get a buddy to drop her off in a Jeep and go running to Charlie.

Many weekends Charlie had to work most of Saturday. After all, he didn't want to take too much advantage of being the boss's son. During that time, Amy would stay at his apartment studying. Sometimes, though, he would take advantage of the fact that he *was* the boss's son, and he and Amy would have the whole weekend to spend together. One of her favorite things to do was to go to the Mall, which in Washington, DC, doesn't mean shopping. They would stroll along the walkways between the Congressional buildings and the Washington Monument, exploring the various Smithsonian museums at length. Charlie's favorite was the Museum of American History, but Amy's was the Air and Space Museum. She just loved imagining what the great explorers must have felt like to fly for the first time or to venture out into space. The fact that her dad had actually introduced her to a couple of the astronauts made the museum come alive for her.

Saturday nights, Amy and Charlie would explore Georgetown, trying out various restaurants and bars, meeting other young people, and having the time of their lives.

Soon, however, it was time for Charlie to return to Boston to begin law school and for Amy to begin her journey to becoming a psychologist. At least they now knew that they would have their summers in DC, since Charlie would intern at his father's firm there each summer until graduation. But leaving was hard.

The Post-Grad Years

Charlie's first day of law school found him sitting in a class next to a young woman who looked remarkably like Amy. As he noticed her, he thought how nice it would be if it were Amy sitting there, going through this experience together. He knew that never could be, but he daydreamed anyway.

After class, the young woman tapped him on his arm as he was getting up to leave. She introduced herself as Julia and asked if he had a study group yet for the class. When he told her he did not, she invited him to join hers. She and two other students had already agreed that they would study together and share notes, and they were looking for a fourth. Charlie felt a shiver go down his spine, feeling as though he was cheating on Amy by spending time with this doppelganger, but he hesitantly agreed since he needed a study group.

Charlie was oblivious to Julia's motives in inviting him to join the group, and he continued to ignore her flirting and longing glances as he told everyone about the love of his life who was working in Maryland. Once everyone (including Julia) realized that he was absolutely taken, they all continued as good friends.

For the next three years, both Charlie and Amy earned the respect and admiration of those in charge of their lives. Amy's superiors recommended her for a promotion to first lieutenant after the obligatory eighteen months, and Charlie was named editor of the *Harvard Law Review* in his third year, a prestigious honor.

Somehow, Amy managed to work full time and take online classes toward her master's degree in behavioral psychology. She and Charlie were determined to have it all, and they knew that these would be the toughest years.

They both racked up the miles on Amtrak as they trekked between Boston and Bethesda for three years, studying along the way, but finally they could see the light at the end of the tunnel—again. Charlie's father had agreed to take him on in the Washington, DC, office permanently, providing he passed the bar exam, and Amy and Charlie would be able to finally be together full time.

At the beginning of Charlie's last year of law school and Amy's last year of graduate school, Charlie and Amy set the date for their wedding. They would be married on June 13th, just a few days after Charlie's graduation. When they announced the date to their parents, Charlie's mother offered their summer place on the coast of Maine. Having visited this picture-perfect spot on numerous occasions over the years, Amy loved the idea immediately; however, she did not want to hurt her mother's feelings by accepting without first talking it over with her. So she politely asked Mrs. Donnelly if she could let her know soon and went home to talk it over with her mom.

At first, her mother dismissed the suggestion, saying that it was the bride's family's responsibility to host the wedding. Tradition-bound as her family was, Amy had known this would be her reaction. Amy pointed out, though, that her mother had already planned and executed the perfect wedding for Amy's older sister, Susan.

"Mom, you've already had the wedding of your dreams for Susan. Would it be okay if this time around it was the wedding of my dreams for me? The first time I visited Charlie's Maine house I actually cried because it was so beautiful. I can't imagine a more perfect location for a June wedding."

How could her mother refuse that heartfelt plea? Even though she had not really been able to host Susan's wedding since it had been held on a college campus, three hours from Duxbury, how could she refuse Amy's wishes? Of course it was okay with her. Amy hugged her, told her how much she loved her and that she would need her help a lot during the coming year because there would be times when she couldn't leave Maryland but would need something done in Boston or Maine. Her mother agreed and said that she would do whatever she could to make sure that Amy and Charlie's day was perfect. The unspoken words, though, were, *Are you sure you know what you're getting yourself into? Are you sure that you and Charlie will be able to handle the military life? He's a child of privilege and doesn't know our ways, no matter how many times you describe them to him.* But these thoughts she kept to herself. She worried endlessly about the daughter she loved with all her heart and the young man who had become like a son to her. She wanted everlasting happiness for them, but she was concerned that a happily ever after might not be in the cards for them.

"Only time will tell," she muttered every time she thought of their future.

The Wedding Plans

The year before the wedding was a blur of train trips, magazines, fittings, discussions with Charlie's mother, her mother, Charlie, her father, Charlie's father, her sister, e-mails, texts, telephone calls, faxes, Skype, and work, work, work. As she was trying to plan her wedding, she was being entrusted with increasing responsibility at her job at the hospital since she now was a full-fledged psychologist working with patients. She had decided to specialize in patients with post-traumatic stress disorder and there were many of them. Everything was coming together to truly test her strength.

Amy and Charlie had less time to simply be CharlieandAmy as their every minute together was spent creating guest lists and table arrangements and choosing cakes and flowers and music. His mother was insistent that it would be the society event of the summer season in Ocean Point, while Amy and Charlie just wanted to get married and get on with their life together. Toward the end of spring, as Amy was sitting on the front porch of their Duxbury home with her mom, her mother said, exasperatedly, "Amy, this is what you bargained for when you agreed to be married at their summer place in Maine. We lost control!"

Realizing that the control issue was really where the problems all stemmed from, Amy made a command decision. The next day, at a planning luncheon attended by her bridesmaids, sister, mother, and mother-in-law to be, held at the Sun Tavern in Duxbury, she picked up her white linen napkin and waved it in the air. She said quietly with a smile, "I surrender." Looking from face to startled face, she continued, "From this moment on, my mom is in charge of every decision. You tell me when to show up, and I'll be there. For the next month, Charlie and I are going to enjoy our time together, and it will be up to all of you to make that happen. That is the wedding gift I want from you. So long as Charlie is standing at the altar and I am walking down an aisle of some sort toward him and at the end we are husband and wife, I don't care about anything else."

Every face wore a shocked expression. Following a couple of minutes of stunned silence, she was bombarded with questions:

"But how many rows should be reserved for your family?"

"When should the orchestra play?"

"Do you want a receiving line?"

"What color should the waitstaff wear?"

"We can't seat Uncle Freddy with Aunt Jane. They don't get along."

"In which papers should the announcement be placed?"

"If the florist can't get yellow roses, do you want another yellow flower or another color roses?"

"Should the gardeners come the day before or do you want them to come a few days before?"

"What color tents do you want?"

"Do you mind if the chairs are white or black?"

The questions came tumbling out of everyone's mouths simultaneously, but Amy just smiled. "You're not listening to me," she said quietly. "I'm serious. I really don't care anymore about the details. I thought I did, but I don't. Charlie and I are no longer in charge. I don't care if we show up at the house in Maine on our wedding day, let everyone stand while we say our vows with a backdrop of the bay, dance in our bare feet on the grass to the playlists on our iPods played over the outdoor speakers, and eat pizza. We would be very happy." After a dramatic pause, she added, "I am deadly serious."

And with that, Amy stood, gave everyone a peck on the cheek as she moved around the table, thanked them profusely for coming to the luncheon, and left, giggling to herself as she walked out the door. She desperately wanted to look back, but she knew that she couldn't because she would laugh at their astonished faces. Charlie was sitting in his Jeep in the parking lot reading a book as she approached, and she tumbled into the passenger seat overcome with laughter.

"Whoa! I didn't expect you for a while yet," he said as he kissed her. "What happened? Did you tell them to forget the wedding, that we're going to elope?"

"Nope. I told them that you and I were finished with spending what precious little free time we have together planning this wedding. I told them that I would be perfectly happy to email our friends with invitations, walk barefoot across the grass, say our vows on the cliff with the ocean behind us, dance to our iPod music, and order in pizza." As she finished, she grinned mischievously and then threw her head back and laughed until she could barely breathe.

"You didn't!" Charlie exclaimed, laughing, knowing that if she said she did, then she did. "Wow! I would love to have seen the look on my mother's face!" And he, too, threw his head back and laughed until tears came to his eyes. "Let's get out of here before they come out with pitchforks and chase us down," he said, pressing the accelerator and speeding to the beach for a quiet afternoon.

The Harvard Graduation

Sitting proudly in the audience, Amy beamed as Charlie accepted his diploma and became a graduate of Harvard Law School. As he strolled across the stage, he looked out, found Amy, and winked. She heard several women in the crowd audibly gasp, as if they thought he was winking at them, which made her laugh, knowing that he was all hers. At the graduation celebratory dinner that night, to which Amy's parents, sister, and brother-in-law had also been invited, the conversation threatened to turn to the upcoming wedding. Each time the subject was broached, however, Amy and Charlie had agreed before the dinner to break in and say, "This is Charlie's day. No wedding talk."

If Amy said it, usually whoever had transgressed would stop immediately and turn to Charlie with some glowing compliment about his achievements. If Charlie said it, though, whoever had committed the faux pas would laugh hysterically, probably because of the pouty look that accompanied the seemingly self-centered comment.

Everyone drove back to Duxbury following dinner and gathered around the Donnellys' pool. Charlie and Amy excused themselves after a little while, though, and drove to Amy's, where they sat on the porch swing, legs entwined, Amy leaning on Charlie's shoulder as they slowly rocked back and forth.

As they heard Amy's folks' car coming up the driveway through the trees, Frank Sinatra crooning out the open windows that he would do it his way, the spell was broken. Amy whispered to Charlie, "Well sir, your day is officially over. Starting tomorrow morning, we are into our countdown to W-Day."

Charlie stood and said, "Ma'am, yes, ma'am," clicked his heels, saluted her, turned and marched away, stopping at the bottom of the porch stairs to turn back and say, "Soon you'll be Mrs. Charles Donnelly."

Amy, not missing a beat, replied, "That's First Lieutenant Mrs. Charles Donnelly, the Second, to you, sir," and she saluted and laughed as Charlie shrugged his shoulders and jogged to his Jeep, throwing out a quick hello and good-bye to her parents as he left.

Amy rose and went into the house, spying an envelope sitting on the foyer table addressed to her. She opened it, read its contents, frowned, and went upstairs to bed, clutching it in her fist. It promised to be a long, sleepless night.

The Wedding

The wedding day dawned sunny and warm, a perfect June day in Maine. With the gardens resplendent with decades-old azaleas and fragrant wisteria, a white rose-covered arch was positioned on the edge of the cliff with the ocean glimmering behind. White chairs had been set up on the sprawling green lawns in neat, tidy, military rows—two hundred fifty in all—and a long, white, silk carpet had been placed over the closely cropped lawn, defining an aisle for the wedding party to walk down. On the side lawn, a shining white canopy had been erected under which glimmering white tables and chairs sat proudly under their yellow cloths and yellow-and-white floral arrangements. A large teak dance floor waited patiently in the center of it all, positioned in front of the silent risers where the ten-piece orchestra would later fill the air with music.

Amy was using the guest suite by the gardens as her dressing room. As her mom, bridesmaids, and two little nieces fluttered around making sure everyone was ready, there was a tap on the door. When the door opened, Amy's father stood there, resplendent in his Army dress uniform, hat in hand, a radiant smile on his face.

"Just let me look at all of you for a minute," he said. "What a room full of beauties!" He beamed proudly, knowing then and there that he was a lucky man to have such a bevy of females looking up at him with love and admiration in their eyes. He cleared his throat and managed, "They tell me it's time."

Amy's mother gave her a kiss, told her how beautiful she was, and slid out the door, brushing a kiss on her handsome husband on her way out. Then each of Amy's bridesmaids giggled, told her what a beautiful bride she was, and slipped out of the room. Left with his two daughters and his two adorable granddaughters, George got a little choked up.

He croaked, What a lucky man I am. What a blessed life I've led. How beautiful you all are." He then composed himself and added gruffly, "Susan, shouldn't you and the girls get out there and make sure everything is ready? You've had your day. This is Amy's."

Susan mock saluted him, squeezed her sister's arm, and said softly, "Enjoy it, Ames. Dad's right. It *is* your day." And she ushered her little chicks out the door in front of her, their yellow-and-white chiffon dresses floating around them.

Amy looked at her father and tried not to cry. All she said was, "Daddy, I didn't tell Charlie. Please tell me it will all work out."

To his youngest daughter, her father said simply, "It will, honey. It will. After all, Charlie is your Noah." Amy smiled at that. Ever since her mom had made him watch *The Notebook* with her, he had referred to Charlie as Amy's Noah. No matter what took them apart, they always found each other again. He reached out his arm, cradled Amy's in it, and they proceeded to the garden doors. He had reassured his baby girl that everything would work out for her, but in his heart he wasn't so sure.

The wedding ceremony was an elegant combination of New England tradition and military pomp. The bridesmaids drifted down the aisle in bright-yellow silk tea length dresses, escorted by Charlie's buddies in black tuxedos. Charlie's fraternity brother, who had become over the past few years like a real brother to him, stood by Charlie's side under the yellow and white rose arbor while Charlie's cousin's eight-year-old son exuded a solemn air no one had ever seen in him, wearing a miniature black tuxedo and carrying the rings tied to a small white pillow with white satin ribbons. Amy's five- and seven-year-old nieces pranced along in miniature tea length yellow-and-white floral dresses with layers and layers of chiffon, dropping yellow and white rose petals from dainty white baskets. Susan followed her daughters, dressed in a yellow tea length dress with matching silk Bolero jacket. Then came Amy and her father. As the string quartet played Mendelssohn's "Wedding March," they walked slowly down the aisle,

Amy in an elegantly tailored, simple white silk sleeveless dress that trailed slightly behind her. A shoulder-length veil erupted from a tiny pearl-covered tiara that held volumes of auburn hair in check. She wore wrist-length white gloves and carried dozens of white sweetheart roses in her bouquet, yellow and white ribbons wound through with strings of pearls wrapped around their stems. As she walked calmly on her father's arm to meet her handsome Charlie in his perfectly fitted bespoke black tuxedo, she beamed at him and their smiling gazes never parted. Charlie silently said, *I love you* as she approached, and melted the hearts of everyone who noticed. It was easy to feel the love that flowed between the two of them. Most of those in attendance knew of their long road to the altar and all of the trials their relationship had endured. This was certainly a marriage that would last forever.

Following the short ceremony, the new husband and wife proceeded through an honor guard of swords held high. Amy's friends from the Academy had offered to add a West Point touch to her otherwise civilian wedding.

Then the party began. The tuxedoed orchestra members took their seats and played under the tent, bubbly flowed from several champagne fountains as well as iced bottles at each table, and black-jacketed waiters wearing bright yellow ties served a sumptuous feast of lobster tails and sirloin. As darkness fell, twinkling white lights erupted from shrubbery and trees to create a fairy tale scene. Amy and Charlie were unabashedly in love, and everyone in attendance felt that love in their own hearts on this day.

As the orchestra struck up the music for the bridal dance, to everyone's surprise Amy and Charlie had made an odd choice, but one with deep meaning for them: "Sitting on the Dock of the Bay." It had been a favorite dream of theirs for years to have time to simply sit on the dock with nothing to do and nowhere to go, just watching the tide come in and go back out again, close together in each other's arms like they did during that idyllic summer before senior year of high school. Maybe someday....

The white, six-layered wedding cake stood tall in front of the head table, under the shimmering, twinkling tent, its yellow sugary roses tempting in their perfection. Rather than a traditional plastic bride and groom, sitting atop the cake was a three-dimensional representation of Amy and Charlie in their senior prom attire. Amy's mom had found a company online that would create three-dimensional characters from a photo. As they stood behind the cake for the photographer, one couldn't help noticing that the happiness they felt then was magnified now after years of enforced intermittent separation. They were older, more mature, and, although those who knew them then wouldn't have thought it possible, even more in love.

The Honeymoon

Around midnight, Amy and Charlie disappeared, only to reappear to their guests' surprise wearing khaki shorts and T-shirts, Bass Weejuns bedecking their feet. Amy carried her bouquet, and they mounted the risers where the orchestra still sat. Grabbing a microphone, Charlie thanked everyone for coming and then announced that Amy was going to toss her bouquet and then they would be leaving for their honeymoon—a well-kept secret destination. Amy turned her back to the crowd of young women gathered on the dance floor, raised her bouquet over her head, and threw it with such force that it sailed over the heads of all of the unmarried women waiting for it. The elder flower girl scampered after it and declared that the ring bearer now had to marry her. She ran to find him. As everyone laughed, Amy and Charlie found their parents in the crowd, hugged and kissed them, and ran off across the lawn disappearing down over the cliff.

Hurrying down the stairs to the dock, they paused for a moment to listen to the music and laughter from the ongoing party above. A few people had followed them to the top of the stairs and looked down at them now, laughing and joking with them.

"It was perfect, wasn't it?" Amy purred.

"It was perfect, and you are perfect, First Lieutenant Mrs. Charles Donnelly, the Second," Charlie replied. And they finished their descent to the dock.

Waiting for them was Charlie's dad's yacht, fully stocked. The Donnellys' gift was to loan them the yacht for their honeymoon. Their plan was to sail along the coast for a couple of weeks. Amy felt just like Grace Kelly in *High Society*, one of her favorite childhood movies. As Charlie started up the motor to cruise out of the bay before they anchored for the night on the other side of the island, she threw off the lines. Nestled next to him as he maneuvered them out of the bay across the glistening water, the full moon creating a path for them to follow, she found herself softly singing "True Love."

> "Suntanned, windblown
> Honeymooners at last alone
> Feeling far above par
> Oh, how lucky we are.
> While I give to you and you give to me,
> True love, true love.
> So on and on it'll always be,
> True love, true love.
> For you and I
> Have a guardian angel on high,
> With nothin' to do.
> But to give to you and to give to me,
> Love forever true."

As Amy sang the last line, she snuggled deeper into Charlie, content and happy in his arms.

For the next two weeks, Charlie and Amy sailed leisurely up the coast, ducking into harbors and bays, inlets and coves along the way. They anchored and visited little towns and lay on the deck in the sun reading. They talked with locals who loved their story, and they bought lobsters directly from lobstermen and boiled them on deserted beaches on their camp stove. They ate in little cafes and spent hours poring through general stores. They sailed and motored their way in and out of dozens of harbors, met wonderfully simple, honest folks along the way, and never wanted to return to civilization. They went skinny-dipping in the moonlight after daring each other to brave the icy waters of mid-June Maine and explored uninhabited islands. Amy's favorite part of all, though, was making love under the stars, cuddled under their Hudson Bay blanket, waves gently lapping the sides of the boat. Each night she fell asleep, happy and content, rocked by the sea in Charlie's arms.

On the last night of their honeymoon, as Amy and Charlie were lying on a cushioned banquette, the boat gently rocking under a full moon, Amy tentatively and tearfully told him that she had received a new commission to Germany. He just stared at her in disbelief. Then he got up and went to the bow, sitting with his legs dangling over the sides, head resting on folded arms on the chrome rails. His life bobbed in front of him as he stared across the black water, focusing now and then on a twinkling star dancing on the surface.

Charlie had thought that maybe he could persuade Amy during their honeymoon to give up her military career once her commitment to the Army was over. She really only owed West Point eight years of her life following graduation, five of them in active duty. She had already served three of them. He was sure that her father could arrange for her to serve the remaining years near Charlie. He had waited until they were almost back to shore at the end of their sail to talk to her about it, but Amy had beaten him to the punch with her news. So much for his plans, he thought.

Amy remained in the stern, sobbing quietly, knowing that she should have told Charlie her news when she had received the letter. But she didn't want to spoil the wedding. Just because she had come to terms long ago with the idea that their marriage would have long absences, she knew that Charlie had not. He still thought a miracle would arrive, telling her that she could be stationed in Boston or at least Washington. At any rate, she knew that he was positive that his father's connections or hers would spare them a life of separation. But Germany!

After a while, she slowly arose and slipped up behind Charlie, climbing into his lap on the bow, leaning back against his strong body, and staring out across the dark, glistening water. She waited for his tanned tennis arms to slip around her, and when they didn't, she was scared. His hands stayed gripping the rails tightly, knuckles turning white. When she couldn't stand the silence any longer, she turned to face him, wrapping her legs around his body and leaning back against the rail. As she slowly looked up into his usually strong face, she saw tears escaping from his sad blue eyes.

With a catch in his voice, Charlie said, "It's not going to work, is it?" Even though she had worried that he might utter those horrible words, hearing them was more than she could bear. He was her one true love, the love of her life, and had been since she had discovered him in high school. Ever since she was sixteen years old, she'd only had eyes for him. Other boys paled by comparison. She'd cheered him on as he threw passes for touchdown after touchdown and got caught up in the frenzy as he led their team to a state championship on the basketball court. All of the other girls had tried to get his attention, but he'd only had eyes for her. All through the college years, she had persevered, knowing that Charlie was hers and that someday they would be together forever. When they burned up the rails between Maryland and Boston during law school, she reassured herself that it was okay because when he graduated they would be together in DC. And now here they sat, newly married, their dream fulfilled, and she was losing him.

"We can make it work," she insisted, as tears trickled down her tanned cheeks.

He reached over at that point and said, calmly and pragmatically, "Don't cry, honey. We've made it through a lot, but how can we make this work? I love you with all my heart, but we've already been apart more than we've been together for the past seven years. How can we sustain a marriage with you in Germany and me in Boston? If I tried to follow you to Germany, I would have no career. I can't practice law there. And you have no choice but to go. The Army isn't going to accept that you want to be here with your husband. We knew this would happen someday and just tried to bury our heads in the sand."

Then Charlie thought he saw a glimmer of hope. He tried one more tack. "Amy, your dad could probably change your assignment if you asked him. He has a lot of clout and would surely use it to help us out of this predicament." As he was saying the words, Charlie knew the answer. Amy was too strong and too proud to ask her father to do such a thing. Favors were against military protocol, though Charlie knew that they happened all the time.

Amy sadly shook her head, explaining that she could not ask him to do such a thing. He had a distinguished career during which time he had never sought favor or used his position for his own personal gain. How could she ask him to besmirch his reputation for her?

Amy shook her head, saying simply, "I can't ask him, Charlie." Those five words seemed to seal their fate.

That night, their last on the boat, they made love under the stars, passionately and hungrily, knowing in their hearts that it might be their last time together. The sail back to his folks' place the following morning was a sad one. They were uncharacteristically somber. As they docked, Charlie's dad came bounding down the stairs and out on the dock to meet them, a smile spread across his face. Seeing their demeanor, he stopped short, waiting to discover what could possibly have caused such defeated expressions on their faces after a honeymoon spent aboard the yacht.

As they disembarked, Amy softly murmured, "Thank you, Charles, for letting us use her. It was a wonderful gift, a time I will remember forever." Breaking into tears, she ran up the dock, up the stairs, and disappeared over the top of the cliff.

Turning to his son, the elder Donnelly gently asked, "What happened, son?"

Seeing the tears well up in his newly married son's eyes was more than he could bear. The father hurried across the dock and embraced his son as he had not done since he was a small boy. Holding him tightly, feeling his son's chest heave as he sobbed openly in his father's arms, the father said, "Son, I'm sure it's nothing we can't fix. All newlyweds have their problems. You'll see. It will be fine. Just give her a little space."

As Charlie slowly pulled away, though, the elder Donnelly knew it would not be okay. He could see real pain in his son's eyes. Not used to being helpless, he felt lost. Not knowing what to do, he proceeded to tie up the boat as Charlie simply stood on the dock sadly looking up at the cliff where Amy had disappeared from sight.

"I'm afraid you can't fix this one, Dad," he said sadly. "No one can. Amy is going to Germany. It's over. I can't do it anymore."

The Parting

Charlie and Amy returned to Charlie's Beacon Hill apartment, and for the next week they talked and cried, held each other, and fought. Charlie accused her of lying to him by not telling him her plans. Amy accused Charlie of not caring about her career. Charlie suggested that he go to Germany with her and Amy refused that option, insisting that he continue his rise in his father's law firm. If he went with her, she knew that he would eventually resent not being able to follow his dream. He told her that she only owed the Army eight years, three of which could be in the reserves. Since she had already spent three in Maryland, she would only have to be in Germany for two years and then she could come home. Amy tried to explain to Charlie that she had chosen the Army as her career and didn't plan to serve only the required five years and then leave to serve out the remaining three in the reserves. They went around and around, and in the end there was no real solution.

At times Amy felt guilty for marrying Charlie, knowing that it probably would not work. She spent many hours alone in the bathroom with the shower running, just crying about their impossible situation. But by the time she'd found out about her assignment to Germany, plans were in full swing, everyone was excitedly talking about the wedding, and she was caught up in the momentum. How could she tell them that all of their planning, enthusiasm, expectations, and money spent were for naught? She had buried her head in the sand and hoped a solution would appear, even though all of her training in psychology told her that she was simply trying to escape reality.

Neither Amy nor Charlie could face the prospect of seeking a divorce. They knew they were meant for each other and no one else. She refused to leave the apartment for the entire week she was there, simply going through the motions of preparing for a life separate from Charlie's after spending so much time planning for their life together. It had all happened too fast. She had difficulty coping as anger and sadness alternated in her being. Aloud, she repeatedly said, "It isn't fair." Finally, the day came when Amy had to leave. Charlie took her luggage to the car and drove her to the airport. Her parents met them there. After a tearful farewell, she and Charlie parted.

Although she could have flown for free on a military transport, her father had arranged for her to fly commercial to Germany. She didn't want the first impression she made on her new colleagues to be as a lovesick newlywed. As the plane rolled down the runway, she was bound for the Landstuhl Regional Medical Center in Landstuhl/ Kirchberg. Charlie sadly drove his Lexus, a law school graduation present from his parents, out of Logan and headed for the South Shore home that was supposed to have been a big surprise for Amy—the home where they would raise a family and live happily ever after. After he discovered that she was leaving, he didn't want to make her feel worse by showing her his big surprise—the Powder Point home he had purchased just for her as a wedding gift.

He had known that it was the home for them the day he saw the "For Sale" sign posted on the lawn. With its white clapboards, green shutters, and sloping lawn, the swing hung from a big old maple tree in the yard, the sparkling blue pool, and the view of children learning to sail in the protected, shallow harbor, he knew it was the perfect place to raise a family. His plan had been to drive Amy there when they docked after their honeymoon. They would take long walks on the beach and moor their very own boat off the little white dock in front of their home. They would raise children who would love the water as much as they did, who would play tennis on the court in their backyard and take the train in to Boston to visit museums and go to shows. They would go for long walks on the beach with their black lab, Spinnaker.

But that plan had been shattered by her news.

Now, Amy sat stiffly at attention on the plane, looking out the window at the blue water and her beloved Boston on her way to another country and a life without Charlie. As the plane made an arcing circle after taking off to the west, she watched the South Shore houses pass by under her. She thought how nice it would be to live in one of them. She looked directly down at a pretty white clapboard house with green shutters and a sloping green lawn, sitting on the edge of the bay, a tennis court on the side lawn and a sparkling blue pool smiling at the bay. A lone figure sitting at the end of the dock made her think of her wedding song and she wished that she and Charlie could be sitting there together. She even imagined what might have been if she had chosen to leave the Army. She might have lived in a house like that one day. She sat in silence, wondering where her life would take her now as the plane gained altitude and the American coast disappeared from view.

The Condition

As the weeks passed, Amy and Charlie wrote to each other, e-mailed each other, and even occasionally texted in the deep of night. They dusted off their Skype accounts again and talked to each other. They tried desperately to share their lives from afar, but soon tired of having to live that way. Even though they had been doing the faraway love thing for years, somehow this was different. She was in another country, on another continent. Both were successful in their chosen careers, and the only thing lacking was each other. How could they have made it through going to different colleges, made it through the three years when Charlie was in law school and she was in Maryland, only to have it all end now? It wasn't fair!

A part of Amy longed for the world her mother had grown up in, a world where the husband developed a career and the wife's career was raising children and creating a loving home. Amy thought about whether she would be content living that kind of life and knew in her heart that she would not. Since she was a little girl, she had dreamed of being in the Army like her dad. Since her first psychology course at West Point, she had known that she would enter the field and try to help vets cope with their lives after service injuries. But, looking down on that pretty house and the solitary figure sitting on the dock by the bay, she had wished that she could feel differently.

In the 1970s, Gloria Steinem convinced women that they could have it all. They could be wives and mothers and have successful careers too. After all, if men could do it, why couldn't women? At this particular moment, Amy hated Gloria Steinem. All she felt was torn in half. Part of her desperately wanted a family with Charlie while part of her desperately wanted a military career. Her problem was that she could not design a world in which both existed together. She resigned herself to the fact that she had to give the Army a shot or she would resent Charlie for stifling a dream. She resigned herself to the fact that although she loved him with all her heart, that love would either endure in Germany or not, and if it didn't, then it really wasn't meant to be. Who knew? Maybe after the two years were up and her required service was over, she would feel differently and would run back to Massachusetts and the man of her dreams to live happily ever after. After all, she could probably get a civilian job as a psychologist. For now, she needed to focus, establish herself as a professional, and serve her country.

While Amy was jetting across the Atlantic, torn by the two parts of herself that could not coexist, Charlie sat on the end of the dock until well after the stars came out. With the first twinkling, he found himself muttering aloud, "Star light, star bright, first star I see tonight, I wish I may I wish I might have the wish I wish tonight," and he wished with all his heart that Amy would return to him.

Charlie regretted not having Amy by his side when he passed the Massachusetts bar. He was sad when he went to court for the first time and won his case, and she was not there to tell. He was lonely each night when he returned to his Boston apartment, wondering what he should do with his Powder Point house as it sat idly waiting for Amy.

Amy was sad that she couldn't tell Charlie the feeling of accomplishment when she talked a vet with PTSD through his torment. She was miserable going back to an empty townhouse every night, and she ate her way through the long, lonely evenings. In fact, her best friends these days were Ben and Jerry. After a few weeks, she started noticing that her uniforms were getting tight and worried that she had better find some new friends. She felt awful and realized that she was actually making herself sick with longing for Charlie. Worried that she would start to lose her ability to function at her job if she kept up like this, she made an appointment with the doctor.

Sitting in the doctor's office following her exam, Amy nervously chewed on her fingernail. When the doctor came in, he sat behind his desk and looked across at Amy.

"Well, Lieutenant," he began, "what do you think is going on with you?"

This question annoyed Amy. If she knew what was wrong, she would fix it herself. She wouldn't need this officious man. Surprised by this uncharacteristically nasty thought, she composed herself and replied, "Well, I was briefly married before I came here… I guess I still am married, actually. Anyway, I know I sound like a silly, emotional female, but I really miss my husband. He's in the States, establishing himself in his father's law firm in Boston, and we agreed that we would end it, but I just can't turn off my feelings for him, can I? I do a good job here, but when I'm all alone, I just miss him so badly it hurts. First, I tried to fill my nights with ice cream, but now I've made myself so sick that I just feel sick all the time. I have little energy and I'm sore all over. I even have started getting physically sick. That's why I'm here." Embarrassed by her lengthy explanation, she added, "I'm sorry. I didn't mean to go on like that. It's really not like me." Much to her surprise, she had to fight back tears.

Suddenly, the doctor, who had appeared cold and professional moments before, smiled a fatherly smile and gently said, "Don't worry about it. I'm not surprised at all. You've been through an emotional few weeks. Add to that your current condition and I'm not at all surprised. I've seen it all before."

Condition? Oh, my God, Amy thought. *I have a condition. Well, he didn't say life-threatening illness or malady or disease. Condition? Does he think I'm crazy? Good grief. I'm a psychologist. I'm not supposed to use the word* crazy. "What 'condition' is that, Doctor Gray?" she asked.

With that same smile, the doctor quietly told her, "Lieutenant, the condition you're in will pass in about seven more months. It's nothing to worry about. Quite the opposite. It's actually exciting. Lieutenant, you are pregnant. Actually, you are approximately eight weeks pregnant.

Pregnant! Alarm bells went off in Amy's head. *But I can't be pregnant. I'm in Germany and I'm an officer and Charlie is in Boston and my mom is in Duxbury and Susan is in Portland.* But as she was denying the fact, and establishing the geographical location of everyone she loved, her heart began to swell. She began to "feel" pregnant. Aloud, she quietly asked, "Are you sure?"

"I am as sure as can be. Actually, your blood test came back a strong positive. You can expect to feel even more sick for the next few weeks, but then it should subside, and I have no reason to believe that you will have anything other than a totally healthy pregnancy."

Amy was suddenly excited but terrified. She politely thanked the doctor, smiled, and walked almost a mile back to her home, blindly opening her door and sinking onto the brown leather couch in her tiny living room. Since she had forgotten to open the drapes this morning, the room was dark, and Amy found the darkness comforting. She lay down on the couch, clutching Charlie's picture, which she had absently picked up on her way through the room, and began to "talk" with him. As she had done for years, she began to compose a mental list of pros and cons:

Pro: This baby would be a constant reminder of Charlie.
Con: This baby would be a constant reminder of Charlie.
Pro: She would not be alone anymore. Someone would need her.
Con: She would have to put the baby in childcare and would not be able to raise it herself. She would need a lot of help.
Pro: She had so much love to give that the child would feel wanted and loved even if it didn't have a father.
Con: She was thousands of miles away from her support system.
Pro: The baby had been lovingly conceived aboard the *Grace* on her honeymoon.
Con: She wouldn't be able to tell Charlie because he would either run to her side, leaving his life and thoughts of his future career behind, or insist that she leave the Army and come back to him.

After hours of mental ping-pong, Amy was exhausted. She glanced at the clock on the wall and was surprised to see that it was eleven already. Starving, she hoisted herself off the couch and padded into her kitchen. Too tired to make anything but too hungry not to, she grabbed some cheese, a bottle of juice, an apple, and one of the boxes of Boston Baked Beans that arrived from her mother the day before and moved to her bedroom. Falling onto the bed, propped up by three pillows, she absently picked up the remote and turned on the television. Nibbling on her "dinner," she flipped through channels, not able to settle on any one of them.

After satisfying her hunger pangs, Amy slipped off into a fitful sleep during which she had a dream.

In her dream, Amy was alone in a large room. There were no windows or doors, and the only furniture was a bed that was bobbing around on waves. On one wall was a photo of Charlie and on the opposite wall was one of her. They were each in their wedding attire but did not look happy. Suddenly, Amy heard a voice. Looking up, she saw a bright light shining across the ceiling and heard a deep voice say, "You know what you must do. No one can make this decision for you. You are a loving, caring human being who has made difficult choices before. You'll make them again. Now make a decision." As the voice stopped speaking, a crib appeared in the room and a beautiful baby boy was lying in the crib smiling up at her. His face looked like Charlie's, and he was reaching up to her. Suddenly, Amy awoke as she heard a loud ringing.

Startled and confused, Amy realized that the sound she heard was her telephone. She ignored it, letting it ring, knowing what she must do. Her career would be hard with a child, but she knew she had to keep this part of Charlie. And she decided not to tell him—yet. There would be plenty of time for that later, once she had figured it all out. She rationalized this decision by telling herself that Charlie had worked too hard to get where he was and was on his way to a happy, successful, uncomplicated life. Somehow, she even convinced herself that he was probably happier without her. Whether it was her hormones doing the persuading or whether she was just taking the easy way out, she was not sure, but she knew that she must not tell Charlie. As the ringing stopped, Charlie's voice came over the speaker of her answering machine.

"Hi, Ames. I know it's the middle of the night there, but I miss you and just wanted to hear your voice. I guess I'll have to settle for your recording. Sleep well, my love. Sweet dreams."

Oh, Charlie, Amy thought. *If you only knew....*

The Top-Secret Project

After getting ready for work the next morning and running through her checklist of what she needed to accomplish that day, Amy shut the door of her small townhouse behind her and turned to walk to her office in the hospital. It was a little less than a mile, and the walk always offered her a chance to think. Today was no different. As she walked, she planned what she would say to her commanding officer. Obviously, she had to tell him that she was pregnant. He'd know soon enough, if he hadn't guessed already, she thought with a smile as she trotted along, glancing at the growing shadow walking along with her.

"Don't you agree?" she jokingly asked her shadow, nervously laughing at her silliness.

As she entered the major's office, a lump formed in her throat. Although she had rehearsed what she would say on her way in, it was going to be awfully difficult to actually speak the words. He stood. She saluted. He told her to be at ease and to take a seat in front of his desk. As she sat, she could feel her skirt tug at her sides, and she had to pull it down over her knees.

"What can I do for you today, Lieutenant Donnelly?" Major Brush asked coolly.

"Well, sir," she began, "it is a personal matter." Amy wasted no time getting to her point. "I believe that I should inform you that I am two months pregnant and that I will be requesting a leave of absence in seven months' time." She could feel the beads of perspiration forming along her hairline and the nape of her neck, and that damnable Irish heritage pushing the pink into her cheeks as she spoke. She had applied extra foundation this morning because she knew what would happen when she got nervous, and the last thing she wanted was for her superior officer to see her blush. She had total control over her emotions—usually—but during the past couple of months, that control had waned.

Major Brush interrupted her silent reverie, asking her if she was okay. Suddenly, the usually severe military man's demeanor had become almost fatherly.

"Don't you worry about a thing, Lieutenant Donnelly. This sort of thing happens all the time. We're the Army. We have a policy for everything." He actually chuckled at his own joke. "You just stop by the corporal's desk on your way out and pick up the appropriate forms," he continued, as he stood to usher her out. "And take care of yourself," he added kindly.

And just like that, in only a couple of minutes, she had jumped the first hurdle of her military pregnancy. *That wasn't so bad*, she thought as she turned to leave. *Not too bad at all.* And with that knowledge, she began to believe that everything would be okay for her and her unborn child.

As she walked home that afternoon, Amy mulled over what she should tell her mother, her sister, her friends back home, her new friends here. In the short time it took her to walk from her office to her front door, she had decided. She would not tell Charlie anything. That decision would stand. He would run to be by her side, and she could not bear the responsibility of his later remorse at leaving behind a successful career in the law. No, he had worked too hard for it to have it ripped from him. Charlie must not know. She waved absently to her next-door neighbor, Beth, who was out on her front lawn, playing ball with her little boy, Zack, and unlocked her front door. Pausing on her front porch, she watched mother and son for a few minutes and then resolutely said to herself, "No, Charlie must not know."

As she was thinking about Charlie, her phone rang. She absently picked it up, and it was, of course, him. They talked with each other occasionally, but this was really bad timing. Totally flustered, Amy stammered something about being really busy. She couldn't talk with him now. She didn't trust herself not to blurt out the fact that she was carrying his child. She held the phone silently. Uncharacteristically, Charlie became immediately annoyed.

"Amy, we haven't talked to each other for days, and now I call you from across the ocean, and you don't even have time to talk with me for a few minutes? I called you last night, and you didn't even pick up the phone. His voice rising in anger, Charlie continued, "Fine, then. If that's the way you want it. I won't call you again. If you want to talk with me, you call. Okay? Until I hear from you, I'll leave you alone since you're so busy. Oh, and by the way, I won a huge case today, in case you're interested. I wanted to share my big news with you, but I guess you're too busy to share good news. Then he sarcastically added, "Are you too busy to say good-bye to me?"

Hormonal tears streaming down her cheeks, Amy spluttered, "No, of course not, Charlie. Congratulations on your case. I can't believe your father let you argue a case so soon. You must be very proud." That was about all she could say before starting to cry again. It was enough, though. Charlie's tone softened. He assumed her tears were because he had gotten angry with her.

"Ames, I'm sorry I got mad. This is so damn hard. I miss you like crazy, and I don't know how long I can live without seeing you. Would you mind if I came to visit in a couple of months? I can get away in October or maybe during Christmas. Hey, how about I come during Christmas and we spend New Year's together?

Amy panicked. She was feeling puffy already. In two months, she really would be showing, and by Christmas, she would be six months pregnant. Oh no! Charlie could not visit her now. Instead of being reasonable, though, she blurted into the phone, "Charlie, I'm really, really busy and I wouldn't have any time to spend with you if you came. Charlie, you can't come!" She sounded crazed, which scared Charlie.

"Amy, are you okay? You sound totally freaked out. Is something wrong? Maybe I should come over now." Charlie had always been able to read her moods.

Forcing herself to calm down, Amy said in as normal a tone as she could muster, "Charlie, I'm fine, really. I'm sorry I sound so crazy, but I've been working long hours, trying to get by without you here, and now I have a huge, ah, top-secret project that I'm working on day and night that has me totally stressed. You just caught me at a bad time.

But, seriously, you really shouldn't come. I won't have any free time for months. Maybe next summer. Let's plan on that." And Amy fell apart, covering the mouthpiece of her phone so Charlie wouldn't hear her sobbing.

Charlie was confused by this suggestion to not see each other for almost a year. Not wanting to hear her answer but needing to ask the question, he softly ventured, "Amy, is there someone else?" Amy was flabbergasted. It hadn't occurred to her that he might think that.

"Oh, Charlie," she spluttered. "Of course there's no one else. You know that you are the love of my life. Trying desperately to regain her composure, she continued. "I really do have a top-secret project I'm working on." The secret meaning of that comment made her grimace. "I can't go into details, but it will keep me tied up for months."

"Aw, come on, Amy. You mean you don't even have time to see your husband? This is bullshit." He then softened his tone, knowing that she was as upset as he was about the situation. He continued more calmly, "Okay, Amy. I guess. If you're sure you're okay, I'll stay here. I don't want to stress you out more making you find time to be with me. I know what it's like to work all hours of the day and night. Julia and I have been at it until midnight every night. But we did win our case today."

Amy's antennae were raised. She thought, *Julia, huh? Okay then.* To Charlie, she said, "Well, congratulations again on your case. Congratulate your partner in crime for me also. I need to run. Bye, Charlie. I love you."

"Bye, Amy. Good luck with your top-secret project. I'll talk with you soon. You know I love you too." And they hung up. Amy sat down on her couch, running her hand over her little top-secret project and weeping.

After recovering from the phone call, Amy realized that she hadn't figured out how to tell her family. Of course, she had to tell them. They would absolutely kill her if they found out that she had kept such a huge event from them. But could she trust them not to tell Charlie? Sure, she could. She could trust them to do what she asked them to do. Her father was in the business of secrets, and the three women had always been close, holding many secrets large and small for each other.

"But this one is a doozy, aren't you, little one?" Amy said aloud with a little chuckle despite her pain over the phone call with Charlie. "Okay, then, I tell Ma and Daddy and Susan, but I swear them to secrecy," she continued. "Okay, little one, now you have me talking to myself," she said as she softly rubbed her growing belly. "So far you've made me throw up every time I smell spaghetti sauce, laugh uncontrollably at the silliest things, cry over commercials on television that I wouldn't have even noticed before, and get this stupid rosy flush in my face at the least provocation. What's next?" As if on cue, she felt a stirring inside, a bubbling, like something was tickling her from within. She stood looking down at her belly, mesmerized.

"That was you, little one, wasn't it? No, it couldn't be. It's way too soon to feel you. Still..."

The Anger

Charlie was miserable after the phone call. He had been so excited to tell Amy all about his case, and she hadn't even seemed interested. In fact, she hadn't even wanted to talk with him. Charlie couldn't figure out what was going on. He and Amy had been so in love for so long, had been so sure that theirs was a love that would last a lifetime. How could it just end so abruptly?

After hanging up the phone, he wandered from room to room of the house he had bought for her as a wedding present, imagining what their life would have been. He had pictured them decorating the house together, making it their own. Now, he had no interest in doing anything with it. Grabbing a bottle of beer in the kitchen, he opened the paneled pocket doors and walked across the glistening hardwood floor of the dining room, picturing the family gatherings that should be taking place there. Now it was just an empty room with sunny views to the bay. Passing out the side doors into the living room, he sauntered across to the open patio doors and just stared at a lone sailboat as it lazily floated across the bay in the late summer breeze. A scene that usually brought him such joy and peace now filled him with pain. He had pictured teaching his own son to sail on this bay as his father had taught him. He stood, gazing at the water, feeling lost.

Now, Amy was thousands of miles away, had ended their marriage before it even had a chance to get started, and he would never have that son with her, the son he had longed for since first meeting her all those years ago. Charlie shivered. The chilly evening air usually invigorated him but today it just made him shiver. He walked back into the house and closed the patio doors behind him.

Sipping his beer, Charlie wandered into his first-floor office, noting that it was the only room in the house that looked lived in. Here, his books lined the cherry shelves, a large desk filled the windows that looked out onto the sprawling front lawn and gardens, and his Harvard-embossed chairs paid tribute to his success. Files sat on the credenza and the top of the filing cabinets, and a radiant Amy smiled at him, glorious in her wedding dress and smiling just for him from the corner of his desk as he slipped into his leather chair.

"Ames, why won't you talk with me? Why are you shutting me out? We have never shut each other out before and we have already been through so much—your time at the military academy and mine at Colgate, then your time in Baltimore and mine in Boston. Through it all, we knew that we would make it work. Sure, this is a little harder, but with a little imagination, we can still make it work. But you don't even want to see me."

Charlie made a note to himself to talk with his father about the possibility of opening a European office in Germany. He knew it was a long shot, but he had always believed in nothing ventured, nothing gained. After a few more gulps, he even considered visiting Amy in Germany, getting her pregnant, and making her come home where she belonged. That thought didn't last, though, because he knew it was not the way he wanted her. He would not force her to return to him. No, if she came back, it would be her choice or not at all.

Charlie rose and returned to the kitchen, passing the closed French doors to what should have been Amy's home office. He had no desire to open the doors because he could see through the glass that what lay behind them was emptiness. He grabbed another Sam Adams and headed for the circular staircase in the foyer. As he ascended the stairs, his heart sank as it did each time he approached the bedroom that was supposed to have been such a retreat but only served as a reminder that he was all alone.

At the end of the open hallway, the master bedroom whose French doors opened up onto a balcony overlooking the lawns and the bay sat bare, with a bed on one wall, a dresser on another, and his clothes in one of the two walk-in closets. There was no artwork on the walls, no draperies on the windows. No thick rugs softened his steps, and no one called his name, softly beckoning him. Charlie shook his head as if to rid himself of his sad thoughts, but when he opened his eyes, he was still alone. He wondered why he had decided to move into this house instead of staying in his Beacon Hill apartment.

"Amy," he cried out to the empty room, "I have waited for you, cried for you, and done everything I could think of to make a happy life for us. If you don't want it, then fine. I get the message. I get it loud and clear." And with that, Charlie's pain turned to anger. He began to be angry for the years he had waited. He became angry for the way Amy sprung on him that she was leaving at the end of their honeymoon.

After having been in denial for so many years, Charlie was suddenly consumed with anger. He railed at the walls, repeating, "How could she do this to us?" In minutes, all of the hurt and loneliness of the past seven years while they maintained a long-distance relationship, knowing that in the end it would be worth it, emerged, and Charlie could barely contain his anger.

Finally, after hours of bemoaning the facts and dredging up every good-bye they had to say, every night they went to bed alone, every time they swore to each other that they would get through this and be together forever, Charlie stormed out of the bedroom, tromped down the stairs, and slammed himself into his desk chair.

"I am done, finished. From now on, I have work and nothing but work. I will become the best, most successful damned lawyer in Boston, and you will be sorry you left me, Amy." And with that oath taken, he shoved Amy's picture into a drawer, grabbed a file from his desk, and went to work.

The Dinner Party

Charlie did, in fact, become a very successful lawyer very quickly, and it had little to do with his father's influence. With a keen mind, analytical skills, friendly personality, and determination, he immediately overcame the stigma of nepotism at the firm. People soon realized that he deserved to be there on his merit. With no personal life, Charlie spent more hours in the office than anyone else. When his father told him he needed to go home and relax a little, he agreed readily and worked from home. Putting in hundred-plus-hour weeks was the norm for him during the next few months.

As Charlie worked nonstop, people noticed his rising star. One ambitious young associate, in particular, decided to attach herself to that star.

Charlie had known Julia in law school. She was bright, hard-working, and beautiful. And she was there. She always seemed to be assigned to the same cases as Charlie. They found themselves working together late into the night, grabbing meals when they could, and talking about their work. Little by little, Julia managed to insinuate herself into Charlie's private life. Soon she was sleeping over in his guest room when they had been working late at night at his house. And soon after, the guest room bed remained made up as she moved into his.

Charlie's mother was worried about him but knew that he had to come to terms with his problems in his own way. Probably the hardest thing she ever did was to step back and not help him through the pain of losing Amy. In the early days, she didn't see much of him, knowing that he needed some space and time. After a few weeks, she didn't see him because he seemed to have come to terms with his loss and was working hard at becoming a successful attorney.

Well, she thought, *working is often the best medicine. If his mind is on his work, the pain of losing Amy won't have a chance to take over his life.*

She began stopping by his house on Sunday mornings with a basket of muffins and a thermos of coffee and the two of them would sit—often in silence—eating and reading the Sunday paper. It was her chance to check in on him and gauge his well-being. Charlie knew what she was doing and appreciated her love—a mother's love. He tried not to think too much about it, though, because he would then invariably think of what a great mother Amy would have been. Working hard and falling into bed mentally exhausted usually kept those thoughts at bay, but in relaxed moments like his Sunday mornings with his mom, they seeped in and took over.

One Sunday morning, many weeks after Charlie had decided to throw himself into his work, he looked over the top of his *New York Times* and quietly told his mother, behind her *Boston Globe*, "Mom, I know why you come over on Sundays. Don't worry about me. I'm fine. I will always love Amy. I will always miss her. And I will always mourn the loss of a life with her. But life goes on. I will go on. You have helped me to do that just by quietly being there for me and not lecturing me." With that, he put the paper down, and surprised his mother by rising, walking over to where she sat, and hugging her.

His mother, usually calm and collected, the epitome of sophistication, leaned her head back and looked up at him, tears escaping from her lashes. She said, "I know, Charles. I know you will be fine. We will all be fine. But we will all miss what could have been."

She then picked up her pen and returned to her crossword puzzle. Mother and son returned to their silent nearness, and it was fine.

One Sunday morning, Grace Donnelly arrived, papers and muffins in tow, rang the bell, and was greeted by a young woman who bore an amazing resemblance to Amy. Grace's mind knew that it was not Amy, but her heart skipped a beat thinking that maybe it was. When she heard the dripping voice, though, she knew better.

"Oh, good morning. You must be Charlie's mom. I'm Julia Arnold. I work with Charlie." Julia smiled and reached out to shake Grace's hand. Never one to be taken aback, Charlie's mother shook her hand briefly and pushed her aside as she strode into the foyer.

"Charles," she called out. "Are you here?" She wanted an explanation and she wanted it now. Furthermore, she was not interested in hearing it from this tramp. "Charles," she called again.

Julia informed her that Charlie was in the shower but invited her in to have a seat in the living room. This infuriated Grace, but she smiled cordially and strode to the kitchen where she placed the muffins and papers on the cool granite of the center island. Then she opened the cabinet, took out two coffee mugs, filled one for herself and one for Charlie, placed muffins on two plates, and said dismissively to Julia, "I assume that you were dropping off some work for Charles. You may go now. He and I have brunch every Sunday morning, and this is our time." She smiled demurely at Julia who simply stood her ground and smiled back.

Julia considered her options. On the one hand, she did not appreciate being treated like a messenger when she was so much more to Charlie. On the other hand, she didn't want to alienate Charlie's mother and, by extension, his father—her boss. In an instant, she recovered her composure and calmly replied, "Of course. I wouldn't think of interfering with your mother–son time. I was just leaving. It was wonderful to *finally*"—emphasis on the word—"meet you, Mrs. Donnelly. Please let Charlie know I left." With that, she turned, picked up her bag from the foyer table, and strode out the front door. She folded herself into her Mercedes and drove away just as Charlie came into the room, shaking his hair dry.

"Mom, I didn't hear you come in," he said as he looked around the room.

"If you are looking for that woman, she has left," said his mother. With that pronouncement, she placed the plates and coffee on the table, handed Charlie his copy of the *New York Times*, and sat at the table as though Julia had never been there at all.

"Uh, Mom," Charlie began. "What do you mean 'she left'?" Charlie waited for an explanation and, when it didn't come, repeated, "Mom, what do you mean 'she left'?"

Grace sipped her coffee and replied that she assumed the woman was merely dropping off a file or something and had told her that she could go.

In other circumstances or in earlier years, Charlie would have been infuriated. Instead, he laughed. "Mom, you are a piece of work. Do you know that? 'That woman,' as you called her, is Julia Arnold. She is an associate at Dad's firm, and we have been working a lot together. Since Amy and I will never get back together, and I am tired of living alone in this big house, Julia has been staying here with me most of the time for a couple of weeks now. I would have told you sooner, but I never had the chance and wasn't sure where the relationship was going."

Charlie's mother feigned surprise and asked Charlie if he was telling her that he was serious about 'that woman,' turning her nose up a little as she said it.

"Mom, Julia is a very nice woman. You'd like her if you gave her a chance. We were friends in law school. In fact, Julia said that she liked me way back in first year, but she knew I was taken so she steered clear."

Grace saw through Julia and knew exactly what she saw in her son—his good looks, connections, and money. To him, though, she simply said, "I see" and returned to her paper.

Charlie had been expecting an argument from his mother, or at least a lot of questions. When neither came, he was relieved and decided to let it go. He sat down at the table, took a bite out of a raspberry white chocolate muffin, and picked up the paper. As they had every Sunday for months, they sat in relative silence for the next few hours, each lost in reverie, questions unanswered.

The next day at work, Julia was not happy. As soon as Charlie went into his office, she appeared and shut the door behind her. Gathering her composure, she began her well-rehearsed speech. "Charlie, did you and your mother have a nice morning yesterday? I'm sorry I had to leave so abruptly without saying good-bye, but I didn't want to interfere with your time with your mom. That time is sacred. When I am a mom someday, I only hope that I can have such a warm and loving relationship with my own son. Your mother is charming, Charlie. We really should invite your folks over for dinner this weekend. We could have our first little dinner party and I could get to know your folks and they me. Don't you think it's time? Your mother knew that I didn't really drop off files, I think." Finishing her speech, she smiled at Charlie and slipped into a leather armchair in front of his desk, crossing her legs and letting her skirt rise up her thigh. "We could cook together and make something wonderful for your folks. It's about time that big old house felt more like a home, and a dinner party is just the way to christen it." She said the last as a pronouncement, not a request, and Charlie sensed that the decision had already been made for him.

"Sure," Charlie replied. "We could do that. But I didn't know you could cook."

Julia laughed softly, calculating how she would tell him that she would cook the entire meal by herself to show him that she could really cook. He could go play golf with his father and return for dinner. Then she could order the meal from a local restaurant, pick it up, put it in her own pans, and come off as a master chef. When his parents saw what a wonderful Susie Homemaker she could be, she would be well on her way to becoming the next Mrs. Charles Donnelly, II. Julia smiled at the thought, and Charlie told her he'd give her a penny for her thoughts. She left her plan in her thoughts and cooed, "I was just thinking how nice it will be to stop hiding that we are a couple now." That said, she rose and crossed to Charlie behind his desk, leaned over, and kissed him. She then turned on her Jimmy Choos and sashayed out of the office (sensing that he was watching her leave) and back to work, knowing that she had planted her garden well and was about to reap the benefits.

The elder Donnellys accepted Charlie's invitation readily. His mom's brief meeting with the woman had whetted her curiosity and, while she was pretty sure she had her number, she wanted to see Julia in action with Charlie to be sure. When Saturday evening came around, Grace and Charles walked over to Charlie's house, a chilled bottle of Pouilly-Fuisse in hand.

As they listened to the doorbell chiming inside, Grace turned to Charles and simply said, "Watch and listen and let me know what you think when we get home. And I don't mean as her boss, but as a father." She then smiled and warmly greeted Julia and Charlie when they came to open the door. The dinner party was lovely. Julia had "made" a delicious dinner. They started with blackened scallops, followed by a simple mixed greens salad. The entree was an ambitious coq au vin accompanied by sweet asparagus tips and a wild rice medley. For dessert, she had "made" a lemon cheesecake with raspberry coulis and tiny chocolate truffles.

"My goodness," Charlie exclaimed when the meal was finished. "I had no idea you could cook like that! You're just full of surprises, aren't you?" and he softly kissed the top of her hair as he passed her to open a bottle of brandy he had purchased just for this occasion.

"Yes," purred his mother. "That was every bit as good as what I have had at the Mayflower House." Of course, she knew that the coq au vin and cheesecake were *exactly* what she had ordered two weeks earlier at the Mayflower House. And her friend Marion had raved over their tiny truffles. Grace did not overtly let on that she knew. To Julia, she merely said, "Julia, everything was delicious. You must give me your recipes."

Hmmmm. The tiniest furrow briefly appeared on Julia's brow. Could Mrs. Donnelly know that she had ordered the food from the Mayflower House? Furthermore, the possibility that Grace might ask for recipes had not occurred to her. She was not worried, though. She would simply Google the meal's items and give the resulting recipes to Grace. No one would ever know her secret.

"Of course," she said calmly. "I would be honored to give them to you. I'm so delighted that you liked the meal."

The rest of the evening was consumed with idle small talk, and when his parents left, Charlie picked Julia up and whirled her around the foyer, exclaiming, "I'm glad that's over, but you passed with flying colors! I have never known my mother to ask anyone for recipes before. She must have really liked your cooking. I know I did. Now that I know you can cook like that I'm going to keep you in the kitchen all the time." With that, he laughed, grabbed her close to him, and kissed her as she cringed at the prospect of proving her culinary skills again and again.

The Announcement

"Hello, Mom?" Amy timidly spoke into the phone.

"Amy, is that you? George, come here! Amy is on the phone!" As her mother called to her father to come quickly, Amy gulped. Could she do this? What would they think of her? Would they think that she was a terrible person for not telling Charlie? Would they tell her that she shouldn't keep the baby? Would they understand?

"Amy, are you there?" her mother asked.

"Yes, Mom, I'm here. And do I have some news for you!"

"George, Amy has some news for us," she heard her mother relate to her father.

"Mom, either tell Daddy to get on the extension or wait until I hang up to talk to him, please," Amy asked, irritated that her overseas call was being consumed by her mother's comments to her father.

"Oh, sure, Amy." And to her husband, she said, "George, go pick up the extension phone. Amy has something she wants to tell us."

"Okay, Amy, I'm all yours." As she said it, Amy heard a click and then her father's deep voice said sternly, "Hello, Amy Lynn. How are you? It's too soon for a promotion, and you haven't been there long enough to have received new orders. What kind of news do you have for us?"

"Hi, Daddy. I love you too," Amy replied, smiling. "Actually, I have some big news. Are you both sitting down? I think you're going to want to be sitting down for this one." Suddenly she felt like she did when she brought home her report card in the third grade with an "Average" in effort. She had been ashamed that she had only given average effort, knowing that her father always expected her to try her hardest at everything she did. Well, here goes, she thought.

"Ma, Daddy, you know that Charlie and I have been in a long-distance relationship for years. Now, with him in Boston and me in

107

Germany we've taken long-distance to the extreme. But we really loved each other when we got married. We didn't know it would be so hard. We didn't know that we would have to live thousands of miles from each other. It was a lovely wedding, wasn't it?"

"Ah, yes, dear, it was lovely," her mother replied, a note of concern in her voice. It wasn't like her youngest daughter to ramble.

"Well, I guess there's no easy way to say this." Amy paused. "I'm pregnant. It's Charlie's baby, conceived on our honeymoon, and I am going to keep it and I am not going to tell Charlie, and you can't either." With that, she paused again, waiting for her father to bellow at her for her selfishness, her foolishness, her carelessness.

Instead, what she heard first was her mother saying, "Oh, Amy, darling, that's wonderful news. You can worry about the details later. Just worry about staying healthy and be happy and…oh I have so many questions and…."

At this point she heard her father interrupt with, "Amy, are you sure? Have you thought about all of the consequences of your decision and are you sure?"

"Yes, Daddy, I have and I am."

"Well, then, congratulations, pumpkin. We will be there next week. It will take me a few days to make arrangements, but I know that your mother won't leave me alone until she sees you with her own eyes and makes sure that you're okay. I don't want to hear any arguments," he added gruffly. "You and your mother work out the details and we'll see you soon." And he was gone. But from his last few words, Amy could hear his voice breaking a little and could tell that he was uncharacteristically emotional. What she didn't know was whether he was disappointed in her or happy for her. After she was sure that he had hung up, she asked her mother, "Mom, are you and Daddy disappointed in me?"

"Amy Lynn Sweetser!" her mother exclaimed. "How in the world could you think such a thing? If you are excited, then we are excited too. You heard your father. We're coming to see you. And I didn't even have to twist his arm for a week to get there. He's the one who wants to go. He's really an old softie under all that bravado. You know that. You don't think I would have stayed with the old grouch all these years if he wasn't, do you?"

"I guess not, Mom. It's just that Susan did the marriage and work and travel and then kids thing, and she's such a great mom and wife and seems to have it all. And then there's me. I'm living in a foreign country all alone with a husband in name only. I've only been married for three months and I'm pregnant. I was afraid you and Daddy would be disappointed in me, would think that I messed everything up."

"Amy," her mother said. "You know, you sweet girl, that you could never do anything to disappoint us. You are our pride and joy. You and your sister are very different people. She's more traditional like me, and you're more headstrong like your father. But you are both the pride and joy of our lives. You have done things differently from the day you were born. Susan came into this world with a smile on her face while you entered screaming and punching yourself in the eye. One of my favorite pictures in my room is that frame with the two newborn pictures of you and your sister. Hers is sweet and scrunchy and there you are looking out at the world through a swollen, black eye." With that remembrance, she laughed fondly. "Amy, I knew from the day you were born that you were a scrapper, that you would survive anything. And you always have. For goodness sake, you used to beat up little boys who made fun of your sister even though they were older and bigger than you were. That didn't stop you. And when you met Charlie, you didn't care what you had to do to be together. You were determined to make it work. Amy, I have always been very proud of that side of you, the side of your father I fell in love with, and something I don't have myself. To be honest with you...." Her voice lowered to a whisper. "...I can hear your father getting down the baby book in the other room. He's a softy and I'm tough, and he's the big macho Army guy and I'm the tame housewife. Amy, we are all lots of different people. And you're about to become the best of both. Of course we're happy for you."

By now, Amy was sobbing quietly, and little one was soothing her from within, tickling her gently. As she sat, listening to her mother, she realized that what she said was true. She was about to become both mother and father to this child, and she actually did have the strengths of both her mother and her father to draw upon to do it.

"Oh, Mom, I love you guys so much," she said. "And I absolutely would love to have you come to visit. I don't know how much time we'll actually be able to spend together, but I would love to have you here. And, Mom, please don't tell anyone, okay? I need some time to figure that one out. I really don't want Charlie to know. I don't want to mess up his life."

"Amy, how could knowing that he has a child on the way mess up his life?" her mother asked. "You know that he still loves you and always will. You two are soulmates."

"I know, Mom, but I just can't tell him. You've got to accept that even if you don't agree, okay? Please? For me?" she begged, panic sneaking into her voice.

"Of course, dear. I won't say a word," her mother reassured her. "And I'll tell your father he's not to speak of this either. You can count on us, Amy." And Amy knew that she could. She could always count on them.

Hanging up the phone, her mother sat at the kitchen table and stared out the window at a momma bird feeding its baby a worm. *Oh, Amy,* she thought. *You have no idea what you're getting yourself into.* Then a wistful thought crossed her mind. *Maybe somehow this will bring you and Charlie back together. Everyone knows you belong together, and maybe this little one will help you to make it happen.* She rose from her chair and padded into the living room where her husband of thirty years was turning the pages of Amy's baby book and coming to terms with his baby having a baby. She walked to him, kissed the top of his head, and settled into his lap like she used to do when they were court-ing. Together they took a wonderful trip down Memory Lane and made plans to visit their daughter.

Amy took a break after talking with her parents to process the conversation. It had gone far better than she could have hoped. With each positive step, she felt more secure in her decision to keep this baby, this piece of her love for Charlie. Now it was time to call her sister.

Susan answered the phone on the third ring, shouting, "Hello!" into the receiver. "Hi, Suze. Did I call you at a bad time?" Amy asked.

Realizing that it was Amy on the line, Susan quickly yelled, "Everyone go out back and play. This is Aunt Amy calling from Germany, and I need to hear her." Amid complaints that they wanted to talk to her too, the girls reluctantly did as they were told, and a few seconds later Susan was back on the line.

"There. Hi, Amy," she began again. "What's new?"

The question, for some reason, delivered giggles to Amy, and she couldn't stop. Finally, with Susan wondering what she had said that was so funny, Amy blurted, "Suze, there's something pretty big that's new! I'm pregnant."

"You're what?" Susan exclaimed. "Amy, does Charlie know? Who's the father?"

It had not occurred to her that Susan might think anyone other than Charlie could be the father, so Amy quickly replied, "Susan! Charlie is the father, of course. I've never been with anyone else besides him."

"Oh, of course," Susan apologized. "I'm sorry Ames. I just was surprised. When are you due? What did Charlie say? What are you guys going to do? Are you coming back to the States? Do Mom and Dad know?"

Susan rattled off the questions that Amy was asking herself. Amy took a deep breath and said, "Susan, I need you to keep this to yourself. I'm not telling Charlie. I don't want him to turn his life upside down."

Susan interrupted, blurting, "Turn his life upside down? Amy, darling, having a child *does* turn your life upside down under the best circumstances. Nothing is ever the same again. You can't keep this from Charlie. He would be a great dad, and it's about time the two of you were actually living in the same place as a family. Daddy could get you an assignment closer to home, I'm sure. Why are you being so stubborn?" She then realized that Amy was sobbing on the other end of the line. "Oh, Ames, I'm sorry. I've done it again. Open mouth; insert foot. Why couldn't I just say, 'Congratulations Amy. I'm so happy for you' and leave it at that?"

"No, Suze, it's okay," Amy managed to say. "I know that you're right, but I just have to do this my way. I'm helping a lot of hurt people here and really feel needed. Charlie is doing great with the firm. He even told me that his dad let him argue a case, and he won it. How can I disrupt that? And I swore I wouldn't use Daddy's influence the day I applied for West Point. I can't be a hypocrite and use it now just because it would make my life a little easier."

"Amy," Susan ventured in a motherly tone, "it wouldn't be hypocritical to let your father help you bring your family together. We use what strengths we have in life, and one of yours is Daddy. Why not let him help you?"

Amy thought for a minute and said, "Well, Mom and Dad are coming here next week, and I'm sure that will come up. I'll have to do a lot of thinking between now and then and decide how to handle it. In the meantime, though, please just be happy for me. You are such a great mom. I just hope that I can be half as good."

As she spoke, she heard the girls burst through the screen door back into the kitchen and Susan yell at them to get out of the house or she would send them to their rooms. "Yeah," she said to Amy. "I'm a great mom. Can't you hear the greatness in my yelling?" This broke the tension, and both sisters laughed.

"Well, Ames, you take care of yourself and you know that if you need me I'm on a plane. John can manage the girls for a few days."

"I'll keep that in mind," a grateful Amy replied. "There may come a time when I take you up on the offer. Until then, though, even though you disagree with me, please don't let Charlie know about the baby. I really need some time to figure this out on my own."

Reluctantly, Susan agreed, saying that she would tell John but not the girls, and John could certainly be trusted to keep Amy's secret. She and Amy hung up after a few more stories about the girls, life in Portland, and Amy's reassurance that she was healthy and taking care of herself. Susan promised to send her some books on pregnancy and some of her maternity clothes, reminding Amy that she would need them when she wasn't in uniform. An appreciative Amy thanked her, and each hung up the phone, sat back, and reflected on the conversation.

Susan sat in a kitchen chair, looking out the window at her beautiful girls and couldn't imagine raising them alone. Her husband was her strength and her love, and one of her favorite activities was simply watching him play with his daughters. Whether they were riding bikes together, racing into the waves, playing dress-up, having a tea party, or playing hide-and-seek, the joy that those little girls brought to him was unsurpassed by anything else in his life. She couldn't imagine how Amy could deny that joy to Charlie. Her little sister had always had a mind of her own. But she had never been selfish, and Susan thought this was a selfish decision. It wasn't Amy's to make unilaterally. Charlie had a right to know that he was about to become a father. Unfortunately, it wasn't Susan's right to tell him. She had given her word to her sister and would honor that word. That didn't mean she had to like it or agree with it. Maybe she could change Amy's mind over the next several months.

As Susan was considering how she could change her sister's mind, Amy was slouched back on her couch, becoming more determined to keep this news from Charlie.

The Visit

A week later, Amy was returning from work, walking leisurely down her street, when she saw a strange car parked in front of her townhouse. Quickening her step, she recognized the heads peeking up over the backrests as her parents'. She didn't realize that they were arriving today but was thrilled to see them. She practically ran the final block to her house where she breathlessly rapped on the driver's window, startling her father from his nap.

"Hi, you two!" she exclaimed as they unfolded themselves from the tiny car they had rented at the airport. "Why didn't you tell me you were coming today? I would have picked you up."

"Sweetie, we didn't want to add any more stress, figured we could just drive out here. Your father has his ID to get us onto the base, and this way we could surprise you. Surprise!" her mother cried out as she ran around the front of the car to look at Amy. "Honey, you look just great! Are you happy? Are you eating okay? How are you feeling? Are you taking vitamins? Have you been to the doctor? Can we see your place?" The questions fell out of her mother in rapid succession until Amy finally stopped her by giving her a big hug and whispering in her ear, "Thanks for coming, Mom. I didn't think I needed to see you guys, but I sure am glad you're here."

By that time, her father had straightened up and was approaching her with arms outstretched. "Amy, you look just great," he exclaimed as he enveloped her. "Your mother's right. Why don't we take this road show inside the house before the neighbors decide to sell tickets?" He grabbed their bags out of the car and followed the women into Amy's tiny, but tidy house.

For a week, Amy felt totally spoiled. Her mother cooked for her, cleaned for her, did her grocery shopping, and even made the beds in the morning. Her father insisted on driving her to work each morning and picking her up each afternoon. In reality, she knew that it was his way of eking out some private time with his baby girl. And she loved showing him around the base. He talked about how it fared compared with other bases, what they should be doing better, and what ideas he could take back to the States. She proudly introduced him to her superior officers, who were impressed that he was her father. She never talked about her military father, never used his status to get ahead. So far as anyone had known here, she was just a girl from Massachusetts and not the daughter of one of the finest military minds of the century. He was responsible for the safety of the troops in many ways through his research work at the Natick Labs. But no one had made the connection between the brigadier general and Amy until they stood face-to-face, thrilled to be meeting him in person.

One morning, as he drove her to work, her father said, "Amy Lynn Sweetser *Donnelly....*" He emphasized her last name. "...you know that it is not best to raise this child of yours without Charlie. This is his son or daughter, and he really does deserve to be a part of its life. In my many years in the Army, I have never used my position for personal gain. I just want you to know that I am ready to do so now. You say the word, and I will have you back in the States with that husband of yours."

Amy had been expecting this at some point but wasn't ready when she heard the words. She bristled. "Daddy," she began, "I know you mean well, but this has to be done my way. I will not use people to get what I want any more than you used people to get what you wanted. Let's just enjoy our visit and let it drop. If I change my mind, I know where you live. I'll ask." Much to her father's sorrow, the conversation was over. He wished he had just intervened without asking her if it was what she wanted.

Far too soon, her parents decided that she was fine, had carved out a nice life for herself, and was healthy. They had been pleased to meet Beth, her next-door neighbor, and were comforted that an experienced mom lived close by in case Amy needed any advice or help. It was time for them to head back to Massachusetts.

Amy stood by the car saying her last good-byes through the open windows, reminding them once again not to mention any of this to Charlie. Then her father gruffly said, "We're going to miss our plane if we don't get going," and they were off.

Amy stood and watched, waving as they drove away, standing in the street long after their little car had turned the faraway corner. As she stared after them, she thought, *Well, Amy, you're all on your own now.* Then she patted her slightly bulging belly and said, "Little one, it's you and me against the world." And she turned and walked silently back into her quiet little house, humming the Helen Reddy tune.

The Secret

When Amy's mom and dad returned home, there was a message from Susan asking how Amy was doing. Mary called her even before unpacking their bags. Susan answered on the first ring and listened attentively as her mother described Amy's life.

"Mom," she asked, "is it okay if the girls and I come down tomorrow? John is out of town, and I would love to talk with you. We need to figure something out here. Ames just can't keep this to herself. She has to tell Charlie."

"Susan," Mary replied, "you are always welcome, and you know we would love to see the girls, but it's Amy's decision whether or not she tells Charlie about the baby."

"We'll see," Susan muttered. "The girls and I will leave Portland around nine so we can avoid the traffic, and we'll see you around lunchtime. Is it okay if we spend the night?"

Mary assured her that it was always okay for her family to stay overnight and that she would have lunch ready for them when they arrived. She would just make sandwiches so if they got delayed, lunch wouldn't be spoiled. The two women hung up, each thinking about Amy and her secret.

The next day, Susan rose early and packed an overnight bag for herself and the girls. She then got them ready for their two-and-a-half-hour drive from Portland to Duxbury. She packed their travel bag with books, music, toys, and snacks, rushed them through breakfast, and loaded them and their stuff into the car.

"Here we go, girls! We're off to see Nana and Grampy!" Inwardly, though, she was thinking of how she and her mother could conspire to persuade Amy to tell Charlie about his child.

When Susan arrived at her folks' house, they both knew that she needed to talk with her mom. Her father emerged from the house and grabbed a granddaughter in each arm, carrying them effortlessly into the house.

"Come on, munchkins," he whispered to them. "Grandpa has a surprise for you out back. We'll go through the house so that your mother thinks we're just going into the kitchen, but we'll go straight through and out the back." He winked at each of them as they tried to get him to tell them his secret. They soon discovered that he had erected a play structure in the backyard complete with swings, a slide, and a clubhouse for them to enjoy.

"Oh, Grampy!" they both exclaimed, "It's great!" And they ran to play on it.

Meanwhile, Susan and Mary settled in on the front porch for a talk.

"Mom," Susan began, "what is Amy thinking? How can she keep this from Charlie? Can you imagine if I hadn't told John about Rachael or Jennifer? They are his world. He absolutely worships those little girls. And Charlie would feel the same way about his child, too."

"I know, Susan," her mother calmly said. "But Amy is not you, and Charlie is not John. Those two have to work out their own lives. Even though we want to fix everything for them, we can't. It's up to them to figure it out."

"But, Mom," Susan complained, "how can they work it out when Charlie doesn't even know there is something to be worked out? I'm afraid he's going to get pretty sick and tired of always having to work things out long-distance with Amy. She's so damned pigheaded and selfish leaving him like this and now not even telling him he has a child on the way."

Her mother sat for a few minutes and then gently said to Susan, "Sweetheart, your sister is not you. She is stubborn and determined to make the Army her life. I don't understand it any more than you do. She saw what we all went through as your father moved from post to post. She probably decided to join the Army long before she fell in love with Charlie. She just didn't realize it. I don't get it either. But where you and I put family and our men first, she can't do that. She feels the same calling your father felt for the Army. It's in her blood, and she can't help it. Neither of you is right, and neither of you is wrong. You're just different. You're more like me, and she's more like your father."

"But, Mom," Susan whined, "this is just wrong. Amy doesn't know if she should be married to the Army because she hasn't given being married to Charlie a chance. She doesn't know the joy of having someone by her side through thick and thin, having someone come home at night from a hard day's work and give her a hug and kiss and ask her about her day. She doesn't know how comforting it is to see his face lying next to hers when she wakes in the morning and to watch him as he plays with his children, smiling in a way only a dad can smile. When we moved to Portland, I wasn't sure that I would like it there, but John made me see that it didn't matter where we lived so long as we were together. And when we moved to this new house in Falmouth, I wasn't sure how the girls would adapt to the move, even though it is such a short distance from Portland. But John made everything okay for everyone. He made it an adventure, and the girls were fine. Ames doesn't know that feeling yet. How can she decide to string Charlie along for so many years only to deprive him of his child? Mom, she can't do that!"

"Susan," her mother continued, although she knew it was going nowhere. "We don't need to agree with Amy. We just have to respect her decision and keep her secret. After all, she would do the same for us, right?" With that, her mother shot Susan a knowing look. "It seems to me that she kept a pretty big secret of yours, sweetheart."

Susan's face flushed as she remembered the whopper Amy had, indeed, kept for her a few years ago. She and John had been dating and foolishly had unprotected sex. Susan had become pregnant and was not in a position to have the child. She was in college and unmarried, and she decided to have an abortion. She told her mother and Amy, but no one else in the world ever knew—not even John. When she and John married and she was ready to have children, they had the two girls and, so far as John knew, they were his only children. Amy had kept her secret and, as she thought about it, Susan realized that she would, of course, keep Amy's.

"Mom, that was a low blow," she quietly whispered to her mother.

"I'm sorry, honey," her mother replied. "I know it wasn't fair to bring that up, but you didn't seem to understand just how important this is to Amy. You girls have the right to live your own lives as you see fit, whether I like it or not."

"Mom," Susan began timidly. "Were you ashamed of me back then? I never asked you because I didn't want to know, but now I am older and wiser, and I really need to know."

Mary rose from her chair and knelt on the porch in front of her firstborn. "Susan, I could never be ashamed of you. There is absolutely nothing you could do that would make me feel that emotion. We all make mistakes in life, and we all live with the consequences. We make tough decisions and should never even think about whether anyone else thinks our decisions are the right ones or the wrong ones. All that matters is that your decision was right for you at that point in your life. All that matters now is that Amy's decision is right for her at this point in her life. We just have to trust that it is."

With that, she got up, leaned forward, and kissed her daughter on the top of her head. Now, let's go see what your father and those girls are up to. He had a surprise for them in the backyard, and I'd love to see whether they liked it. Come on. We can talk some more later if you want to." With that, she walked through the front door, leaving Susan to ponder life and the decisions that change its course.

The Pregnancy

Amy's pregnancy was an easy one. She was never sick after the first three months, felt strong and energized, and with the exception of her burgeoning belly, was in the best shape of her life. She walked everywhere she went on the base and doggedly ate more healthy foods than she ever had before. Like everything else she had ever done, if something was worth doing, it was worth doing right. If she was going to have a baby all alone, she was going to do it right. She ate fruits and vegetables, lots of fish and chicken, drank milk and ate cheese. She stayed away from sugar of all types, saying a polite "no thank you" whenever a birthday cake was passed around or someone arrived with doughnuts. She never ate candy or cookies. And she stayed away from potato chips and pizza. Hers was a model pregnancy. As the beach ball grew on her belly, the rest of her looked even slimmer and more toned. Her doctor remarked every time he saw her that she should teach classes on how to have a healthy pregnancy, but she declined the suggestion, perfectly happy to spend her evenings preparing for little one. When asked if she would like to know the sex, following an ultrasound, she didn't even think about it.

"Absolutely not," she replied. "I want to be surprised," even though after the dream she'd had early on, she was positively certain it was a boy.

She tried to call Charlie at least once a week but found herself preoccupied with little one and sometimes forgot. When she did talk with him, he often seemed distracted. They talked about the weather, their work, and not much else. Amy agonized over whether or not she should tell Charlie, but each time she heard his voice and he told her about how much he loved the law, she bit her tongue and kept little one to herself.

So, as the months flew by, before she knew it, she was only two weeks from her due date. Her parents and her sister, Susan, would be arriving in a week to make sure they were there for the delivery. Amy went into nesting mode. She folded the baby blankets, hung the tiny clothes in the closet, placed diapers in the new changing table, and made up the bassinet Beth had loaned her. She moved the bassinet from one side of her bed to the other, put it in the spare room, the living room, and even in the hall. Finally, she settled on the corner of her own room near the foot of her bed. That was the perfect place, she decided— close by in case little one needed her in the night, but far enough away not to be tempted to lie awake all night and watch little one sleep. Her house began to look decidedly like that of a new mother, with pastel colors appearing everywhere: afghans on her couch, rocking chair, and the foot of her bed; bottles lined up on her kitchen counter; a monitor on her bedside table and end table in the living room (although her place was so small that she really did not need a monitor at all); diaper bag hanging on a hook by her front door that she installed for just that purpose; tiny clothes in her closet; and a food processor and fifty tiny jars on her kitchen counter for the baby food she planned to make herself in a few months. Hidden behind her door were two signs she made last week: "It's a girl!" and "It's a boy!" One of them would grace her front lawn when little one was born. Amy had surprised even herself by deciding to wait to discover if she would have a daughter or son until the moment of delivery. Yes, Amy was ready.

Just when she thought she had run out of things to do in preparation, Amy felt a muscle spasm in her lower back. "I must have worked too hard getting ready for you, little one. I'll take it easy today." Lucky for her, it was a Saturday. Her parents and Susan were arriving later. She had opened the couch in the den for her sister and freshened up the guest room for her parents. She had fluffed extra pillows and folded extra blankets. Everything was ready for their arrival. *I'm glad I did everything ahead of time*, Amy thought. *I really don't feel like doing anything today.* As she grabbed an apple from the refrigerator, her back hurt again. "Ouch!" she cried. *Geesh! All these months of doing everything right, and I hurt myself the week before little one is due,* she thought as she dropped to the couch to watch some television. Soon, she was asleep—until she turned and her back hurt again. *I'm glad Dad didn't want me to pick them up at the airport this afternoon*, she thought. *My stupid back really hurts. I shouldn't have done so much.*

Amy tried lying on her bed, but her back hurt. She moved down to the living room couch, but her back hurt. Just when she thought she had found a comfortable position, it hurt again. Mid-afternoon, her neighbor Beth stopped by. When Amy opened the door, Beth took one look at her and asked tentatively, "Are you okay, Amy?"

"Oh, I'm fine, Beth. It's just that I hurt my back getting ready for my family to arrive." As she spoke, it hurt again and she winced, against her will.

"Amy! What was that?" Beth asked, alarmed.

"Oh, just my stupid back again," Amy answered.

Beth suggested that Amy sit down, and she followed her into the living room. They talked for a few minutes about what Beth could do for her while her family was visiting and after little one arrived, when Amy winced again.

"Uh, Amy, was that your back again?" Beth asked.

"Yeah. It's really hurting more now."

"Amy, I don't mean to frighten you, but I think you might be in labor. With Zack, my second, I had back labor. All of the pain was in my back. Sweetie, why don't we go to the hospital just to make sure? Bill is home this afternoon, so I can go with you."

At first Amy resisted the idea, but as another pain washed across her back, she relented. "Fine, Beth. I guess it can't hurt to check it out. It really hurts now." Standing was tough, but Amy walked to Beth's car and fell into the passenger seat. Beth quickly scribbled a note to Amy's family and taped it to the front door, and then ran to the car, yelling to her husband who was trimming the hedges, "Bill, I'm taking Amy to the hospital. When her folks get here, send them over, okay?"

Without waiting for an answer, she jumped into her car. Seeing the pain in Amy's face, Beth knew that it was almost time, so she drove quickly to the hospital, all the while trying not to alarm Amy, chattering about what to expect while in the hospital, how Amy's family would be here in just a couple of hours, and joking about how nice it was to be away from the house by herself—even if it was going to the hospital with Amy. By the time she had crossed the base, Amy was obviously in pain, but determined not to show it. Pulling up to the emergency door, Beth jumped out and ran inside, calling for someone to help her get a woman in labor into the hospital.

The Baby

Settled in a hospital bed, a hospital gown draped over her and a cold cloth resting on her forehead, Amy waited for her doctor to arrive. Beth stood by her side, chattering and trying to keep Amy from being scared.

"Hey, Amy," she said. "Bill just texted me and told me your folks arrived and are on their way over here. Their plane got in early. Hold on. They'll be here in just a few minutes."

"That's nice," Amy replied mechanically, another pain gripping her.

"Sweetie, I'll be right back. I need to check on something," Beth said, hurrying out of the room. Once in the hall, she grabbed the first white coat she saw and said menacingly, "Look, my best friend is in there about to give birth. She's scared, in pain, and no one is paying any attention to her. Now either get your sweet little ass in there and take care of her or find someone who can. I don't care if her doctor is here or not, and, frankly, neither does that baby. It's coming like it or not, and she better not have to deliver it herself!" With that, Beth smiled a sweet Southern belle smile and coldly added, "What are y'all waiting for?"

As she finished threatening this unsuspecting intern, Amy's doctor came hurrying down the hall.

"Dr. Gray! Thank goodness!" Beth exclaimed. "Amy really needs you! She's about to pop, and no one has even checked her yet.

"I'll decide that," Dr. Gray said officiously.

"Well get in there and decide, then," Beth replied, unaffected by his arrogance.

As the two of them entered Amy's room, she was in the midst of a big contraction and barely noticed them.

Dr. Gray rushed to the door and called, "Nurse, I need you in here *now!*" Not two seconds later, a young nurse appeared, flushed and eager to please. As Dr. Gray sat on a stool, he rolled it up to Amy's bed, pulled the sheet back, and saw a little blond head trying to enter the word all on its own. He lost no time telling Amy to push, that her child was about to emerge. Beth held Amy's hand as she swabbed her head with a cold cloth and cooed to her that she was about to become a mother, all the while telling Amy how proud she was that Amy had done this on her own with no medication. Amy looked up at Beth with gratitude before she grimaced one last time, pushed with all her might, and felt little one enter the world. Listening for its cry, she held her breath. Seconds later, she heard a strong wail and Dr. Gray's announcement, "Amy, it's a boy!"

She waited while the nurse cleaned her son's eyes and nose, wiped him off, and scored him on the Apgar scale. Then it was the moment she had waited for all these long months. As the nurse handed her the little squirming bundle that was her newborn son, the door opened and in rushed her mother, father, and sister, looking scared and then immediately ecstatic. Beth said a quick hello and silently slipped out of the room to give the family time to meet the baby. Amy smiled at them and then looked down at a perfect replica of Charlie. She gazed at his face and through her tears, whispered, "Welcome to the world, Charles. You look just like your daddy."

Her mother gasped when she saw Charlie's face looking up at her in this little one's body. "What are you going to name this little angel, Amy?"

"Charles," Amy replied simply.

"A good, solid, respectable name," her father replied, coughing to hide his emotion.

"He looks just like his daddy," Susan gushed. "Amy he's gorgeous!"

At that, Amy laughed. "Oh, so you think my husband is gorgeous, eh, big sister?"

Embarrassed, Susan spluttered for a minute before realizing that Amy was teasing.

Her folks stayed for a little while, and then her mother sternly directed everyone to leave and give Amy time alone with her son. Amy silently mouthed, *Thank you* as her mother turned to take one last look before shutting the door behind them.

Alone at last, Amy looked at her new son and decided to have a little talk with him.

"Charles," she began, "you and I are going to be just fine. We really are. Your daddy would love to know you, but we can't tell him just yet. I hope he'll forgive me someday for keeping you all to myself." Charles looked up at her with eyes filled with wisdom, or so Amy thought. "Little one, someday we'll tell your daddy about you. Someday you'll know him and love him. But you have to give me time to figure out how to do that." And she held little Charles close to her breast, hoping with all her soul that somehow this would all work out.

The Homecoming

Since the day after his birth was a Sunday, Amy and Charles stayed in the hospital until Monday morning. First thing, though, Amy demanded to be allowed to go home.

"Doctor Gray, I am perfectly fine, and Charles is perfectly fine, and there is no reason for us to be staying in this hospital for one more minute."

Dr. Gray chuckled and agreed that Amy and Charles should go home and begin their new life together. He quickly signed the discharge papers and Amy called her house. Her mother answered the phone on the first ring and, hearing that Amy was being discharged called to her husband, "George, Amy and Charles are coming home. Go get them—*now!*" to which Amy heard her father reply, "Ma'am, yes, ma'am," and Amy smiled at the memory.

"Your father is on his way, Amy," her mother told her.

"Okay, thanks," Amy replied before hanging up the phone, clutching her son tightly and whispering, "That's what your daddy used to say to me, little one. Whenever I told him to do something instead of asking him to do it, he would say 'Ma'am, yes, ma'am.'" After a moment of reverie, she continued, "Well, let's get you ready to go home," and she rose, dressed first herself and then her little boy, and sat patiently waiting for her father to arrive.

The short drive home with Charles was wonderful. George kept glancing lovingly in his rearview mirror to watch his daughter with her son in the backseat. *She's a natural mother*, he thought. *What a shame that Charlie can't be here with them at a moment like this. I'll have to see what I can do about changing that stubborn girl's mind.*

As they approached her little house, Amy was shocked to see the welcoming committee on the front lawn. Her sister had posted the "It's

131

a Boy!" sign by her mailbox, and jumping up and down with excitement were her mother, Susan, Beth and Bill, and their little boy Zack. Seeing the car arrive, several other neighbors emerged and came over to offer their congratulations. Before she knew it, Amy and little Charles were the center of attention in this tableau that had been played out millions of times all over the world.

"Okay now, folks," her father bellowed after a few minutes. "These two need some rest. Let's let them go inside." Amid good wishes and many kisses on her cheeks, Amy made her way into her home, Charles in her arms.

The next two weeks were a blur. Amy fed Charles, slept, talked with her parents and sister, accepted visitors, received flowers and baby gifts, and learned how to take care of a baby. The first time her mother showed her how to give Charles a bath, she was sure she would drown him, but she discovered that she was able to wash his squirming little body and soothe his fears, and he did survive.

Amy's visit with her family was much too short, though, and before she knew it Susan had left. A few days later, her parents left as well, telling her how proud they were of her, how much they adored Charles, and that she was going to be a terrific mother. Unspoken by agreement were the admonitions that she should tell Charlie and let him be a part of this time in her life.

As her parents climbed into their rental car, she stood on her front lawn with little Charles in her arms. She waved his little arm at them and the last thing she saw as they drove away were the smiling tears on her mother's face. And then she and Charles were alone.

During the next few weeks, Amy learned that she loved being a mother. She loved pushing Charles's carriage along the sidewalks of the base as everyone she met cooed over him. She adored burying her face in his growing head of blond hair after a bath and smelling that unique baby smell—a mixture of baby shampoo and powder—kissing his little belly and seeing him smile up at her, and just holding him propped against her knees as she sat on the floor talking with him about life and love. His unwavering gaze and furrowed brow gave him an old soul's appearance as she talked, and she was sometimes sure that he understood her.

Amy talked about Charlie, telling little Charles all about how his mommy and daddy had met, fallen in love, and defied the odds for so long before realizing that they just couldn't do it anymore. She assured him that Mommy and Daddy still loved each other very much and that someday he would meet his daddy, who would love him with all his heart. She showed the pictures in her photo albums to Charles, explaining each one, and marveled at the little guy's eyes following the turning of the pages.

As the weeks passed, Charles grew and developed a personality all his own. He was a good-natured baby, hardly ever crying but rarely sleeping either. He was alert and attentive, happy just to be with her. She carried him everywhere, choosing not to use the Baby Bjorn she had been given. She liked to feel his little body in her arms and know that she could protect him from harm. She talked with him about the sky and the birds, the neighbors' cats and dogs, read her magazines aloud to him, and let him sit in her lap when she watched *Jeopardy*. In fact, Charles became so accustomed to going to bed after he heard the *Jeopardy* music at the end of the show that he rarely fussed when she deposited him in his bassinet and returned to the living room for the evening.

Amy infrequently called Charlie now, and he began calling her less and less. They were coming to terms with the fact that they just were not going to make it as a couple. She was afraid that Charles would make noise when she was on the phone, so she usually stepped onto the front porch to talk with Charlie once Charles was sound asleep. Their conversations, though, became stilted and formal—not the carefree ones they used to have. Amy was afraid she would slip and say something about Charles, and Charlie was afraid he would hurt Amy's feelings by telling her that he was seeing more and more of Julia. So they talked less and less.

The Phone Call

Finally it was time for Amy to return to work, and she was forced to leave little Charles behind in day care. For the first time in her life, she wished that she had not chosen a military career. She was conflicted between serving her country and being what she considered to be a good mother. Even though hers was a military family, her mom had always been a guiding force in her life. It was her father who had come home repeatedly over the years and announced that they would be making yet another move to another base. Her mother was her divining rod, always there, always the same, always smiling and excitedly researching the new place where they would live, relating stories of the great fun the family would have in their new location. Amy always knew that wherever her father's career took them, their new house would soon be their home.

Her mom always orchestrated great adventures in their new area so that they would look upon it as a wonderful place to be. She would pile Amy and Susan in the family car and head out, taking a right turn and then a left, a right and then a left until they were totally lost and would have to find their way back to their new home. It was an adventure they had with each move and one they looked forward to. Once they had been driving around for a couple of hours when they stopped for lunch. Amy's mom asked the waitress how they could get back to the base only to be told that it was a block away! Amy and Susan and their mom laughed and laughed. Mary always immediately joined the PTA and volunteered at her daughters' new schools, paving the way for Susan and Amy. Yes, Amy always knew that hers would be a close family because of her mom. Her mom would make every new quarters a cozy home. She always knew that wherever she lived, her room would be her own, her mom making sure that it reflected Amy's current passions.

Now Amy was feeling as though she were failing her son by not providing that life for him. She could not be everything for him, though, no matter how hard she tried. She was the one who had chosen to follow the Army life, but that meant that Charles would be alone, raised by virtual strangers while she served her country. Maybe she should call Charlie after all and let him know that he had a son. She shouldn't be so selfish. If the news disrupted Charlie's life, so be it. It had sort of disrupted hers, too, although she was thrilled with the disruption.

She no sooner decided to call Charlie, though, than she would remember again that he had no life here in Germany. There was no work for him. He was not the type to be satisfied as Mr. Mom while she left for work each day. No, sadly, she would always determine that it was better for Charlie if he did not know.

The months passed, and then one Sunday afternoon, as Amy was relaxing with a good book and little Charles was napping, Charlie called.

"Hi, Ames," she heard. *Something is wrong*, she thought as she listened to those two words. *Wow! How can you know someone so well that you know when something is wrong just by hearing two words?* Her internal reverie was broken, when she again heard her name. "Ames? Are you there?"

"Er, of course I am, Charlie," she stuttered as cheerfully as she could muster. "It's been ages since I've heard from you."

"How are you, Ames?"

She choked back her surprise, told the butterflies that always arrived when she heard his voice to settle down in her stomach, and cheerfully replied, "I'm fine, Charlie. How are you?"

"Okay, I guess. But I really miss you. Is there any change in your status? Any chance that you might be coming back home soon?"

"No, I'm afraid not."

Without making small talk or wasting any time in idle conversation or remembrances, Charlie blurted, "Ames, I will always love you and wish that we could be together forever, but you know that won't happen now. I can't just stay all alone forever, and you don't seem to be coming home any time soon. I need to have someone who needs me and loves me and wants to be with me. Julia does."

With the mention of a real name, the reality of what Charlie was saying burst upon Amy's psyche.

"What?" she exclaimed. "What did you say? What are you saying?" Amy began to panic. *No! You and I have a child!* she wanted to scream. But she remained quiet.

Charlie hesitated and then quietly and calmly said the words Amy had hoped never to hear but knew that she would someday: "Amy, I need for us to get a divorce so that Julia and I can get married. Is it okay if I send the papers to you? They're all made out, and all you have to do is sign them. I've been very generous."

Amy was dizzy, heard Charles waking from his nap, and did not want Charlie to hear the intermittent calls of "Mama" coming from the other room. Without hesitating, she stammered, "Well, if that's what you want, Charlie, of course I will agree. I hope that you will be happy with her. But I really have to go now." And she hung up the phone.

Charles's happy "Mamas" eventually changed to insistent ones and then to tears. By the time Amy actually heard him again, he was wailing, feeling abandoned and alone—much like Amy, herself, was feeling. She ran to him, whipped him into her arms, smothered him with kisses and tears, and promised him that somehow she would make a good life for him, knowing now for sure that she was all he would ever have. "I brought this on us, little one. I am so sorry. I decided what your daddy needed to know, and now you will never have a real family. How could I have been so selfish? How could I have kept you a secret from your own daddy? Oh, Charles," she wailed, "how could I have done this to you?"

A few days later, the papers arrived in Amy's office, and she absently looked at them. She regretted the unfairness of never even having a chance to make a life with Charlie before it was over. She took the papers and dropped them on her desk, promising herself that she would look at them later. And she got back to work.

A week passed and Amy still had not signed the papers. Once again, on a drizzly Sunday afternoon as Charles napped, the phone rang.

"Hello?"

"Hi, Amy. It's Charlie."

"Oh! Hi, Charlie. I know I should have sent those papers back to you by now, but I've just not been able to bring myself to do it yet. I promise I will get to it tomorrow."

"Thanks, Amy. And…Amy?"

"Yes?"

"Do you have a few minutes just to talk? We've been together too long to let it end like this. I'm hoping that we'll always be friends."

Friends, she thought. *I don't want to be your friend.* But then she said, "Sure, Charlie. I want that too. You're the only one who really gets me. Some of the guys here in the Army think I'm soft, and civilians think I'm tough, but you're the one who knows both sides." Her voice trailed off as she debated telling Charlie about Charles. She knew that she might not get another chance. She also knew that if she told him now, there would be no divorce. "Charlie…." she began, determined to tell him once and for all. As she spoke his name, though, he was also speaking.

"Amy, my friends have been teasing me because Julia looks a lot like you. She's an associate at the firm and works crazy hours like I do, so we started grabbing a late dinner together. We've been friends for years, ever since law school. You probably remember her. We were in study groups together all through law school. I'd never tell her, but it was the fact that she looks like you that initially drew me to her—not then, now!" he hastily added. "I felt as though I had a piece of you with me. I later realized that was crazy, but by then I had discovered her many facets and realized that we could have a good life together. She's always around for me and understands my work."

"That's nice," Amy absently muttered, becoming frantic.

"No, really, Ames. You can't expect me to wait forever for you. We tried for a lot of years to make it work. It's just time we grow up a little and realize that it isn't going to work. You used to think that faraway love was romantic. Well, enough is enough. It isn't. People just don't get their happily ever afters."

"I know, Charlie," Amy tried again in an uncharacteristically small voice, attempting to remain calm. "But there's something I have been meaning to tell you for a long time. About a year ago I should have told you, but now I just don't know how to say it."

"I know what you mean," Charlie interrupted. "There are so many things I have wanted to say since you left and just couldn't figure out the way to say them. Don't worry about it. I know what you mean."

Amy sat staring out her window at the bird on the bush outside her window, listening to Debussy playing in Charles's room. He loved listening to piano music. It calmed him whenever he fussed, which was rarely, and she always played it as he napped.

"Amy, are you still there?" she heard.

"Uh, yeah, sure." She managed. She tried one last time. "Charlie, I really do think I should tell you something before I sign these papers."

"Don't worry, Ames. You don't have to say it. I know you still love me. I love you too. But it's different now."

Wow! He was making this really hard. Maybe she shouldn't tell him after all. As she questioned her decision to tell him about Charles, she heard Julia's voice in the background: "Charlie, are you coming? Your mother and father are expecting us in a few minutes. We'd better not be late!" What a voice! It was like dark maple running over steaming pancakes, slow, dreamy, syrupy. It made Amy's skin crawl.

"Uh, yes. I'll be right there. Just give me a minute," she heard Charlie answer, muffled by his hand over the phone.

"Ames, I really have to go now. We're going over to my folks'. Remember to send the papers, okay? And whatever you think you have to tell me can wait until later, okay? Gotta go. Bye." And with that the phone line went dead, much as her hopes for ever living a life in a pretty white colonial in Massachusetts, little Charles playing on a manicured lawn that sloped its way to the shore. A picture came to her mind of herself in a flowery sundress, tanned and lithe, sitting at a pristine white table, a tall gin and tonic in her hand and laughing as Charles played badminton on the lawn with Charlie, her Adonis in white, having just returned from a tennis game with friends.

"Mama!" brought her back to the present. Looking around, she saw a tiny, tidy, functional house and heard her little boy calling for her to go to his side. She dragged herself out of her chair and plodded into his little room. Absently, she thought that the den had made a nice bedroom for him. Seeing his smile, she resolved to let his daddy have the life he had dreamed of. She was the one who had taken that life away from him, after all. It was her responsibility to try to give it back to him—even if it were with someone else. She was definitely big enough to do that for him, and she loved him with all her heart— and always would. Charles had never known him and could not miss him. She would continue to tell him about his father, knowing that someday it would come back to haunt her when Charles would insist on meeting him. But she could live one day at a time and worry about that later.

Her decision made, she picked up her squirming child and twirled him around in the air, clutching him at the end of the arc and smothering him with wet kisses. As he giggled and returned his own version of kisses—an open mouth placed repeatedly on her cheek—a smile spread across her face. Sometimes a decision made, whether right or wrong, is easier to live with than no decision at all.

The next morning, Amy dropped Charles off at the day care center and walked to her office. When she arrived, she picked up the divorce papers and signed them, staring at her signature on the page for quite a while before folding them and placing them in an envelope. She addressed the envelope and dropped it in the office mail to be sent to the States. Charlie should have them next week. A single tear trickled down her cheek, a tribute to love lost.

The Dandelion

Months passed and Amy didn't hear anything from Charlie. Her family didn't mention him. Her friends didn't mention him. When she asked them how he was doing, they would mutter, "Okay, I guess," and change the subject.

Amy busied herself with her work and her little boy, who was growing every day. Before she knew it, he was walking and talking. Every day, he reminded her of his father in the confident way he moved, his love for sports, and his gentle nature.

Amy and Charles created a nice life for themselves and a rhythm that worked for them. Amy received promotions at work and made more friends now that she had a child. She became active in a Mommy and Me group and found that she had a knack for throwing themed parties for children. Charles was extraordinarily social and loved being surrounded by other children, usually becoming their leader in whatever game they were playing. Because of his growing circle of friends, Amy planned birthday parties, Halloween parties, and even St. Patrick's Day parties for Charles and his friends.

One afternoon, as Amy and Charles were walking in the park, he proudly picked a bouquet of dandelions for her and presented them clutched in his chubby fist. She smiled and thanked him, remembering the day her mother had told her the story of the dandelion. She said, "Charles, these are very special flowers, especially for people like you and me. Would you like to know the story of the dandelion that my mother told to me when I was just about your age?" Charles grinned broadly and nodded his head.

"Come on over here and we'll sit on the bench and I'll tell you the story.

"Dandelions will grow almost anywhere, and they are very hard to destroy. They aren't a showy plant, but they are very pretty. People tend to like them a lot. They are survivors and will live in almost any climate. Like dandelions, children whose parents are in the military bloom everywhere the Army sends them. They are hardy and have strong roots in the Army, but they are always ready to fly wherever they need to go having new adventures and making new friends in new lands. Military children learn that home is where their hearts are and that good friends can be found anywhere. They learn that they can adapt and that when the Army sends them to a new place, that is simply the end of one chapter and beginning of another in their lives. With every move come new and exciting adventures, new friends, and new experiences."

Charles thought about that for a while and then asked, "Mommy, are we going to fly on the wind like the dandelion and go to a new place?" His brow was furrowed in much the same way his father's would wrinkle when he was deep in thought.

"No, Charles, we are not going anyplace right now, but someday we probably will. That's just how the Army works. Haven't you had to say good-bye to some friends and make new ones?"

"Yeah, I guess so," replied Charles. Then he brightened. "I made a new friend with Joey, and he wasn't here last year. Did he fly like the dandelion to here from someplace else?"

"Yes, he did," Amy told him, impressed with her toddler's ability to make sense out of new information.

"Okay," said Charles and he took off running ahead of Amy.

When Amy wasn't doing something with or for Charles or working, she began dating again—occasionally going out to dinner or a movie with a colleague. She could never bring herself to consider any of these relationships as serious, though. At the end of every evening spent with a man, she found herself comparing him to Charlie, and he paled by comparison. She would say a polite good night, thank him for a pleasant evening, and fall into her bed—alone.

The Plan

Back in Massachusetts, Charlie and Julia were married in a quiet ceremony with friends and his family in attendance. After honeymooning in Italy, they moved into the home Charlie had bought as a wedding surprise for Amy. He never told Julia that. As far as she knew, it was simply Charlie's house. Julia loved having one of the prettiest houses on Powder Point. She loved being able to play tennis in the side yard and swim grueling laps each morning of the summer in her own pool. It was her dream come true. One summer morning, as she sat on the patio sipping her coffee and looking out over the bay, she mused that she had come a long way from the blue-collar world of South Boston.

How Julia had worked to rid herself of her past! After graduating from high school, she had attended Middlebury College on a scholarship. She'd worked at the Middlebury Inn during the school year and at different Boston restaurants during the summers, jobs she had selected because she knew she would make lots of money in tips. She never spent any of the money she earned, saving it for the day when she would have to impress someone.

Julia was a woman with a plan. During her senior year in high school, she had sat on her bed in the tiny, dark bedroom that she shared with her younger sister and written her plan in her "My Life" notebook. She wrote:

1. Graduate from a prestigious New England college
2. Attend Harvard Law School
3. Find a husband at Harvard, preferably someone who has family ties to a law firm, thus assuring an appointment as a partner in the firm

4. Live happily ever after in high society, never again wearing hand-me-downs or living in a crummy apartment in a crummy town

All she had ever wanted as a small child living in the shadows of Boston society was to one day be a high-powered lawyer working in one of the big firms and being respected and admired by rich and powerful people. She had settled on law after watching television shows with lawyers and seeing the respect and admiration they garnered. She also liked their fancy offices and beautiful clothes.

Growing up, she had studied the ways of rich people and determined that she would live as one of them someday. She studied hard in high school and got lots of scholarships and financial aid from her number one choice, Middlebury College in Vermont. When she went online, looking at pictures of all of the different colleges and universities, Middlebury looked like the kind of place rich kids would go. It kind of had that country club feel to it. She applied for early decision and was accepted.

While at Middlebury, she carefully observed the way the privileged kids dressed and walked and talked. She paid attention to where they went on vacations and what kinds of cars they drove. Working in the restaurants, she observed their table manners. Julia wanted nothing more than to fit in among them.

When she graduated from Middlebury, Julia headed back to Boston—to Cambridge, actually, to Harvard Law School. She knew that if she went to Harvard Law, she would be able to meet someone well connected in society, and she would never have to shop in discount stores again. She would live in a big fancy house and drive a fancy car, and people would respect her. She would leave her roots far behind her, even if they were only a few miles from her success.

Unfortunately for her, Julia never was able to snag anyone at law school, but she did become friends with a young man who had a father who was a senior partner in one of the city's most prestigious firms. This young man was totally unavailable as a boyfriend because he was madly in love with his high school sweetheart, but Julia and he became friends, studying for exams together, occasionally attending parties together, and discussing their plans for their lives (although Julia never told him her true plan). One night, Julia told him how much she hoped she could find a job at a firm in Boston. (She thought if she couldn't go into a firm on the arm of a husband, perhaps she could do it with a well-placed friend.) Julia prickled with excitement. She thought that maybe she could steal Charlie from his fiancée, but after a while, realized that was not to happen. She then determined that she would simply maintain a close friendship with Charlie and hope he would put in a good word for her when she applied to his dad's firm.

Her plan worked, and Julia received an offer from the firm of Donnelly, Winslow, and Adams. She worked very hard and, whenever possible, volunteered for cases she knew would involve working with Charlie. She figured that when it came time to name partners, Charlie could once again put in a good word for her.

Julia's plan worked better than she could have hoped. During late night research sessions with Charlie, listening to him talk sadly of his wife, of how much he missed her and how confused he was, Julia slowly inserted herself more and more into his life. She managed to get invitations to parties he attended, telling him that since his wife wasn't there, she would be happy to go with him—just as his friend. Little by little, Julia would make suggestions like, "Charlie, let's pretend that I'm your wife and see if we can fool people." Always one to love a good joke, Charlie would go along, wrapping his arm protectively around her, looking lovingly into her eyes on the dance floor. Julia was making progress. Fake it until you make it, as her mother used to say.

For more than a year, she worked beside Charlie, attended social events with him, and listened attentively as he cried on her shoulder about the wife he missed so much. She occasionally made offhanded comments about how she would never treat him as callously as Amy had, how she would always worship him and keep him close to her if he were her husband, how Amy was foolish for choosing her career over him. Little by little, she persuaded Charlie that he should not remain married to a woman who had discarded him. Finally, one Saturday night, as she and Charlie were seated in the back of a limousine, he escorting her home to her apartment from a gala they had attended following a long day of work in the office together, Charlie leaned over and kissed her. She acted surprised, while inwardly celebrating victory. Charlie apologized, but Julia quickly turned her face to his and kissed him.

Shortly thereafter, Charlie decided that he could not remain married to someone who did not love him enough to be with him. He asked Julia to marry him and asked Amy for a divorce. Julia quickly accepted his proposal, seeing partner behind her powerful new name. She told Charlie that her parents were dead and that she was an only child. She only invited friends from law school and the office to their wedding—no family. She was convinced that if she had she invited her family, Charlie would never have married her. That was more than five long years ago.

Hearing Charlie coming across the patio, Julia was shaken from her reverie. She had so much now, and in just a short time she and Charlie would be named partners in the firm. Then she would have it all. She just had to keep from getting pregnant.

Charlie really wanted to start a family, and she certainly did not. A screaming baby was not in her plan. She just had to hang in there long enough to make partner. *Who knows?* she thought. *Charlie is a really nice guy and it's nice being known as his wife. Maybe I'll just say that I can't have children and then get my tubes tied. He never has to know.* She smiled sweetly at Charlie as he planted a kiss on her lips and sat to read the paper.

Charlie and Julia had a good life. But every time Charlie brought up the subject of starting a family, Julia would smile coyly and change the subject. Or she would tell him that there was plenty of time for that. Or she would suggest that they could start a family after these tough associate days were over. Once they were partners, she would have more flexibility to become a mother. And Charlie waited, not knowing that Julia never planned on having children.

Often Charlie thought of Amy and wanted desperately to call her, to hear her voice. Even though he was married to Julia, he missed Amy in a way only she would understand. He would find himself looking out the window in his office, seeing a boat sail by, and remember their wonderful, carefree honeymoon—until Amy had shattered its tranquility with her news. He would be sitting quietly on the front veranda of his home or on the patio, watching children learning to sail in the shallow bay and think of his plans to watch his own children doing just that, with Amy by his side, proudly smiling at their son as he trimmed the sails perfectly, and came about with ease. Then he would hear Julia call him and would realize that this was his life now. It was a good life with his beautiful, intelligent wife. Soon they would begin a family. He would have to remember to talk to Julia about that again. She had a way of brushing off the conversation and distracting him every time he brought up the idea of starting a family. He would say, "Jules, how about we try making a baby tonight," and she would change the subject or remind him that they were working fourteen hours a day to make partner. There would be plenty of time for children. But he was beginning to wonder....

The Partner Decisions

The day dawned foggy and chilly, a typical New England March morning. This was a big day for Charlie and Julia—the day when they would officially become partners in the law firm. They drove in to Boston together, chatting about how they would celebrate their big day. They agreed to leave work early and head to Drink for celebratory champagne. Julia decided that they would then have a sumptuous dinner at her favorite Boston restaurant, the exclusive, five-star Menton.

After a long morning, trying to be absorbed in their work, it was time for new partners to be announced. Everyone gathered in the atrium, a long-standing tradition of the firm. With pomp and ceremony, Charlie's father spoke of the hard work put in during the past few years by members of this "class." He actually cited a specific example of exemplary work done by each and every one of the nine associates who were due for a partnership decision. Then he began welcoming new partners into the firm. After each name was announced, every-one applauded politely and the new partner would step forward to shake Mr. Donnelly's hand, as well as those of the other senior partners. Three people's names were called, and each of them proceeded through this ritual. Then Charlie's name was called. Julia gave him a soft kiss of congratulations with everyone watching, and he strode forward to shake his father's hand.

Once Charlie had been welcomed by each senior partner, his father turned to the group of new partners and said, "Welcome to the family, ladies and gentlemen." Without another word, he turned and walked back to his big corner office, closing the door behind himself. Charlie looked at Julia in disbelief. He hurried to her side and whispered, "There must have been a mistake, Julia. I'll take care of it."

Julia looked at him with venom in her eyes. "You'd damn well better," she hissed.

And with that he stormed into his father's office, demanding to know why his wife had been passed over for partnership.

His father sat quietly behind his polished mahogany desk, listening to Charlie rant and rave at him for a few minutes; then he slowly put his hand up to quiet his son.

"Charles," his father began, in his thick, Brahmin-bred accent, "Julia is a lovely girl and a fine lawyer; but you and she have been married now for five years and it is high time you begin a family. If you are not going to make it happen, then maybe you need a little push. Julia is a powerful woman. If she becomes a partner, you will never make me a grandfather. She will work day and night. If she is refused partnership, perhaps she will realize that there is another option—the fine old occupation of motherhood. Maybe now I will have a grandson to spend time with, to take to Sox games and teach to sail like I did you." With that said, he sat back in his chair, obviously daydreaming about spending time with his future grandson.

Charlie sat open-mouthed, not believing what he was hearing. It took a few minutes for the news to register, but when it did, he was furious.

"You can't do that! You can't control peoples' lives like that, Father!" he roared.

"Ah, but I can, Charles," his father replied gently. "You have never completely grown up. Everything has been pretty easy for you, and as a result you haven't become a man and started a family." More to himself than to Charlie, he added, "Amy would never have let you get away with this. If you were with her, I would have a grandson by now."

Not to be pacified, Charlie yelled, "Father! I am not with Amy and that was not my choice. If you recall, that was her choice. I'm with Julia, and I love her. She is my wife, and my own father is preventing her from pursuing the career she wants." Then more quietly, he added, "What am I supposed to say to her?"

"Tell her whatever you need to tell her. Tell her that we could only name four partners. Tell her that her work was not up to par with the others who were named. Or tell her the truth. Maybe she'll see the light. She must have a maternal side in there somewhere," his father replied, a smirk forming on the left corner of his mouth. "You'll both soon realize that this is for the best."

With that, he stood and made it clear that it was time for Charlie to leave his office.

"Don't you have work to do, Mr. Junior Partner?"

Charlie obediently stood, turned, and replied, "Yes, I do. But first I need to see Julia. She was devastated when you omitted her name just now. I honestly don't know how to tell her that you are trying to orchestrate our life for us, trying to force her to have a child so you can be a grandfather." Charlie just stood there looking at his perfectly polished Johnston Murphys. "How can I tell her that, Father?"

More sympathetically now, the elder Charles said, "You just tell her that maybe this is the best thing that could have happened. Now the two of you will be able to start a family and fill up that big, sprawling house of yours. It's time to make it a home." With that, he got up and walked over to his son, putting his arm around his shoulders, and guided him to the now open door.

Once Charlie had left, he turned and walked to the windows. Staring out over Boston Harbor, he said to himself, "Now maybe you will truly see the stuff that girl is made of. I'm sorry, Son, but this is for your own good." When Charlie had started dating Julia, his father had asked the firm's investigator to find out about her. His wife suspected that Julia was not who she said she was, and Charles decided to follow up on her intuition. It usually was spot on. Once the elder Donnelly had all the information on her background, he had a pretty good idea what she saw in his son. Rather than confront her, though, he had wisely decided to bide his time and let her show her true colors. He hoped that his son would not be hurt by her, but he needed to stay out of it. The only interference he ran was making sure that the prenup she signed was ironclad.

Charlie walked down the hall, waited for the elevator, and took it down three floors to Julia's office. As he rapped on the door, she smiled and gestured for him to have a seat. She was on the telephone talking with a client but wanted him to wait. As she finished her conversation, she looked up expectantly.

"Well?" she asked. "Was it just a simple misunderstanding?" As she asked the question, though, she could see the answer on Charlie's face before she heard the words.

"Jules, it's not that simple," Charlie began.

"What's not that simple?" Julia asked, her voice rising slightly as she spoke. "Your father is the managing partner here, and we have paid our dues. Now it's our turn to start sharing in the big pot." She was beginning to worry that all of her plans were about to disintegrate.

"Jules, I just spoke with my father, and he and the other partners have decided that I will be joining the firm but that you will remain a senior associate." He hurriedly added, "They think your work is incredible, but there were just too many people up for partnership this year, and they didn't want it to look like nepotism to name both of us at the same time." *So what if it's a little white lie? It might save her from having hurt feelings. Maybe she will accept that reason better than the truth as my father explained it.*

"You have got to be kidding!" she exploded. "I have been working my ass off in this firm for seven long years, playing the perfect little South Shore wife, and now when I finally might get a personal payoff, I get screwed?" Now she was on fire.

"Do you honestly think I married you because I loved you?" she seethed. "I thought it was a lock to make partner if I was your wife! Now I don't even get that?" Suddenly, she realized what she had said and softened. "Oh, baby, you know I don't mean that. I'm just angry. You know what they say, "You always hurt the ones you love.""

But as Julia tried to backpedal, Charlie's world came crashing down around him—again.

As Julia stung him with her words, all he could think of was Amy and how much he needed her right now. She was his soulmate and the one he always wanted to turn to when he needed someone to talk with or had some exciting news to share. If he heard a great joke, his first thought was to call Amy and tell her. If he saw a funny movie, he longed to talk with her about it. Whenever he was sailing with Julia, it was Amy who was trimming the jib for him in his mind's eye. It really didn't come as a big surprise when Julia told him that she had used him to get ahead in the firm. If he was honest with himself, he had used her too—to get over the horrific loss of Amy's love.

All he said to Julia at this moment, though, was, "I'll have Stan draw up the divorce papers and we can go our separate ways." Thank goodness his father had insisted that they sign a prenuptial agreement. Each would leave the marriage with what each brought into it, as well as 50 percent of anything gained during the marriage. He would keep the Duxbury house and his beloved sailboat. Under the circumstances, Julia agreed to move out immediately and, in fact, left the office to pack up her personal effects and move that very day.

Charlie dragged himself back upstairs to his father's corner office and just stood outside the closed door. After a few minutes, Mrs. Braxton, his father's long-time assistant, asked him if he was okay.

"Oh, yes, of course," he replied absently, and rapped on the door.

"Enter," barked his father.

"Seeing his son's fallen features, he knew the outcome of the partners' decision.

"I'm sorry, Son. I take it Julia took it hard?"

"You might say that," Charlie sarcastically replied. "Stan will be drawing up the divorce papers tomorrow."

"It's all for the best, Son," said his pragmatic father, but that was not what Charlie wanted to hear right now.

Sadly, Charlie asked, "Father, how can you be so cold? My life is overturned again and all you can say is, 'It's all for the best.'"

"Son, I have been on this earth a great deal longer than you and have seen many kinds of people. Julia was not the type of woman you need. She would never have supported your career. She would not have given you children. She is a taker. And she is a liar. I had Joe do a little digging, and it seems that her family is alive and well and living in South Boston. Her father is a union man, works on the docks. Her mother works as a maid at the Holiday Inn. She has a sister in Chelsea who is married and has six kids. Evidently, she didn't think she would catch you if you knew where she came from." Charles Donnelly hated to be the one to tell all this to his only son, but he felt he deserved to know now that Julia had shown her true colors to him.

Seeing Charlie diminish before his eyes, sinking into the wingback chair in front of his desk, head in hands, his voice softened. "Son, why don't you take a few days off and go on a little trip somewhere? It's been many years since you've been to Europe. Remember that trip we took to London when you were younger? That was the last real family vacation before you headed off to college. And, as I recall, you had a pretty nice time in Paris a few years back. Maybe this would be a good time. Take a couple of weeks, pack a bag, grab your passport, and just head out. See where your heart takes you."

"Maybe I will at that," Charlie muttered, immediately thinking that maybe it was time he saw Amy face to face. It had been too long. He missed her terribly and needed to see her, to talk with her, to find out if there was any way they could make life together work. After his experience with Julia, maybe he needed a dose of Amy to mend his heart—or break it again. At any rate, it was certainly worth the risk.

Charlie smiled sadly and looked up at his father, who had been watching him for the few minutes of thoughtful contemplation. "You're not as dumb as I used to think you were," he said. "Manipulative, but not dumb." Charlie's father stood up from his desk at that, walked over to where Charlie sat, leaned over, took Charlie's hand in his own, and as Charlie stood, embraced him rather than shaking his hand, much to Charlie's surprise.

"Your old man's got more than a few tricks up his sleeve, young man," he told Charlie. "As I said, I've seen all types, and Amy's a keeper. Whatever it takes, go find her," he said, as though he knew what Charlie had been thinking. "A lot of water has gone under the bridge, and you are very different people today than you were seven years ago. See what happens. If she hasn't found someone else, maybe you could work something out."

"I think I will," agreed Charlie. And he turned and left his father's hopeful smile behind.

The News

While Charlie's life was being shattered, Amy received the shocking news that she was headed to Afghanistan. Although she knew that she would probably see combat duty during her time in the Army, she never thought that it would be while her son was so young. Of course, the Army didn't care if she was a single mother. *That isn't their problem*, she thought, bitterly. *But it sure is mine. I'm the only parent Charles has ever known. What can I do? What if something happens to me? Charles will be all alone in the world. Oh*, she thought, *I shouldn't have kept him from his whole family for so long. That has been selfish. Seeing them a couple of times a year was not at all fair to him or to them. I just wanted him all for myself. He has been my North Star, and I have been his. But now it's time to be practical. I can't put him in the position of losing the only parent he has ever known and get sent to his grandparents or to my sister without ever really knowing them.*

So, without another moment's thought, Amy decided to take the two weeks' leave owed to her and return to Massachusetts where she and Charles could spend time with her parents. Maybe it would be easier for him to stay with them if she spent some time there with him as they got to know each other. They had seen so very little of each other over the years. She picked up her phone and placed a call to the States.

"Hi, Mom!" she said cheerily. "How'd you like some company?"

"What are you saying? Are you coming here?"

"Would you believe tomorrow, Mom? Can you or Daddy pick us up at Logan? I'll let you know when we're arriving as soon as I make reservations. We're flying commercial."

The Internet being the wonderful tool it is, Amy went online and found Charlie's address. Oddly, the listing was just in his name. She was surprised that Julia's name was not listed as well. She would assume that a high-powered Boston attorney would at least insist that her name be listed in the white pages. She cringed when she realized that his address was on Powder Point. He was, apparently, living her dream. He must have bought one of the houses near his parents', or maybe he was living with his parents.

"Oh well," she said to herself. "You could have had that life if you had allowed your father to pull some strings, but you were too proud to do that." As she said the words, a thought began forming, but she was too busy to allow it to fully emerge. She had reservations to make, a house to close, movers to call, and packing to begin.

When Amy picked Charles up from school that afternoon, they walked home together. He chattered about getting an A on a spelling test and how he was the best reader in the whole class. He asked her excitedly if he could sign up for baseball, told her about his best friend's antics that day, and then ran ahead to play with a dog sitting in a driveway waiting for him to walk by. Every day he stopped for a couple of minutes and played with the same golden retriever. Amy often thought that she really should get him a dog of his own. He so loved animals and had never met a dog that didn't fall in love with him.

After Charles finished playing fetch with the dog, he rejoined his mom to continue their walk home. As he started talking again about all his exciting news of the day, Amy laughed and interrupted him.

"Charles, are you going to let me get a word in this afternoon? I have some pretty exciting news myself, you know."

Charles looked up at his mother then and saw her whole face smiling back at him.

"Oh, Mom! What is it? Your mouth says it's good news but your eyes aren't sure."

As she had many times before, Amy marveled at her son's ability to read people. Aloud, she said, "When we get home, I need you to go to your room…"

At that, Charles sobered, thinking that he had done something wrong and wondered why his mother's face had lied to him.

"I need you to go to your room," she continued "and take out any clothes and books and toys that you think you might need at Nana and Grampy's house for the next couple of weeks and put them on your bed."

Charles stopped walking and looked incredulously up at his mother.

"Are we really going to their house? All the way across the world? Are we going to be dandelions?"

Amy assured him that they were, indeed, going across the world together the very next day. They hurried the rest of the way home, Charles asking questions faster than she could answer them.

"How will we get there? How far is it? Is it hot there? Do they know we're coming? Can I call my friends? When will we be back? Can I take Gruffles (his stuffed dog)? Will I have a room there? Will Aunt Susan be there? Can I go to the ocean? How about baseball? Will I meet my cousins? What about school?" The questions tumbled out of him one after another.

Opening the front door of their house, Amy told her son to go take out his favorite things, those things he couldn't live without, and leave the rest. She assured him that there were lots of stores in Boston—"way more than here"—and that his grandmother and grandfather would probably want to take him shopping anyway. He ran off to decide what to take on his first big adventure of his young life. Amy went to her room to pack and to think about how to break the news to him that she would be leaving him there with his grandparents while she went to far-off Afghanistan.

The Confusion

In true romantic comedy fashion, and with the lack of timing that Charlie and Amy's relationship had always had, while Amy and Charles were packing, Charlie was booking the next flight to Germany.

When Charlie arrived in Landstuhl the next morning, he found an empty house, with no one answering the doorbell. As he turned to leave, a neighbor arrived home. Getting out of her car, she approached the handsome man who looked so confused in her neighbor Amy's front yard.

"Hi, y'all," she cooed in her sweet southern drawl. "I'm Beth. And you are?"

"Oh, hi. I'm Charles Donnelly, Amy's hus…um, a friend of Amy's." As he uttered those words, he tripped over the word "friend." "You wouldn't know where I could find her, would you?"

Beth put a hand on her hip and looked at Charlie from head to toe. *Donnelly, huh?* she thought. *I wonder what relation this gorgeous man is to you, Amy.* She flipped her long blond hair over her shoulder and replied, "Well, sure I do, darlin'. You just missed them. I drove them to the airport to go to the States. Their flight isn't for hours, but she hates to be late."

Charlie's heart dropped, thinking that "they" meant that Amy was now married to someone else. Not wanting to make the situation awkward, he merely thanked the woman and turned to leave. As he was about to get into his car, Beth didn't want her time with this handsome man to end, so she offered, "I think Amy was heading to the States with her son to visit her folks. I don't know why they had to leave so early. My little one kept me up all night." At this, Charlie stopped dead in his tracks, his back to Beth. He turned slowly and stared at her, not believing that he could possibly have heard her correctly. *Amy has*

159

a child? He had always thought that they would someday raise a family together. Now he found out that she had another man's son. His heart began to pound in his chest.

"Is her husband going with her?" he asked as casually as he could.

"Husband? No, she don't have a husband. It's just her and little Charles," answered Beth, happy to be engaging with the handsome man once again. "And Amy never talks about her son's father. In fact, I don't think she's had a serious date the whole time she's been here. She just lives for that boy. It ain't natural, but that Charles is one lucky six-year-old. She just worships him."

Suddenly Charlie could no longer hear her voice. His world was spinning. She named him Charles. That was no coincidence, he thought. Gathering his wits about him, he asked, barely above a whisper, "How old is the boy? Did you say he's six?"

The neighbor replied, "Yeah. We had a fun birthday party for him. My son Billy and him are good friends, even though Billy's younger. We had balloons, and cake and ice cream, and played games…

"Hey, mister, are you okay?" As Charlie slumped to the ground, she approached him nervously. Sitting right on the tarred driveway, he hid his face in his hands and wept. Nothing Beth could say or do could console him. All the stress of the past seven years erupted from him, its lava spilling down his shirt and wetting the land around him. As he cried, he kept repeating, "No. No. No."

Even though she thought he was pretty good-looking, Beth wasn't looking for trouble with a total stranger who would cry in her neighbor's front yard. What kind of man was this anyway? About to call for the MPs, Beth made one last attempt to comfort Charlie. After all, he must be some kind of relation to Amy. It wouldn't do for her to be rude.

"Mister, would you like to have a glass of water or some sweet tea? Coffee? How about a stiff drink? Hey, calm down, mister. What did I say? And then, after a brief pause, she asked, "Who are you anyhow?"

Gathering his wits, Charlie sat up straighter, his Cole Hahn loafers planted on the damp earth beneath them. He took his monogrammed handkerchief from the pocket of his powder-blue pinstriped shirt and wiped his eyes, his face, and blew his nose. He looked down at the wet stains on his wrinkled khakis and brushed at them with his hand as he got up, gathered himself to his full height, and smiled as best he could through his embarrassment.

"I'm really sorry, ma'am. I didn't mean to alarm you. Believe me. This is not like me at all." He couldn't quite believe the extent of his public reaction. "This has all come as a bit of a shock. That's all."

Always the nosy neighbor looking for some good gossip for tomorrow's coffee klatch and really getting a kick out of this guy's New England accent, Beth couldn't help asking, "What has?"

"I just didn't know that Amy had a son, that's all."

Beth couldn't understand why such news would hit him so hard. Never one to be shy about asking questions when she wanted to know something, she boldly asked, "Well, why should that be such a shock to you? "

Charlie really didn't want to get into it with her, but Beth was insistent. She now stood, hands on her hips between him and his car. He figured that he would have to tell her something in order to leave.

"It's just that Amy and I used to be married. But we never had any children."

Excited now that she might be getting some really good stuff, Beth said, "Well, I didn't know that. Amy is probably my best friend here, and I didn't know that. Hell, I was the one who was with her when her son was born. And even I didn't know she'd been married." As she said this, Beth made a mental note to ask the other ladies if any of them had known that the pretty young neighbor had been married. All this time they had thought that she had Charles as the result of some one-night stand or something. They knew she never dated much, and they had never been able to figure her out.

"Well, she was," Charlie replied, interrupting Beth's thoughts. "I am Charlie Donnelly, Amy's husband. We were married almost seven years ago. Well, actually, I'm her ex-husband, I guess," he added more to himself than to the neighbor.

As the synapses fired in her brain and Beth did the math, she began to understand the implications. "Oh my," she uttered. "Oh my."

Looking at this gorgeous blond man, Beth could see Charles's tiny features reflected in his strong ones. She was pretty sure that she was talking with Charles's father.

As she was about to ask yet another prying question that was really none of her business, the baby monitor in her hand came to life with a series of insistent cries. *Damn*, she thought. *I was just about to get to the bottom of this mystery.* Always the good mom, though, she quickly turned and tottered off on her three-inch mules to her front door. As she approached her doorway, she turned and called to Charlie, "Well, I need to go now. Jimmy will make himself sick cryin' if I don't pick him up when he wakes up from his nap. If you want someone to talk to, though, I'm right over here, and I'm a real good listener." As she spoke, she flipped her blond hair again and gave Charlie a come-hither look. And then she closed her door and was gone, leaving Charlie standing in Amy's driveway with nothing but his thoughts.

"I don't believe it," he muttered. "I don't believe it. How could she not tell me?" And with that thought, he became angry.

"How could she not tell me?" he yelled into the empty air. "How could she not tell me?" he repeated more quietly. "How could she not tell me?" he practically whispered.

Energized, Charlie's legally trained mind began to kick into action. "Okay. First, I have to find her," he said. Hadn't the woman said that Amy and her son—their son—had gone to the States to visit her folks? That meant they were on their way to Duxbury—where he had just come from. He would call Amy's mom to see if they had arrived yet. Then he would get on the first plane back to Logan and straighten this mess out once and for all.

With that thought, Charlie had a plan. He folded himself back into his rental car and backed out of the driveway, dialing the airline as he drove. He booked the last first-class seat on a plane leaving in two hours. Then he dialed Amy's mom's number. When she answered the phone, he didn't indicate that he knew anything about the boy. No reason to spook her.

"Why hello, Mary. Long time no see," Charlie jovially began.

"Why, is that you, Charlie? My word. Charlie Donnelly, I haven't spoken with you in a long time. I did read that you had married Julia Arnold a while back. Maggie tells me that you bought the old MacDougal place on Powder Point a few years ago. Is that true? I can't believe we never see each other around town. It's not that big a place." With that her voice drifted off. *What a coincidence that he should call her so soon after Amy had told her that she and Charles were visiting. Was there something Amy wasn't telling her?*

"Mary, I was wondering if I could stop by for a visit," Charlie began. "It's been too long. And, yes, I did buy the old MacDougal place. Actually, I bought it for Ames, but that never worked out."

"Oh yes, now I remember. I guess my old memory isn't what it once was, Charlie."

"Mary, as I said, it's been too long," Charlie continued as he approached the drop-off location for his car. "What do you say I take you out to lunch tomorrow? I have a real craving for The Milepost's fried chicken." He gave her no indication that he wasn't sitting in his den across town. "Thank goodness for international cell phones," he thought.

Mary hesitated for a minute and in that hesitation, Charlie knew that Amy was on her way there. "Charlie, I'd love to see you again, but tomorrow is tough. I'm real busy tomorrow."

"Oh, now Mary. I'm always busy, but I'd love to make time for you. It's been a long time since I've had lunch with a beautiful older woman." Charlie was really turning on the old Donnelly charm now and was a little ashamed of himself for doing so. Since he had an idea why she was hesitating, he decided to make it easier for her.

"Mary, how about we just meet at the Milepost? That way I won't take more of your time than you can give. Let's make it twelve thirty tomorrow. Okay, beautiful?" Then he crossed his fingers and hoped that she would meet him.

"Okay, you old charmer. I never could refuse you and you know it. Even when you and Amy were in high school, you had me wrapped around your little finger. My, er, company will have to understand that

I have a former commitment for an hour or so. Okay, I'll meet you at the Milepost. But I'm going to make you buy me a lobster!"

Charlie laughed at that, relieved, and said, "It's a deal. I'll see you then."

He jumped out of the car, grabbed his bag, and ran into the airport, hoping he could catch the flight to Logan on time. As Charlie rushed through the airport, he was grateful that he just had his leather carry-on. He wouldn't have had time to check bags. He heard his flight boarding being called as he went through security, and ran the distance to the gate, arriving just before the door was closed. He slipped onto the plane and into his seat as the door was closed.

Unbeknownst to Charlie, Amy and Charles were only a few feet behind him in coach on the same flight.

The Grandparents

When the plane landed, Charlie jumped up and hurried through the airport, rushed through customs, and ran to the parking garage where he hopped in his Lexus and drove to Duxbury. He had a lot of thinking to do before his lunch with Mary.

Meanwhile, Amy and Charles waited as passengers disembarked in front of them and then made their way through customs and to baggage claim where her parents would be waiting.

"Mom!" Amy spotted her mother standing by baggage claim. She grabbed Charles by the hand and rushed forward to greet her mother.

Meanwhile, her mother, seeing Amy talking animatedly with the young boy, thought, as she did every time she saw him, "My, God! He looks just like Charlie!"

Amy let go of Charles's hand and hugged her mother, feeling like a little girl again, safe in her mother's arms. For an instant she felt so safe that she never wanted to let go. Tears welled in her eyes as she realized how long it had been since she had enjoyed loving human contact with another adult. Did she really have to let go? Reluctantly, she released her hold on her mother and stepped back, the two women's teary eyes meeting each other.

Charles tugged at his mother's jacket, as if to remind her that he was still there. Bending down, Amy tucked his little hand in hers and said, "You remember Nana, Charles. Isn't it nice that she came to pick us up? We're going to visit Nana and Grampy at their house, remember?"

Charles was going through a shy stage and absolutely refused to even look at his Nana. He tucked his face into Amy's side, and there it stayed as they waited for their luggage. After all, he only saw his grandparents a couple of times a year. He needed some time to warm up to them again.

"Where's Daddy," Amy asked while she was pulling their bags off the carousel, but she no sooner asked the question than she saw her big, strong, handsome father striding toward them.

"Well, it's about time," he bellowed, as he approached them, working hard to hide the emotion he felt as he saw them. "Did you bring everything you own, Amy?" he asked as he began piling the suitcases onto the cart he had rented.

"I love you too, Daddy," Amy replied as she made him stop what he was doing long enough to give her a big hug, letting go of Charles's hand again as she did so.

"And who is this big boy with you?" her father asked, a twinkle in his eye. "It can't be Charles. He's just a little guy. This one's almost all grown up!"

That's all it took to get through to Charles, who replied in a tiny voice, "It's me, Grampy. Don't you remember me? I'm Charles."

Kneeling down as if to get a closer look, her father said, "Well, now that you mention it, I guess it is you, after all. What has your mother been feeding you, young man? You've grown a foot since I saw you last. I was planning on doing little boy things with you while you were here, but I think we're going to have to plan some man stuff, don't you?"

Charles's face broke into a freckly grin as he expressed his approval of that idea. Braver than Amy had ever seen him, he walked up to his grandfather and asked, "Do you think we could go to the beach? Mommy says you have a really nice beach, and I've never been to a beach before. She showed me pictures, though, and it looks like a lot of fun."

"Young man, we will definitely go to the beach. In fact, if you get a good night's sleep tonight, we will go to the beach tomorrow. What do you think? Just you and me?"

Charles nervously looked at his mother who was smiling and nodding and agreed that he would like that idea very much. Amy marveled at her father's ability to make Charles feel welcome and loved so quickly.

"Well, then, let's get this show on the road, shall we?" And with that, Amy's father picked Charles up and deposited him atop the luggage, then pushed a smiling Charles and the cart of luggage ahead of them all, asking Charles to let him know if he was going to run into anything or anyone.

"Grampy, there's a post in front of us!" Charles exclaimed, as his grandfather deftly swerved at the last minute to avoid it, knocking over a giggling Charles and annoying his daughter and wife.

"George, you stop fooling around with that thing," warned Amy's mother. "You're going to knock Charles off and hurt him."

Winking first at Charles, he turned, saluted, and sheepishly said, "Ma'am, yes, ma'am," then proceeded to career through the doors and out onto the sidewalk, as Amy and her mother shot looks at each other that said, *He's never going to listen to us, is he?*

"Grampy! Grampy! The street is coming! Stop!" Charles yelled, and the luggage cart abruptly stopped inches from the curb.

"Well, do you want to come with me to get the car, young man, or do you want to stay here with the ladies?" As he said this, he scrunched his nose as though smelling something bad.

Charles looked first at his mother who was smiling and nodding her head in her father's direction; then he smiled and said, "I want to go with you, Grampy."

"Well, then, let's get a move on," George said, holding out his hand for Charles to take. Off they strode, the older grandfather and the little boy who had just discovered what fun it could be to have a man around.

"Well, dear," Amy's mother started, when the two guys were out of earshot. "It's lovely to have you home, but is there another reason why you're here? You look tense."

"Ma, this really isn't the place to discuss it. Let's wait until we get home. Then we can sit on the porch and have a good talk."

Something in Amy's voice worried her mother, but she held her tongue. After all, she had her own secret, didn't she? She was having lunch with Charles's father and the love of her daughter's life tomorrow. She didn't want to have a heart-to-heart before the lunch because she was afraid she would tell Amy. "Well, honey, you must be tired after your long trip. I think we should go to bed when we get home and have that little talk tomorrow afternoon."

Now Amy was really confused. Ordinarily, there would be nothing that would keep her mother from sitting and talking with her, especially when she had returned after being away for so long. What was she not telling Amy? Her mother had never been a very good dissembler, and this time was no different. She was up to something, all right. But what was it? She decided not to push it. She'd find out later. What she said was, "Okay, then. When we get back, I'll unpack and put Charles to bed. Geesh! I've been gone for all this time and, when I get home I get to be Cinderella instead of having a nice long chat with my mother." Even though her voice evidenced her annoyance, she smiled and gave her mother another hug for good measure. If she wanted to keep her little secret, then fine. All in good time.

"Oh! Here they are!" she heard her mother say, interrupting her pity party. And, sure enough, there they were, with her little man sitting proudly in the front passenger seat next to his grandfather.

"You get in back right now, you little devil. You know better! You aren't old enough to be sitting in the front seat and you know it," Amy scolded, wiping the smile off Charles's face. She was immediately sorry for spoiling his fun, and tried to recover by saying, "That seat is for Nana. You sit in back with me. I missed you while you were gone."

Charlie took the bait and whined, "Mooooommmm. I was only gone for a few minutes. Me and Grampy had man stuff to do. We got the car for you ladies." Amy cringed as her son and her father high-fived each other before Charles got out of the car and moved to the backseat. She held her tongue, though, and didn't even correct his grammar. He was just too happy for her to burst his bubble—again.

The ride from Logan back to Duxbury was full of family chatter. Charles read road signs, since he now knew how to read and couldn't get enough of it. Amy talked about their trip and how excited Charles had been to fly for the first time. Her father made faces at Charles in the rearview mirror, making him laugh. But Amy's mother sat in front uncharacteristically quiet, gazing out the window at the passing scenery. She occasionally muttered, "That's nice" or "My, my, really?" But she was definitely preoccupied. She kept looking at her watch and asked her husband when they would get home. Amy had no doubt, as they passed the Duxbury town line sign, that her mother was up to something, and she planned to find out what it was.

As they pulled into the driveway, Amy looked at the house and felt she was truly home. This was the house she had lived in when she met Charlie, the house where she had sat on the front porch swinging and talking and making out with him, the house where she had packed up her things and moved away from the only man she had ever loved. As she reminisced, a movie playing in her mind of all the moments that make a life worth living that occurred in this house, she heard from a distance, "Mom! Mom! Are you listening to me?" And she was back in the present. Her excited son was itching to get the car unloaded so that he and his grandfather could begin their adventures. "Mom! Grampy says as soon as we get the car stuff in the house and I go to sleep, tomorrow we can go to the beach. Pleeeeeeeease hurry."

Amy looked out of the car to see her little man half carrying, half dragging a huge suitcase all by himself.

Well, you are in a hurry if you're helping out so much, she thought. *That's nice. I was hoping that you would be able to bond with your grandparents. You're going to need to love them and trust them to take care of you while I'm away.* Out loud, she said, "Hey, bucko! Wait for me. Let me help you with that" and she ran to catch up with him, taking the suitcase from his tiny arms. "Why don't you go back to the car and get my carry-on for me, okay?" And off Charles ran to do his part in unloading the car.

As Amy walked up the three steps to the front porch, she looked to her left and saw the old porch swing right where she remembered it. She and Charlie had spent many wonderful, hopeful, romantic, silly evenings next to each other on the old wooden swing, laughing and talking of their future, and kissing. Amy lost herself in her memories long enough for Charles to catch up with her, carry-on bag clutched in his arms.

"Why do you look so funny, Mommy?" he asked, confused by her melancholy expression.

Hearing his little voice broke her trance and she jumped a little as she answered him. "I guess 'cause I'm funny looking," she said, crossing her eyes and sticking her tongue out to one side, a face that always made Charles roar with laughter. This time was no different. She opened the screen door to the house and booted him lightly in the fanny as he walked in ahead of her.

Suddenly Amy felt as though she were seventeen again. She was home. She was safe. Nothing bad could happen to her here. Charles would be safe here. She just hoped that her parents were up to the task. If not, then she would ask Susan to take care of her little boy. Susan would love it, and her husband, John, would have a great time with a surrogate son. The two girls were girly girls, and while he loved them with all his heart, he was left out of a lot of their activities as Susan went shopping with them, was den mother for their Brownie troop, curled their hair, and tied their ribbons. She was usually the parent of choice for dance lessons and room parent at school. Sometimes he felt kind of lonely and even joked that he was going to get a male dog just so that he would have another guy in the house. He would definitely have fun with Charles doing boy stuff. And Charles would definitely love having someone to do boy stuff with him.

But Amy had decided that the best choice while she was in harm's way would be for Charles to be with her parents. Her mother would nurture and love and cuddle and fawn over him. Her father would teach him to fish and take him to the dump (actually a social destination in Duxbury). He would take him to the base and show him fighter planes and "cool stuff" as Charles would say. He would have their undivided attention, something he would need without her. Up until now she had been his entire life.

Stop thinking about that, Amy, or you are going to start crying, she cautioned herself. Suddenly she realized that Charles was just standing there in the foyer wondering which way to go. The confused look on his face made her smile at him.

"So what do you think of the old farmhouse, buddy? Pretty cool, huh? Want a tour so you know where everything is?"

Just then her father came in carrying the largest suitcase. "Out of my way you two!" he shouted, huffing a little under its weight. "I have to take these bricks upstairs."

Charles looked even more confused, which made Amy laugh. "Don't worry. I didn't bring any bricks. It's all our clothes—well mostly yours, little man. Come on, let's follow Grampy and I'll show you where your room will be. It's right across the hall from mine." And they each picked up what they had been carrying and followed her father up the stairs. Unbeknownst to anyone but her, everything Charles owned was in those suitcases. She wanted to make sure that he had everything he could possibly want while she was away.

When they arrived at the guest room, Amy was shocked. It looked nothing like the last time she had seen the green gingham-and-lace room. It had been a pretty country guest room when she left. Now it was enough to take her breath away. Her parents had redecorated the room for their grandson. Amy realized that her dad must have gotten a heads up about her transfer and assumed that she would bring Charles to stay with her parents.

Charles's eyes grew to twice their normal size as he looked around. The first thing he noticed were the airplanes seemingly flying all around the room. (George had tied them to hooks in the ceiling with fishing wire to make them look like they were suspended in midair.) The ceiling had been painted light blue with fluffy white clouds floating across it. The window seat that looked out onto the side yard had been enclosed with a navy curtain that was pulled back with bright red tiebacks now to reveal a red cushioned seat just right for a little boy to sit on and dream of flying as he gazed out the window. Across one wall was a floor-to-ceiling bookcase, and on it were many of the games and toys Amy had loved as a child—Chutes and Ladders, Candy Land, Checkers, Life, Monopoly—as well as her old comic books—*Archie, Little Lotta, Nancy, Richie Rich*—and her Tinker Toys and Legos and Lincoln Logs. A small pine table with two little chairs sat in one corner by the bookcase, and in the other was a wonderful child-sized pine rocking chair. Across the room, she saw the new bed—a pine double bed with lots of pillows shaped like military airplanes and a comforter that looked like the cloud-filled ceiling. Sitting on one of the two bedside tables was a B-52 alarm clock, and on the other was a lamp with little airplanes flying around the top.

"Wow! What did you do?" she exclaimed as she gasped at the sight. Then, because she was emotional these days, she began crying.

At that, her father's beaming face clouded and her mother (who had run into the house ahead of them to turn on the lamp and make sure everything was just right) worriedly asked, "Don't you like it?"

"Like it? It's amazing! How? Why? When?" Amy's words came tumbling out of her mouth as she tried to catch up.

Suddenly, they all just stood and watched as Charles ran across the room, leapt up on the bed, and began jumping up and down in excitement.

"Is this really my room?" he asked, disbelief plastered on his face. "I love it!" He then added, eyes wide, "It's *huge!*"

"Yes, dear, it is your room—all yours," answered Mary. We hoped that someday you would be able to visit us, and when you did you'd need a room of your very own. We never had a little boy, so it was an awful lot of fun for us to do this for you. Do you like it?"

Up to this point, Charles had been infatuated with his grandfather but shy with his grandmother. When she told him this, he jumped off the bed, ran to her, and hugged her with all his fifty-pound, six-year-old might, excitedly saying into her side, "Nana, it's the bestest room I ever saw in my whole life!"

Hearing that, the adults all laughed, and George said in mock seriousness, "In your whole life? Are you sure? You mean you have never seen a room better than this one?"

Charles did not understand the joke and replied in all seriousness, "No, Grampy. I've *never* seen a better room."

"Well, then," his grandfather teased. "I guess you don't want to go to the beach tomorrow. You can just stay here in this great room."

This worried Charles. He really did love the room, but he really did want to go to the beach. He'd seen pictures in his mother's albums and seen beaches in movies. He couldn't wait to see one in real life.

"Grampy, can we go to the beach and then when we get back I can be in my room?"

"You've got it, big man. That sounds like a plan. Who knows? I might even hang out in here with you. This is a fun place. We could play one of those games. But it's getting late. You need to get ready for bed."

Amy hugged first her mother and then her father again, amazed that they would go to this much trouble for her little boy. They must know what she was about to ask them, and she would make sure that they understood just how much she appreciated the fact that they had made Charles a special place where he could retreat and be a little boy.

As she was about to become emotional again, her mother suggested that they all go to Amy's room so she could see what had happened in there. The door was closed, and when she opened it she discovered a country retreat—the most warm and welcoming room she could have imagined. With touches of her favorite things still there, her mother had redecorated to make it a grown-up room instead of the teenager's room she had left. Overstuffed chairs upholstered in pastels of pink and blue flowers sat welcoming by the windows, while a white four-poster, queen-sized bed stood sentry where her little twin bed had been. A dotted Swiss bedspread peeked out from under pink, powder-blue, and pale green shams and pillows. White ruffled curtains fluttered at the open windows as a small breeze welcomed her to her new safe haven. Across the room was her old desk, refinished and painted white to match the bed. On the bulletin board over the desk, her teen years said hello to her—homecoming corsage, high school ID, beach pass, photos of friends, ticket stubs from movies and concerts, and a picture of her with Charlie at the senior prom. Charles didn't think much of the room, but when he saw the pictures he asked, puzzled, "Mommy, who is that boy with you? He looks like me."

Amy's heart stopped for a second, the room swirled, and she almost fell over. How in the world could he have noticed that? Sure, they have the same hair and eyes and nose and smile and dimples. Sure, their freckles are placed in all the right places to make them look boyish and adorable. And Charles had noticed! Amy had not thought of that possibility. She weighed her answer carefully. She would not lie to him, but she was certainly not ready to tell him the story of his birth yet, either. He was only a little boy and not ready for that bombshell.

Actually, Amy had dreaded the day when she would have to tell Charles about his father. She was surprised that she had gotten away with not telling him for this long. After all, most of his friends had mothers and fathers living together on the base. He had often wondered why he didn't have a father, but she usually could put him off by telling him that she loved him enough for two parents, hug him, tickle him, and change the subject. Now, though, as she looked at him, he was staring her square in the eye and had the most befuddled expression on his little Charlie face.

Amy looked first at her father and then at her mother, but they stood silently, as if to say that this was her issue to deal with and not theirs. Neither of them said a word.

Well, Amy thought. *What do I do now?* She knelt down, looked at Charlie, and simply told him the truth.

"That was my high school boyfriend. He was very special to me, and we were all dressed up in that picture because we went to a very special dance together. Don't we look silly in those funny clothes?"

Charles was not buying it.

"But why does he look so much like me?"

It was times like this that Amy did not appreciate her son's precocity. He had been an intuitive child ever since she could remember, always attuned to the world in ways other children were not. He seemed wise beyond his years somehow. In fact, she often called him her great thought thinker and joked to her friends that he was an old man caught in a little boy's body. Sometimes he could be so serious and thoughtful, spend hours just thinking and then come out with an idea or a view of something that even she had not thought of before.

That precocity was rearing an ugly head now. He seemed to know something that he didn't know. He seemed to suspect that there was something about this person who looked like him, but he didn't know what yet. Again, he asked, "Why, Mommy? Is he my twin? My teacher says that everyone has a twin somewhere in the world. Maybe he's my twin!" With that thought, Charles's concern burst forth in a huge grin.

He was proud that he had figured the mystery out all by himself and became excited that he had discovered his twin in the world.

"When we get back home I'm going to tell her that I found my twin!" he exclaimed excitedly. "Can I show her the picture? She'll never believe me if I don't show her the picture."

Dumbfounded, Amy knew she had dodged a bullet. She stuttered, "Um, yeah, sure, Charles. We probably can find a picture or two around here of him where he looks like you. Maybe you can look at some pictures with Nana and find one you like. He was a very good friend of mine, so we have lots of pictures of him."

"Okay," Charles answered, and was on to the next subject—going to the beach. "Grampy, what time are we going to the beach?"

"Well, big man, I have some things to do in the morning, things you can help me with if you want." Charles grinned and nodded his head. "I guess we can go around eleven and have a picnic on the beach unless the women need us for any man stuff around here."

"No, George," his wife replied with a chuckle in her voice. "I think we womenfolk can manage just fine without you around for a while. Besides, I have that errand to run, remember?" And a look passed between the two of them that was best described as conspiratorial. Amy was positive that something odd was up. If they thought that they were going to keep a secret from her they were wrong. She'd tail her mother when she left if she had to.

"What are you up to?" she asked her mother. When she asked the question, she saw her mother's cheeks flush, the Irish curse that gave her away every time. Her mother recovered quickly, though, and said that it was time for everyone to go to bed. With that, she turned, told Amy over her shoulder that she was glad she liked the room, and disappeared. Seconds later, her father followed her mother down the hall to their room.

"Hmmmm," Amy thought. "It would appear that I am not the only one keeping secrets around here. Touché, Mother."

Amy ran a bath for Charles and then tucked him in. She was pleased to see that he looked comfortable in this room. He asked her to sing their song and she began singing,

"When you're down and troubled and you need some lovin' care,
And nothing, nothing is going right,
Close your eyes and think of me and soon I will be there
To brighten up even your darkest night..."

She looked down and saw that the excitement of the day had caught up with him and he was already sound asleep.

The next morning, Amy awoke to the smell of coffee brewing and muffins baking. She went into Charles's room to wake him and found an empty bed. She showered and dressed quickly and ran down the stairs to the kitchen where she discovered Charles and his grandfather sitting on stools at the center island while her mother scurried from refrigerator to counter to cabinet, pulling together a breakfast fit for a king in moments. By the time Amy sat at the table, a plate had already appeared loaded with scrambled eggs, crisp bacon, and a blueberry muffin. A steaming cup of coffee was placed on the table in front of her as her mother kissed the top of her head. "It's good to have you home," she whispered into Amy's ear.

Once everyone had polished off breakfast, George took Charles out to the barn to work on an old car he was fixing up. Charles wasn't sure what they were going to do, but he knew it would be fun because it was man stuff with his grandfather.

Mary washed up the dishes while chatting with Amy, and then took down the old wicker picnic basket. Into it went paper plates, napkins, cups, a Thermos of ice-cold milk and another of iced tea, followed by an egg salad sandwich with lettuce on whole grain bread for Grampy and a ham and cheese on white bread for Charles (cut in quarters with the crust removed, of course).

At about this time, the menfolk returned to the house, covered in grease and dirt.

"Don't you go bringing that dirt into my house," chastised Mary. "You go right out there and wash up." She pointed to the slop sink on the back porch. Her husband grinned, stood tall, and saluted, saying,

"Ma'am, yes ma'am." Charles thought that was funny so he did the same thing, much to Amy's amusement.

When they returned to the kitchen, somewhat cleaner, Mary brought the big crockery jar filled to the brim with freshly baked chocolate chip cookies to the island. Charles's eyes became owl-like again. He had never seen so many cookies in one place before. At his house, if his mother baked cookies (and she didn't do that very often) she only made a dozen or so. Here was a jar filled with many dozens of cookies. His grandfather reached over and grabbed a handful, handing him two of them under the level of the countertop, thinking he was sneaking them. His wife didn't miss a trick, though, and even though her back was turned, she scolded him for giving Charles cookies before lunch. George sent her a "who, me?" look when she turned around, and they both smiled knowingly.

Charles wasn't sure if he should eat the cookies or not, but he wanted to sooooo badly that he gave in and munched on them right in front of his grandmother. She mock scolded him, telling him that he had better eat his whole lunch even if he had already had cookies, and proceeded to fill a zip-lock bag with about ten more cookies— just for the two of them to have on the beach at their special first picnic. Charles couldn't believe his eyes. If this was what having his grandparents in his life was like, he never wanted to leave them. Before he could finish the thought, the wicker basket was buckled shut with two leather straps and his grandfather was telling him that it was time to go.

Just when Charles was about to say that he had to go say good-bye to his mother, she walked into the room. She put her hands on her hips and exclaimed that she couldn't believe he was going to leave without even saying good-bye. Charles was horrified until he realized she was teasing. He ran across the polished hardwood floor to her, jumped up into her arms, and gave her a kiss and a big hug. Could this possibly be the shy little boy who had arrived in the United States just last night? She couldn't believe the rapid transformation. Her parents were miracle workers.

Well, she thought, *let's hope you are miracle workers because I'm about to ask you for a miracle or two.* She smiled at Charles and told him to have a good time. She wanted to tell him not to go in the water, to watch out for horseshoe crabs, to put on sunscreen, to wear a hat, to eat his lunch, to mind his grandfather, to sit in the backseat, to put on his seat belt, but she held her tongue and simply told him to have fun and stood on the front porch waving to him as he happily left the driveway, sitting in the front passenger seat, hatless, probably going to get a sunburn, and definitely (if she knew her father) going to go in the water clothes and all.

The Lunch

The car had no sooner left the driveway than Amy's mother came bustling out the door, a pretty pink sweater over her shoulders. She hugged Amy and told her that she should be back in about an hour. "You just rest up from your long trip, sweetie. It will be good for you to have some quiet time without all of us around here driving you nuts." Her mother said this as she hurried down the front walk to her car parked at the side of the driveway on the worn grass under the big oak tree.

Again, Amy wanted to ask her where she was going, to insist that her mother tell her, to ask why she was being so secretive, but instead she simply told her to have a nice time wherever she was going and that she would see her when she got back. Secretly, though, she was worried.

Gee! I've made some personal progress today in the control department, haven't I? she thought. *I didn't tell Charles what to do, and I didn't pester my mother to tell me what she's up to. Maybe this little trip will be better than I had hoped.* She turned and, instead of going back into the house, she shuffled over to the porch swing and began pushing herself with her toes back and forth and back and forth and back and forth... hypnotized by the motion, relaxing a little more with every swing. For a few minutes, she actually accomplished not thinking about anything serious and simply enjoying the summer's day, the smell of the ocean breeze, the puffy white clouds dancing across the sky, and the sound of the neighbor's dog barking happily as the children played in the yard.

Then her heart yelled at her mind so quickly that she didn't even see it coming.

"This is the life I should have had!" she cried to no one. Then, more softly, she repeated, "This is the life I should have had." Then, with tears forming, she whispered, "This is the life I should have had."

What she also realized, though, was that it was too late to have thoughts like that. Amy had always been a pragmatic person, and she knew we have to live with the choices we make in life for better or worse. Of course, as soon as she thought of the phrase "for better or worse," she began thinking of her wedding and Charlie and their honeymoon sailing in Maine. Those thoughts took her to the night she had told Charlie that she was going to Germany and the long, sad days that followed. Once she had let her thoughts go that far, she took them the rest of the way and relived highlights and lowlights from the past seven years.

Deep in her thoughts, she didn't hear the car or the footsteps on the stairs or even see the woman approaching her on the porch. When her sister touched her shoulder, she literally jumped up from the swing.

"Wow! What's with you?" Susan began. "I haven't seen you that lost in your thoughts on that swing since you and what's his name used to sit there and play kissy-face for hours. Whenever I'd visit, you two would be out here 'swinging' and 'talking.'" She made exaggerated air quotes and laughed.

"Susan! I didn't know you were coming today!" Amy exclaimed.

"That's because Ma and Dad didn't know I was coming either. I decided this morning that I hadn't seen you or that nephew of mine for almost two years and that was ridiculous. I couldn't let another minute pass without seeing both of you. I left the girls with John and drove down to see you guys. So where is everyone anyway?"

Amy laughed. "Would you believe we got here last night and they all took off on me today? Daddy took Charles to the beach for a picnic, and Ma took off on some mystery mission all flustered and blushing. If it wasn't obvious that Daddy knew where she was going, I would have thought she was meeting a man or something. Do you know what she's up to? She isn't sick, is she?"

"Hmm," was all Susan said, which intrigued Amy enough to ask what she meant. Susan told her that she had seen what she had thought was their mother's car in the parking lot at The Milepost, a popular tavern and restaurant in Duxbury, as she drove into town earlier, but that she knew it couldn't really be hers because Amy had just arrived and their mother would be at home.

"Hmmm," Amy replied. Then she had a brilliant idea. She suggested that Susan and she go to The Milepost and snoop to see what their mother was up to. Susan said that she could use a little intrigue in her life. If their mother got mad, they would just blame each other like they used to do, and her mother could never be mad at both of them at the same time. After all, she was just at a restaurant in a public place, and it wasn't illogical that Amy and Susan would decide to go out to lunch. With both their mother and father out of the house at lunchtime, and so much time having passed since they last saw each other, it was reasonable that they would treat each other to a nice meal instead of scavenging in Mom's kitchen. The Milepost had always been Amy's favorite place in town (and Charlie's too, her memory added).

"Hey, Susan, have you had lunch yet?" she asked her big sister.

Catching on right away, Susan replied, 'Why no, Amy, I haven't. You know what I really feel like? I'd love some of The Milepost's famous fish 'n' chips."

"And I would really like The Milepost's famous fried chicken. I remember it as being the best in the world."

With grins on their faces, looking like they were ten years old again and about to get into mischief, they strode across the porch. Instead of heading for the car, Amy stopped and decided to run a brush through her hair and dab on some makeup. Then she asked Susan to wait just a minute while she ran upstairs to throw on some different clothes, yelling over her shoulder that if she ran into anyone she knew, she'd like to look half decent. It had been a long time since she had seen anyone from town and would like to make a good impression. Susan reluctantly agreed to wait for her but gave her only five minutes.

"If you're not down in five minutes, I'm leaving without you!" she called up the stairs.

Geesh! Some things never change, Amy thought with a smile as she ran down, placing a headband in her hair and tying a pale green sweater around her shoulders, her pretty flowery sundress swishing around her legs. It felt good to be wearing real clothes instead of her usual wardrobe of uniforms or jeans.

"I only took three of your five minutes. So there!" she taunted as she ran past her sister and out into the yard.

"Well, Speedy Gonzalez, maybe you want to put on some shoes?" Her sister laughed as Amy looked down and realized that she was barefoot.

"Oops!" She laughed too and sprinted back across the grass and into the house to grab a pair of sandals. As she came back out, her sister was already behind the wheel of her car, having turned it around in the driveway.

"Let's go," she called, as Amy shut her door and buckled her seat belt. Then, in a more ominous voice, Susan dramatically began a monologue that could have been the opening lines of some detective show on television. "The two women, looking dazzling in their summer frocks, slipped quietly down the driveway, the only sound to be heard that of the foreign car's engine. Looking both ways at the end of the driveway, the more beautiful one edged the car onto the country road and headed toward her destiny at the local tavern."

Neither of them could keep from laughing at that point, and they began talking at the same time, wondering what their mother was up to. They decided that when they got to the restaurant they would sneak in and peek around before they asked for a table far away from where their mother was sitting. If she was in the dining room, they would sit in the bar and if she was in the bar, they would sneak past and sit in the dining room. That way, they could quietly spy on her.

Unfortunately, for them, when they arrived, the hostess of The Milepost was an old high school chum of Amy's who recognized the two of them immediately and exclaimed to everyone in the place, "Will you look who the cat dragged in! It's old home week here, I guess. Amy and Susan Sweetser are here." Then, to a table Amy could not yet see from around the corner, as they entered the main dining room, she said, "Mrs. Sweetser, Charlie, look who's here!" and before Amy had time to run the other way, she was standing face to face with Charlie Donnelly, her embarrassed mother fidgeting in her chair at their table.

Charlie didn't miss a beat because he already knew that Amy was in town. He had missed her and pulled her into his arms. He hugged her, not wanting to let her go and kissed her softly on her cheek, smiling all the while, looking at her with those eyes that she had never forgotten—her little man's eyes.

"Well, where are my manners? Hi, Susan!" he said, giving Susan a hug and a kiss on the cheek, as well. "Why don't you two join us?"

Mary was flummoxed. She wasn't sure if she should be happy or worried. She just smiled and decided to let this little luncheon party take whatever direction it would take. She hoped that her daughter wouldn't be too angry with her, though.

Charlie had not told her yet that he knew about Amy's son. As he looked at Amy while the waitress was bringing two more chairs and setting the places for them, his face hid his mixed emotions of anger, sadness, and excitement. It would only be minutes before he would know for sure. With the three Sweetser women sitting at this table with him, he would definitely learn the truth. He warned himself to be patient, make small talk, and act as if he didn't have the most important question of his life bearing down on him. Amy glared at her mother and silently asked her what she was doing there with Charlie. Her mother just shrugged and looked away. Then she and Susan placed their orders. Other people in the restaurant came over and said hello to Amy, chatted briefly about her time in Germany, and moved back to their tables. Soon, it was just the four of them at the table.

Susan was the one to break the awkward silence. "So, Ma, why the clandestine meeting with Charlie? Why couldn't you tell Ames that you were meeting him for lunch? We had all sorts of ideas swimming in our heads. For God's sake, we even thought you might be having an affair." With that, she shot a manufactured look of horror at Amy, who returned the look.

They then, in unison, looked at Charlie and exclaimed, "You're not having an affair with our mother, are you?" That question made everyone laugh and the tension was broken. They moved on to other topics of discussion.

With meals served and everyone seeming a bit more relaxed, they were suddenly aware that it was pouring outside. Charlie jumped up and ran out to put the top up on his car, narrowly missing being hit by a driver skidding on the wet pebbles in the driveway as he pulled into the parking place next to Charlie. Charlie jumped out of the way, hopped into his car, and proceeded to raise the roof to protect the leather interior from the rain.

Back inside, the three women were having a hushed but heated discussion. Amy was asking why her mother was secretly meeting Charlie. Mary was asking why her daughters were spying on her. Their conversation was brief and quickly interrupted by a bounding, wet little boy who put his arms around his mother and exclaimed, "Mommy, this is the absolute best day of my life!"

Amy was horror-stricken. Charles was here! And Charlie was here! All she could think of was getting out of the restaurant. She demanded of Susan, "Give me your car keys. I have got to get this little guy home and dried off before he catches a cold. As she said this, her lips smiled but her eyes betrayed her panic. Susan quickly obliged, and Amy whisked Charles up in her arms, apologized for cutting out so rapidly, and literally ran for the car. As luck would have it, Charlie had headed for the men's room to dry off a little after being outside, so she did not run into him.

By the time Charlie returned to the table, Mary had paid the check so that she and Susan could escape without leaving the bill for Charlie, and meals had been packed in to-go boxes for everyone. George was standing by the table, dripping wet and confused. Charlie remembered his manners and shook George's hand, exclaiming that he didn't realize he was going to get together with the whole Sweetser clan today. George started to explain that he had been at the beach with his....

Mary jumped in and said, "With that silly old metal detector of yours, I bet," horror-stricken that he had almost blown Amy's secret prematurely.

With Mary catching him just in time, George realized he had almost goofed. He had almost said that he was at the beach with his grandson, Charles. Amy would have shot him if he'd said that. For some reason unknown to him, that fool daughter of his had decided not to tell the boy's own father that he had a son. And at the same time, she had deprived little Charles of knowing his father. The boy was starved for male attention, a male role model. Just one day with him had told George that much. He would have a long talk with Amy when he got home. He decided that he had had enough of staying quiet about the whole situation. It wasn't fair to anyone. His daughter usually had a good head on her shoulders, but this time he downright disagreed with her, and had for some time now. Now that she was on his turf, he would bring her to her senses. If all else failed, he would "accidentally" run into Charlie when he was out with Charles. That little boy deserved his daddy and Charlie deserved to know his own son.

Charlie was devastated. What had looked like a sure thing a few minutes ago had been taken over by fate and a heavy downpour. He knew that George had almost spilled the beans and wished that he had. It would have given him the opening he needed to ask Mary and George about Amy's son. Now he would have to wait to find out for sure if the little boy was his.

Always the gentleman, Charlie stood and shook hands with George, kissed Mary and Susan on their cheeks, and said that he would like to all get together sometime soon. Mary agreed that she would like that, too, that she had missed seeing him around their house, and George quixotically said that he wouldn't be surprised if they started seeing a lot more of Charlie very soon. With that, they all ran out to their cars through the raindrops.

By the time Mary and George and Susan got back to the homestead, Amy had relaxed a little, changed into jeans and a T-shirt, and insisted that Charles change into dry shorts and a T-shirt as well. She had piled her curls on top of her head and was sitting in the swing on the covered porch, breathing in the wet leaves and grass and ocean smells as the rain subsided. Charles was playing with one of his newfound airplanes on the floorboards of the porch. Amy decided that she was going to enjoy her visit with her sister and not let her chance encounter with Charlie ruin the day. She would not be preoccupied with thoughts of what might have been. There was plenty of time for that. As she thought of not being preoccupied, her mind wandered to this same scene with Charlie sitting on the porch swing next to her and little Charles playing happily at their feet, a child with both a mother and a father smiling down at him.

Her parents and Susan arrived home, and her mom beckoned Charles to join her in the kitchen. He jumped up to happily oblige her. His mom wasn't much fun right now anyway. He kept trying to talk with her and she just mumbled stuff at him in reply. Mary, George, and Charles went into the house to unpack the to-go boxes and get lunch ready. Susan waited until Charles was out of earshot and then exclaimed, "Earth to Amy! Earth to Amy! Come in Amy!" Her sister stood on the porch in front of Amy, arms on hips. "What the hell was that? Running off like that when you finally had the chance to tell Charlie about Charles. You might be my little sister, but I sure as hell don't understand you. Ames, deal with this! Enough is enough. You can't hide Charles from his father or keep Charlie from his own son anymore. They are both here in the same town, and you have got to get them together. If you don't, I will." With that she went inside to help her mother warm up the lunches and make some iced tea for everyone, slamming the screen door behind her. As an afterthought, she yelled outside, "Wanna join us? Or are you planning some devious plot to continue your Machiavellian ways?"

"I'll be in in a minute," Amy absently replied. She wasn't finished with her reverie just yet. She sat on the swing, gently rocking back and forth. In a couple of minutes, George emerged through the door.

"Mind if I join you?" her father asked.

"Sure," Amy answered, wondering what was up. Her mother had taken Charles in. Susan had yelled at her. This was a plot. She could sense it. Something was going on here. Suspiciously, she asked, "So did you want to talk with me about something Charles couldn't hear?"

With a smile crinkling his eyes, her father commented that she always could see through their plans. "Actually, Amy, I did want to talk with you. I know it's been a tough few years for you. I'm real proud of the way you have handled yourself in the Army. I'm proud of what a good mother you are to little Charles. He's one heck of a great kid. And he has his mother to thank for that."

Amy could hear the unspoken *but* about to fall.

"But, Amy, do you really think it's fair to anyone to keep Charlie in the dark about his son? To not let the little guy know he has a father? To not admit that you still are crazy about Charlie and try to see if you can work something out? Amy, I know I'm butting in where I probably don't belong. You're a grown woman with a child and a commission. You're an adult who should be able to handle her own affairs. But, hell, Amy, you're also my little girl, and I see you hurting and I hurt. Your mother is a mess. She loves you to pieces and can't stand seeing you living a lie. It would be one thing if Charlie was a terrible man. But he's a great guy. He deserves to know. It will be messy, and Charles will probably be really mad at you for a while. Charlie will be furious with you. Let's face it, sweetie. You have been doing a lot of lying to both of them for six long years. Don't you think it's time to stop and take your licking? I'll be here for you to lean on, and I'll intervene if it gets really bad, but don't you think Charlie has a right to know? Both of them?" And he fell silent.

Father and daughter rocked in silence for what seemed like a long time, tears raining down the daughter's face as the tough old father sniffed the air. As Amy reached up to give her father a big hug and lean into him, a car pulled into the driveway.

The Runaway

I t was Charlie.

Waving out the window as he drove up the drive, the sun glistening on the wet car, Amy looked at her father and said, simply, "Yes."

She got up from the swing, wiped her eyes with the bottom of her shirt, sniffled a lot, and opened the screen door.

"Hey, little man!" she yelled through the house. "Can you come out here? There's someone I want you to meet."

Her father wrapped her in a protective hug and then retreated into the house as Charles bounded out and stood in front of her.

"Who, Mom? Who do you want me to meet?"

"Well," she began, "Do you remember that picture you saw of my good friend who you decided was your twin? He just pulled in." The car door slammed shut and up strode Charlie, handsome in simple blue jeans and a green-and-white polo shirt unbuttoned and untucked over a green T-shirt. On his feet he wore ratty brown docksiders, and in his hand he carried a light green sweater.

"I presume this is yours?" he asked Amy, handing the sweater to her as Charles hid behind her, peeking out at Charlie.

Taking a deep breath, Amy replied simply, "And this, I presume, is yours," and gently pulled Charles out from behind her. The meaning of the words escaped Charles but did not elude Charlie. He couldn't believe Amy was so direct about it after hiding the boy for so long.

Getting down on one knee, wrapping her arm protectively around Charles, she said, "Charles, remember the picture of the boy you said looked like your twin? Well, this is him. And you know what? His name is Charles, too."

Amy was afraid that this moment was going to be filled with anger and recriminations. Instead, Charlie knelt down on one knee in front of her and his son and put out his hand to shake hands. "I'm very glad to meet you, Charles. If you think we look like twins, I'm pretty lucky because you are one great looking little guy."

Much to Amy's surprise, little Charles wriggled out from her grasp, stepped forward, and shook Charlie's hand. She heard the father's breath catch as he touched his son for the first time. Knowing him as she did, she knew it must be torture for him not to grab this little guy in his arms and make up for six lost years. But he played it cool. When Charles told him there was a picture in his mom's room that he had seen and that it was really cool that they looked alike and that he was going to take it back to school to show his teacher that he had found his twin in the world, the newly minted father had to turn away, pretending to look back at his car for something.

"I'm not sure if I forgot something in my car," he said. "How about if you go get that picture, and your mom and I will go check out my car? Charles headed off, excited to have a mission, saying that he'd be right back with the picture.

Once he had left, Charlie took Amy's hand in his and pulled her up to her feet, dragging her down the stairs and out toward his car.

"Amy, how could you?" he muttered. "How could you? How could you? How could you?" As he repeated the question, he sadly shook his head from side to side, breaking Amy's heart. He wasn't angry. He didn't rant and rave about the deception. He was just sad. She could have taken his anger. She felt that she deserved his anger. But she was having a hard time dealing with this total sadness. His shoulders drooped. He kicked at the grass as he walked. He repeatedly ran his fingers through his hair. He wouldn't look at her. When they got to his car, he stood facing it, not moving, as she stood behind him.

Amy couldn't stand the silence. She knew that she had hurt Charlie terribly and that it was totally unfair of her to have kept Charles from his father for so long. She kept telling herself that she'd had good intentions. She really did. But even she couldn't believe that as she stood watching Charlie's shoulders shake as he sobbed quietly.

"Charlie, I have no explanation other than that I thought it was best. I thought that you would give up everything to be with me, to be with

190

him, and I couldn't let you do that. I loved you so much that I accepted the fact that I would be a single mother rather than ruin your life."

Then the anger came.

"Ruin my life? Loved me so much? Ruin my life?" Charlie's voice was barely audible, but it was full of anger and disbelief. The anger became quietly white hot. "You thought telling the man you loved that he had a son with the woman he loved more than the air he breathed would ruin his life? You thought that you loved me enough to sacrifice everything to raise this child by yourself but wouldn't even give me the option of sacrificing or not? You made all the decisions. You never gave me a chance. Now this little boy has no father, has spent six years of his life with no father. He probably thinks his father doesn't love him, doesn't want him. Children say cruel things to each other. Someone has probably told him that he doesn't have a father because he doesn't deserve one. Have you ever thought of that? Have you ever thought of the pain you might have caused that child? Have you ever once thought of how you have robbed him of six years of a father's love? Did you think at all of how much a little boy needs a father to emulate? Who teaches him about guy stuff? You? Amy, I will love you until the day I die, but I will never forgive you for this."

Then it was as though Charlie flipped a switch on his emotions. He turned, held Amy's arms with his hands, leaned down, and kissed her. Her knees felt weak, and she leaned into him, holding onto his arms for support. He let go and wrapped his arms around her as she looked up at him, her tear-streaked face silently searching his. She knew he was right and had no desire to argue with him. All she said were three little words: "I'm so sorry."

With that, she melted into him, and he hungrily kissed her, knowing that their lives were about to change again. Amy did not yet know that Charlie had been processing this new information since he'd discovered her secret in the driveway in Germany. It was not news to him. He had worked through disbelief, anger, pain, sadness, elation, and then had run through them all again during his long flight back to Boston. Now, as he stood there, seeing her pained expression, her quiet strength and sadness, her pride and her decision to tell him before he dragged it out of her, he knew he would be okay. He hoped they would be okay.

"Amy, I love you now, yesterday, and tomorrow. I will always love you. If this doesn't prove to you that there is nothing you could ever do to make me stop loving you, nothing ever will."

And he kissed her again.

George, Mary, and Susan were all peeking out through the curtains in the living room, watching the drama unfold as little Charles was searching for the picture. Although they couldn't hear what was being said, they were pretty sure from the body language that Charlie was taking it well. George had been ready to go out and forcibly send Charlie packing if he had reacted violently to the news. He was relieved not to have to do that. As they watched, Amy rose on tiptoes and kissed Charlie again, this time, kissing with love and appreciation and sorrow and apology and gladness and a million other emotions all packed into that kiss that had been waiting for almost seven years to erupt. As she did, her son burst through the screen door, out onto the porch and stopped in his tracks, confused about what he was seeing. He slowly and quietly approached his mother, grasping the photo in his little hands.

"Uh-oh," muttered George, Mary, and Susan in unison.

"I wonder how she's going to explain this one," said Susan, matter-of-factly.

"She'll be okay," George asserted.

"I sure hope so," a worried Mary added.

And they continued to watch.

Not hearing or seeing little Charles approaching, Amy quietly said, "I love you so much, Charlie. I always have. I never stopped. And I've felt so guilty all these years keeping this secret from you. There were so many times I wanted to tell you, tried to tell you. But something would happen or be said, and the moment passed. I don't want there to be secrets between us. As soon as we tell Charles that you are his father, we won't have any more secrets."

As she said this, her son was close enough to hear. He stopped. He gazed at the two adults locked in an embrace in front of him. He looked down at the picture. He remembered all of the things his mother had not told him about his father all these years. He thought about all the things the other kids had said to him and how he never let his mother know because he didn't want to make her cry. He was a precocious little boy and as he looked up at Charlie, he suddenly understood why they were here. This man hugging his mother was his father.

Then he ran.

He ran and ran and decided he would never stop running. He ran down the driveway and as he reached the road, he heard the screen door slam and his grandparents come hurrying down the steps. He heard his mother screaming his name. He heard this new man who looked so much like him because he was his father yelling to him to stop. And he ran. He turned at the end of the driveway, dropped the picture on the road, and ran even faster. He remembered the way to the beach. It wasn't far in the car and he was really good at remembering where he'd been. He decided to run to the water.

As Charles ran, his confusion and anger propelling him faster and faster, he was somewhat aware of a car following him. Unknown to him, however, was that in the car were his mother and father, driving slowly, staying back, letting him work out his anger by running, yet making sure that he was safe. As little Charles ran, his thoughts ran with him. He was in Germany, in school, at home, in his grandparents' house, at the beach today with his Grampy. And finally he was standing on the lawn listening to his mother telling her secret to this stranger, this stranger who was, apparently, his father.

All he could think over and over again was, *How could you? How could you? How could you do this to me? How could you not tell me I had a father? How could you not tell me I have a father and that you love him? How could you let me live all this time without a dad? I hate you! All the times I dreamed of having a father and wishing on the first star I saw every single night for my father to love me and want me and come to me and all the time he was here not even knowing about me. Mommy, how could you?"*

Suddenly, as Charles approached an intersection with lots of cars, he slowed. He began walking instead of running. He walked and walked, and that car kept driving behind him, slower and slower. He turned and saw his mother in the passenger seat and that man who looked like him driving the car. They looked worried. They looked sad. Good! And Charles began running again. Amy didn't know her son could run so far. All the way along Powder Point Road he ran, watching the happy boats playing in the high tide, hearing the seagulls laughing at him, smelling the sea air as it filled his lungs, and feeling hurt and tired. As he approached the little wooden bridge that would take him out to the beach, he turned and saw the car still creeping behind him. A Jeep passed it and then him, filled with teenagers laughing and tanned. As they passed, they noticed that he was running and crying. Much to his surprise, they stopped and one of the pretty blonde girls asked him if he was okay.

"I'm okay," he managed to croak out.

"You don't look so okay, little boy," she said, kindly. Then, to her boyfriend, she said, "Josh, stop. I want to get out." Saying this, the Jeep pulled over and stopped. The pretty girl got out and came over to Charles, getting down on her knees in front of him.

"Hey, little guy, you can trust me. I'm okay. I just want to make sure that you're okay. You look really sad. Can I help?"

From the car, Charles heard her friends calling to her to get back in. She waved them off, never taking her beautiful blue eyes off Charles's tear-stained ones.

"Come on, Brittany! Let's go!" The boy named Josh called out to her, "If you don't get back in, we're heading over to the beach without you."

"Fine," she replied. "Go ahead. I'll meet you over there. I'm going to walk across with my new friend." And she reached down, took Charles's little hand in hers and they began to walk in silence, with Charles calming in her grasp, as she talked about the beauty of the day, the expectation of how nice the water was going to feel when they got to the beach, how she would call his mom and dad for him on her cell phone if he wanted her to. All the while, Amy and Charlie followed slowly from a distance. Brittany didn't suspect that this slow-moving car was following Charles because cars had to drive very slowly as they crossed the little wooden bridge that was barely wide enough for two cars to pass. As far as she knew, this little boy could have come from anywhere. She knew instinctively that she had to gain his trust before asking him the tough questions, though. When she saw a small smile form on his lips as she talked, she figured she could broach the subject of finding out who he was and where he came from.

"You can hang with us, little guy, if you want to, but we have to call your mom and dad and let them know you're okay first. Do you know your number? Do you have a name? Well, that's a silly question. Of course, you have a name. Would you tell me your name? My name is Brittany. If you tell me your name, you can call me Brit like my best friends."

Charlie wasn't quite sure he wanted ever to talk with his parents. He was perfectly happy to be walking with this pretty, nice girl. She made him feel safe. He snuck a glance over his shoulder and saw them driving behind him, concern painting their faces.

"Aw, come on. What's your name?"

By now, they had crossed the little bridge and were standing in the parking lot about to cross over the dunes to the beach. Brittany stopped, got down on one knee, took both of Charles's hands in hers, and said, seriously, "Come on. Your parents are probably really worried about you by now. You look like you ran away from home. I know that look because I did it once when I was little. My mom and dad told me they were getting divorced when I was seven, and I ran away from home. I figured if I ran away they would be so worried about me that they would have to stay together. It was pretty silly, though, because they were worried about me, but once they found me they still got divorced. Did your folks tell you something like that? If they did, don't worry. It's cool only living with your mom or dad. They both love you just as much, and sometimes grownups have reasons that don't make sense to kids, but when you get older they totally do."

As Brittany talked, Charles was thinking that she made a lot of sense. His mom and his twin wouldn't have followed him in the car if they didn't love him. They did look worried about him. They were still there, sitting in the car in the parking lot about fifty feet away. They were letting him make the decision to come back. They weren't chasing him, just making sure he was safe. Maybe Brittany was right. Maybe they did both love him. Maybe it would be okay.

"My name's Charles, Charles Donnelly."

Amy was confused.

"Did you say your name is Charles Donnelly? I know someone with that same name. In fact, my big sister used to have a huge crush on him. You know what? You even look a lot like him…." Suddenly, she stopped, guessing the truth but not sure how it could be so. Instead of confronting the obvious, she decided to ask, "So why did you run away?"

"It's hard to 'splain," Charles said. As he said this, Brittany sat down on the sand, pulling him down across from her, facing her.

"Try me," she said. "I'm a pretty good listener."

The two of them sat there, cross-legged, looking at each other. From Charles's position, he could see his parents watching him. Charles believed her and since he needed someone to talk with, he told her the whole story, as best he could, starting with coming here for a vacation with his grandparents from Germany where he lived with his mom and ending with finding out after six years that he had a father who lived here in Duxbury and who hadn't known that he had a son until today. He even told her what he hadn't told anybody about how the kids teased him sometimes and said that he didn't have a father because he was too stupid to have one or because he was too ugly to have one or because his mother was too ugly to have a husband. (He had fought with the boy who said that one and came home from school with a bloody nose. He never told his mother what had started the fight.)

Brittany couldn't believe the story. Mr. Donnelly had always seemed so sad to her. He was a nice man who had married a barracuda of a woman. Everyone was surprised by his marriage and not at all surprised when it had ended recently. Duxbury was a small town, and everyone knew everyone else's business. But this story was unbelievable! Even though she was amazed, somehow she knew she would keep it to herself until Mr. Donnelly was ready to share it with other people. She liked him a lot and did not want to hurt him any more than he already must be hurting. She said, "So do your parents know you ran away?"

"Well," Charles began quietly, "they're sitting right over there." He pointed to their car fifty feet behind where Brittany sat in the sand. "They followed me all the way from my Nana and Grampy's house to here."

Brittany turned to look and, sure enough, she saw Mr. Donnelly and his first wife sitting in a car, he with a worried expression and she with tears in her eyes but a smile on her face.

Brittany suggested that they walk over to the car and that he talk with his mom and dad the way he had just talked with her. Charles wasn't sure he was ready to do that. He was still really, really mad at his mom. And he had no idea who this guy was. He looked nice enough, and his mom seemed to like him. But he was not ready to talk with them yet.

"Not yet," Charles said.

Brittany looked at him then, picked him up by his arms, faced him toward his mom and dad, and said, "March, Charles Donnelly. You're a big boy, and your mom and dad deserve a chance to explain what happened to you. And you need to listen and give them a chance." She then lifted his little face up to look at her. "Look at me. It worked out okay for me. It'll work out okay for you, too. Now, go!" With that, she gave Charles a gentle push toward his mom and dad who were now standing by the side of the car.

With a look back at Brittany that almost broke her sixteen-year-old heart, Charles bravely walked toward the mother who had lied to him and the father he didn't know. His mom reached out and enveloped him in her arms, while his new father sniffed the air and put a hand on his mother's shoulder.

When Charles was convinced that his mother was going to crush him right there in the parking lot, with the sand blowing in their faces, she let him go, held him at arms' length and scolded him. "Charles Henry Donnelly, don't you ever do anything like that again! You could have been hit by a car or gotten lost or been kidnapped. All kinds of horrible things could have happened to you when you took off by yourself like that. You scared me to death!" Then, just as Charles thought he was going to cry, she hugged him again, sobbing into his hair, "I love you, little man. Don't you ever doubt that or think that running away is the answer." The irony of that last sentence slammed into her consciousness, but she sternly told it to go away for now.

Charlie still could not get used to hearing Amy refer to this little boy by his own name. She had named him after his father even though neither father nor son knew the other existed. Every time Amy called the little boy by name Charlie's heart skipped a beat. *I have a son*, he kept thinking.

Mother and child held each other for a couple of minutes before Charles remembered that his new friend, Brittany, was watching. The last thing he wanted was for her to see him acting like a baby. He pulled free of his mother, swiped his eyes with his sleeve, and said that he was sorry for running away. He looked at his mother with such adoration that his father felt a stab of pain for the relationship he had missed for so long. He wanted his son to look at him that way. He wanted his son—*his son*—it sounded funny to his ears as he thought the words—to love him the way Amy was loved. *Someday soon*, he thought. *Someday soon.*

Just then, Charles pulled his mother along with him over to the place where he had left Brittany standing by the dune.

"Mommy, this is my new friend, Brittany. She's really cool. Brittany, this is my mom."

"Hi," began Brittany, not quite knowing what to call his mother. "I hope you don't mind that I was talking with Charles. He just seemed lost, and I wanted to make sure he was safe. I have a kid stepbrother, and I'd die if anything ever happened to him." Brittany paused as the trio was joined by someone she knew. "Oh, hi, Mr. Donnelly," she said, not quite sure which emotion she should be feeling. After all, she knew his secret, and he didn't know for sure that she knew, and he had just found out himself.

"I was just telling Charles's mom about Parker. This little guy reminds me of him a lot. When I saw him crying, I just had to help him out."

"We really appreciate it, Brittany. I'm sure Amy was relieved when someone cared enough to walk and talk with this little man. But didn't you leave your friends to take care of this guy?"

"Yeah, I did. That's okay, though. They won't miss me much. I'm sure by now they're all zoned out on the sun and sand anyway."

"I can give you a ride down the beach, if you like, so you can join them."

Duxbury Beach is unique. On the ocean side of the dunes is a long stretch of sandy beach, miles long, while on the bay side of the dunes is a sandy "road" that intrepid beachgoers drive down to find the perfect secluded spot on the beach. Half a mile down the beach from this little bridge is a stretch of Jeeps and Land Rovers behind sun worshipers who want to have all of their things with them on the beach instead of carting them over the dunes by hand. This is the land of barbecues and coolers, volleyball and beach football.

"Nah, thanks anyway, Mr. Donnelly. I think I'll just walk. It's such a pretty day today." She turned to little Charles, got down on one knee, and said, "Charles, I hope we see each other again sometime. Maybe we can come to the beach and have some fun one of these days. I could even bring Parker along so you'd have someone your own age to play with."

This elicited a smile from Charles, who said that he would really like to do that. He liked this kind, pretty girl.

"Mom," he asked, "would that be okay? It would be fun to have a friend here to play with at the beach. Grampy is lots of fun, but he can't do some of the stuff I could do with a friend."

Amy's heart was touched at the thought that Charles thought of Duxbury as a place he could stay in for a while, a place where he could have a friend. She spontaneously gave Brittany a hug and told her how kind she was and that she would be calling to set up a play date in the near future. Brittany gave her cell phone number to Amy and bid them all farewell. Charlie shook her hand and told her how much he appreciated what she had done.

"It's nothing, Mr. Donnelly," she said. "I would hope that if Parker ever ran away, someone would care enough to look out for him."

As Brittany set off over the dune to walk along the water's edge to her waiting friends, Amy ushered her son back to the car. Once he was safely buckled up in the back, she climbed into the passenger seat.

Driving back across the little wooden bridge toward Powder Point, Amy was taken back to her teen years. Life was so simple then. Crossing this bridge in Charlie's old Jeep, laughing and holding hands, her long hair blowing in the ocean breeze, Charlie's suntanned face smiling at her, his eyes full of love. Why did it all have to change? Why did they have to grow up? Why did she have to blow it by following some mission of serving in the military as her father had? What did she have to prove and who was she trying to impress? All of these thoughts rambled through her mind as they drove in silence.

About halfway home, Charlie broke the silence as he drove.

"Amy, how about you and this little guy and I go out for dinner tonight? I'll take care of everything. Throw on some jeans and sneakers, bring along sweatshirts, and we'll go somewhere where we can talk and get to know each other again."

Without asking Charles, who by now was almost asleep in the backseat, the emotion of the day catching up with him, Amy agreed. "When do you want to go?" she asked.

"How about I wait for you guys to grab your stuff when we get back to your folks' house and we'll head out now? I don't think that Susan or your folks will mind under the circumstances."

"Well," Amy said slowly, "Susan did drive all the way down from Maine just to see us, and we've only had a little while together. I feel kind of guilty."

"I know you do, Amy, but we have some serious getting acquainted to do."

Amy knew from the sound of Charlie's voice that he was hiding a lot of pain in those few words. She owed him this much, didn't she? Susan would certainly understand. "Okay. But," she added more quietly, "I think the serious talking is going to have to wait. There's no way I'm going to talk about anything serious with you with Charles along. He's had a tough day." As she said this, she glanced back to see the little body leaning over in his seat, sound asleep. He looked so fragile that her breath stopped for a second as her guilt overwhelmed her.

"Amy, what kind of a person do you think I am? I just met this guy and I love him already. I have a lot of catching up to do," Charlie added with the sadness in his voice tinged with subdued anger. "In fact, I have something in mind that I think he'll like."

By this time, they had arrived back at the Sweetser house. Not surprisingly, her parents and Susan were all sitting on the porch, making believe they were busy doing something other than worrying about the current situation. Amy's mother had knitting in her lap, her father had a newspaper lying across his, and Susan had an open magazine resting on her knees as she sat curled up in one of the comfy old Adirondack chairs. As the car drove up the driveway, Amy noticed each of them return to what they were ostensibly doing. Mary's hands began to fly through the yarn as George's newspaper crinkled to life, and Susan's magazine was suddenly mesmerizing.

Getting out of the car, Amy was about to lift Charles out and carry him to the house when she felt a strong hand on her arm, gently moving her aside. Instead, Charlie picked up his son for the first time and, laying his sleeping head on his shoulder, carried him across the lawn and up the steps of the porch, mouthing *hello* to Amy's family as he passed through and into the house, up the stairs, and into Charles's room with the little boy still asleep on his shoulder. Amy quickly tossed the extra shams from the bed and with barely a whimper little Charles nestled into the softness of the down comforter. Amy covered him with an airplane motif quilt she found at the foot of the bed, kissed his forehead gently, and tiptoed out of the room. When she turned to thank Charlie for carrying the little guy upstairs, he was not there. Looking back into the bedroom, there he stood next to the bed, tears silently streaming down his suntanned cheeks, a sad smile on his tortured face. Amy choked back a cry and decided to give him some time alone. She padded down the stairs and out onto the porch to explain the events of the past hour to everyone.

The Walk

After Amy had finished explaining what had happened at the beach, how Brittany had befriended Charles and how he had responded to her, how Brittany now knew that Charles was Charles Donnelly and probably had made the connection as to his parentage, and how she and her two Charleses were going to go out to dinner to talk and get acquainted with each other, Charlie had emerged from the house, looking as though he had been struck by the boom on his boat.

"How is Charles, Charlie?" Mary asked. Then, before he had a chance to answer, she added, "This may not be the time, but do you think we could do something about these names? It's getting confusing for this old brain of mine."

"He's sleeping," Charlie replied quietly as he fell into a white wicker rocker. He looked over at Amy curled up on the swing and at George, Mary, and Susan sitting there on the porch, the sun falling lower in the sky and the breeze hinting at a cool summer evening and wondered how his life had become so complicated. Was it so long ago that he had sat on this same porch with these same people and laughed, carefree, his only worry getting his homework done? He and Amy had their life planned out so differently from what had happened. Was there any salvaging it? Maybe he could persuade her to try to request a transfer to the States, or maybe he could take a leave of absence from the firm and go to Germany with her and Charles. All he knew was that he was not ever going to let those two out of his sight again.

He would do whatever it took to convince Amy that they had to stay together this time. They had run into each other by accident this afternoon, but Charlie didn't believe in accidents. Everything happened for a reason. He said to Amy, "Why don't we let the little guy sleep for a while, and you and I can take a walk and talk. I was going to go home and pack a picnic for dinner, but we probably should talk while we can." To her family he asked, "Would anyone mind if I stole her for a little while?"

All three Sweetsers replied that they totally understood, but before he and Amy stepped off the porch, he turned and said, Mrs. Sweetser, I agree that the name thing is confusing. I obviously am not going to take the little guy's name away from him, so how about if everyone starts calling me 'Skip'? My family used to call me that when I was little. My dad used to let me think that I was the skipper of the boat and started calling me Skipper. It wasn't until I got to school that people started calling me Charlie. It's okay with me if you all call me Skip. At least it's a name I'm used to answering to." He actually chuckled a little. "Amy, do you think you could get used to calling me that?"

With a sad little laugh, Amy said, "I don't think so. You are not 'Skip' to me, Charlie. But I do understand the confusion. We'll have to play that one by ear, I think." Then, with trepidation, she stepped down off the porch and headed out across the lawn. "Are you coming? We may as well get this over with," she called to Charlie.

She and Charlie headed off down the driveway, turning onto the road, retracing the path they had taken in the car earlier that afternoon as they followed a scared, angry little boy two long miles to the beach. George, Mary, and Susan just looked at each other for a couple of minutes, no one wanting to say the wrong thing. Then Mary stood and said, "Susan, come on with me. Charlie mentioned that he was going to pack a picnic for their dinner. If they're talking, he'll never get around to that. Why don't you and I go into the kitchen and see what we can pack up for the three of them? They'll want to spend some time alone with their son when he wakes up." Just saying "their son" sounded good to her ears. She hadn't been able to say those words out loud since the day Charles was born. She had promised Amy to keep her secret and she had.

The Intervention

As Mary and Susan packed the dinner, Amy and Charlie walked and talked, and little Charles slept, George sat sentry on the front porch with his newspaper. He was worried about this situation. Amy didn't know it, but he had been given a courtesy heads up on Amy's assignment to Afghanistan. After days of soul-searching and discussions with his wife, George had made a difficult decision. There was no way he was going to let his youngest daughter go to Afghanistan. He was proud of her determination to go to West Point and follow in his footsteps. But she was not him. As old-fashioned and sexist as it sounded, he just didn't want his little girl to be put in harm's way. He had bitten his tongue and stayed out of it when she had thrown her life with Charlie away and headed off to Germany. He had kept his opinions to himself and let her make her own decisions when she decided not to tell Charlie about the baby. But this was too much. Amy was his youngest little girl, the mother of his only grandson. She deserved happiness in her life. After all, every day she listened to psychologically scarred men and women tell her about their nightmares and their anguish. She was helping returning vets every day. Did she have to do it in a war zone?

George had never pulled a string in his long and illustrious military career, but now was the time to call in any chips he had. For three days, he had made calls and when all was said and done, he had managed to get her posted to the Edith Nourse Rogers Memorial Veterans Hospital in Bedford, Massachusetts. They needed a good psychologist to work with returning vets, and she had several years' experience doing just that. It was high time she came home. He knew that if she ever found out, she would be very angry with him for giving her preferential treatment. But he wasn't sorry he'd called in a few favors to do it. In fact, he was angry with himself for not doing it when Charles was born. She was his little girl, and he was still as proud of her as he was when she had graduated from West Point with honors. He hated what that had meant to her life with Charlie. He blamed himself for that. If he hadn't moved her all over the world as his career advanced through the ranks, she wouldn't have even considered a military career. She would be married to Charlie, living in a nice house on Powder Point, watching her little boy grow up in this Norman Rockwell world on the South Shore.

Never one to let himself get away with an undebated thought, however, he also acknowledged that if he hadn't led the life he had chosen, they never would have ended up in this sleepy little town, and Amy and Charlie never would have met in the first place. Now he was getting sentimental, and sentimentality was something he did not often allow himself. In a sentimental versus rational thought debate, he always sat at the rational thought table. Just as in a fate versus free will discussion of any issue, he would land on the side of free will. People made their own luck, just as they made their own life.

Amy was not in the position she was in because of fate. She had consciously chosen this life. She had set the gears in motion when she had married Charlie, knowing full well that she was heading to Germany. And she had accelerated when she chose not to tell Charlie about his son. Now she was heading at full speed toward a crash if she went to Afghanistan. How could a loving father allow his baby to crash if he could do something to avert it? Everything surrounding that girl was complicated. Of course, he hadn't known until a few days ago that the posting had been changed, but now it was a done deal. His little girl would be living and working in Massachusetts. Whatever became of her relationship with Charlie was now up to them. At least he had given them a chance. That little boy deserved a daddy. George peered over the newspaper he was holding but not reading and watched Amy and Charlie as they walked down the driveway.

It was funny that Amy hadn't caught on when she saw the airplane room. Why did she think that he and Mary had fixed up the spare bedroom as a little boy's dream room? When her father had learned of her posting to Afghanistan, they assumed that she would ask them to care for Charlie while she was gone. They wanted him to feel comfortable and welcomed in their home. If George's intervention had failed, the room would be ready and waiting for Charles. And he had noticed the tears the room had brought to Amy's eyes. It had given her comfort.

Now she was talking with Charlie, explaining her reasons for keeping his son from him for six long years. George knew his strong-willed daughter well enough to know that she would not be able to tell Charlie that she was leaving soon and leaving their son with her parents. Too much had happened too fast today. He hoped that the papers would come through soon telling her of her change in assignment. Should he tell her before she told Charlie she was going away again? Should he ease her mind about leaving Charles behind? Would she ever forgive him, or would she be grateful?

He didn't know which way it would go, but he made a decision to tell her when she and Charlie returned from their walk. He couldn't stand to see her tortured any more than she was by the situation she had created when she kept the little boy a secret from his father. If she hated him for it, then so be it. After all, that is what good parenting is. You do what is right for your child, even if it drives a wedge between you and that child. In his heart of hearts, though, he didn't think that she would be angry. In fact, he imagined that she would hug him and thank him and run to Charlie to begin the life they had always deserved. George almost thought "the life they were destined to have," but if he thought that, he would be admitting that fate played a role in our lives, and George did not believe in fate.

Well, having his youngest daughter return, if only for a brief visit, had been much anticipated. If this was what havoc she could wreak in one day, though, what in the world did they have in store for them for the rest of her visit? When she found out that she had been restationed in Massachusetts, would she want to continue to live with them, or would she and Charles move in with Charlie? Would she never speak to him again, or would she thank him?

Lost in his thoughts, he hadn't heard the screen door open. He was startled when a little hand landed on his arm.

"Grampy, would it be okay if I sit with you?" a small voice asked, and George looked down into the face of his first grandson.

"Why, of course, it's okay, big man. I think this is the perfect time of day for the men to sit on the porch and talk. Sometimes I have to talk to myself out here because I'm the only man around. Lucky for me, today I have you to talk with." Pausing as Charles climbed up into the swing, George continued, "It's been quite a day, hasn't it?"

Charles nodded, saying nothing.

"I think it has been a stupendously fantastical day!" George suddenly exclaimed, much to Charles's surprise. "No, seriously, Charles Henry Donnelly, the Third," George continued, using the full name to let Charles know he was totally serious. Speaking deliberately, he said, "Just think what has happened to you in the last twenty-four hours. You arrived in the good ole US of A for the first time. You went to the beach for the first time with a grandfather you never really knew very well. You got a brand new, incredible bedroom in our house and it's all yours—nobody else's. *And*, most important of all, you got a father today! If that all doesn't add up to a pretty stupendously fantastical twenty-four hours, I don't know what does!" He gave all of that a minute to sink in and watched Charles's worried expression relax a little. As the little gears turned in Charles's mind, he commented, "The third? What does that mean?

George was impressed by just how bright this little boy was. He didn't miss much. Even though his little mind must have been spinning with all the new information he had to process, he had picked up on that. George said, "Well, Charles, you have a daddy whose name is Charles Henry Donnelly too. And you have another grandfather who is your father's father, and his name is Charles Henry Donnelly. So that makes you Charles Henry Donnelly, the Third. Quite a name, huh?" Charles just nodded in agreement.

George thought for a few minutes as they sat there and Charles absorbed this new information. Then he made a decision. If he was in trouble with his daughter for telling her son about her and Charlie, then so be it. He had kept quiet long enough. He was going to be in trouble anyway for restationing her. He may as well let loose on all the ridiculous secrets he had been holding for her all these years. Sometimes you just had to take advantage of opportunities that arose, and this little guy sitting next to him seemed to be ready to hear what was going on. Amy had her hands full with Charlie, so George decided that he would take responsibility for helping Charles to understand how much he was loved.

He began, "After the day you've had, I bet you have a lot of questions, right?" Charles just nodded, his green eyes staring trustingly up at his grandfather. "Well, Charles, I'm going to tell you some family secrets that I probably shouldn't tell you, but they have a lot to do with you, and you're a big boy now and old enough to know."

Charles's eyes grew even wider, not knowing what else he could possibly hear today. But he said nothing.

"When your mom and dad were teenagers, they used to sit on this same swing you're sitting on and swing and talk and even kiss a lot." At this thought, Charles scrunched up his little nose in disgust, which made George smile. He continued, "They have known each other since they were in school. They used to date in high school and in college, and then they grew up and got married…."

Charles exclaimed, "They were married?" at that revelation.

"Yes, sir, they got married, and then your mommy had to go to Germany with the Army right away. Your daddy couldn't go with her because he had a very important job here in Boston. She couldn't stay here because she had a very important job in Germany. So even though they didn't want to be apart, they had to be. They had no choice." George was trying to keep it as simple as he could, knowing that if Charles had questions, he would ask them later.

"Then you were born in Germany and your dad didn't even know it. You and your mom were so far away that he didn't know. In fact, he didn't know it until today.

"But Grampy," Charles ventured in a small voice, "you and Nana knew and Aunt Susan knew. How come he didn't know?"

At this question, George sat back, turned to face this thoughtful little boy who seemed to understand way beyond his years, and said honestly, "Well, Charles, that there is a very good question." Charles beamed. "Your mom and dad love each other very much and they love you very much, but they just had a whole lot of obstacles in their way. Do you know what 'obstacles' are?"

Charles nodded and said, "They're things you have to get over and through on an obstacle course. Mom took me out to show me the obstacle course one time, and there were lots of people running around on it. It was cool. I even got to try a couple of the things." Charles was a very precocious six-year-old, his grandfather thought.

"That's right. Obstacles are things you have to get past in life. We all face lots of obstacles, but somehow we manage to get past them. We are strong and don't let anything stop us. Right?"

Charles nodded. He would believe whatever this man told him. This was not only his grandfather, but also an Army man, and Charles's mom had told him that her father was a very important man in the Army—a brigadier general. Listening to him now, Charles believed it.

"But why would my mom not tell me about my dad and not tell my dad about me? Was she ashamed of me?" Charles added a little more quietly. He had wondered about that ever since Billy Miller had said that he didn't have a father because his mother was too ashamed to tell his father he even existed. He had never told his mother that Billy said that, but he had wondered about it for a long time.

"Of course not," George reassured him. "She was just in a difficult position and tried very hard to do the right thing for everyone. Sometimes we make mistakes when we try very hard to do the right thing. It's not our fault. We love everyone so much that we don't want to hurt them, but then we make decisions that end up hurting them anyway. It's pretty confusing grown-up stuff, but your mom was *never* ashamed of you or of your father. She just got confused. You get confused sometimes, don't you?"

Charles nodded again. "All the time," he said solemnly, making his grandfather grin.

"Well, then, maybe when they get back here, you could give them a break and be a big boy. They want to take you out to dinner tonight— just the three of you like a real family. Maybe you could go along and try to have fun? If you do that, I promise you that everything is going to be just fine." He turned to face Charles straight on and continued, "Charles, did you hear what I said? I promise that everything will be okay."

"I will, Grampy. I promise," the little boy who was wise beyond his years replied. "Honest. I believe you." Charles decided that he would always believe whatever his Grampy said. And he relaxed a little as they sat in silence swinging gently back and forth.

The Conversations

While Charles and his grandfather were having this serious discussion on the porch, Mary and Susan were having one of their own about how convoluted this whole mess was. Susan exclaimed to her mother, "Mom, how have you been able to live right here in town with Charlie for all these years and not tell him about his son?"

Mary did not hesitate in her response. "Susan, I was asked by my daughter to keep her secret. At that point, it was not mine to tell. Regardless of what I felt about it, I had to keep Charles's existence to myself. Besides, I haven't really run into Charlie very much. I grocery shop in Kingston and never really have occasion to go to Powder Point where he lives. Your father and I keep pretty much to ourselves or have friends over here. Except for the occasional meal at The Milepost, going to the Fourth of July parade, and picking up a pizza from Duxbury Pizza, we don't do much here in town. It hasn't been too hard."

Susan replied that she had almost called Charlie several times over the years to tell him about his son. Every year as she packed up birthday gifts and Christmas presents for Charles, she wanted to pick up the phone and call Charlie. But every time, even if she had the phone in her hand, she thought of her responsibility to her sister and changed her mind.

As grandfather and grandson were talking and Mary and Susan were having their discussion over picnic preparations, Amy and Charlie were having one of their own.

Charlie began as they walked down the driveway, "Amy, I unequivocally will not let you take that little boy back to Germany without me. I have a son, for God's sake. He's six years old, which means I have missed his birth and six birthday parties and seeing him learn how to walk and talk and seeing him wave for the first time and watching you nurse him and getting up in the middle of the night to calm him when he cried and walking him in his carriage and taking him to Disney World and seeing the amazement on his face when he saw Mickey Mouse...."

"Hey, hold on there," Amy interrupted. "I thought we were going to talk about the future, not the past."

"You're kidding, right?" Charlie replied incredulously. "I find out I have a son and I'm supposed to not even think about what might have been for the past six years? I'm supposed to say, "Well, thank you very much, Amy, for letting me get to know my son now that you're good and ready." Charlie's anger was nearing the boiling point. He had suppressed it all day and couldn't hold it in much longer. As he continued, he began talking faster and louder.

"Am I supposed to thank you for making a decision that should have been ours to make, not yours? Am I supposed to remain calm and collected and not be furious with you for stealing six years from me? I never got to see you pregnant and rub your belly and run out in the middle of the night for ice cream." Charlie was yelling now, as they walked along the path around the cranberry bog by her folks' farmhouse. No one could hear but Amy and the frogs.

"Of course I don't expect you to thank me!" Amy yelled back. "But at least stop to consider that this was a really hard decision for me to make. I did it for you!"

"Oh no you don't," Charlie bellowed. "Don't you dare tell me you kept me from knowing my own son for my own good."

"Well, I did," Amy replied quietly, feeling defensive and small as she said it, but knowing in her heart that her motivation had been pure. After all, she had tried many times to tell him, but something always got in the way.

Amy's calm reaction to his outburst relaxed him a little. He never could stay mad at her, although this was a bit more extreme than most of their arguments. Charlie stopped short, took Amy's hands in his, and dropped to the ground, pulling her down with him. They sat there holding hands, looking at the berries forming on the vines. Soon this bog would be a sea of red cranberries. As they sat there, deep in the most important conversation of their lives, all she could think about were the cranberries. They were beginning to turn red. Soon the bog would be flooded, and the men would come with the machines to shake the berries off their vines and float them to the conveyer belts that would dump them into big trucks. When the harvest was over, hundreds of cranberries would be left floating on the surface of the water for the neighbors to gather to make their Thanksgiving pies and sauces. She thought of how she and Charlie used to collect these berries in her mother's old colander and take them back to her mother, who would turn them into the most delicious sugared, syrupy cranberry concoction. As Charlie gazed off into space, lost in his thoughts and planning how he would approach the subject of Amy staying in Massachusetts with him, Amy forced herself to think about the cranberries.

It was funny how even during times of emotional stress, one can think of mundane, extraneous things like cranberries. Yet, here they sat, Amy thinking for a few minutes about the cranberry harvest to come in the fall. Soon, though, she returned to the matter at hand.

"Charlie," Amy began, breaking the silence. "I know that you will never believe me, but I really did keep Charles a secret from you because I thought that if you knew about my pregnancy you would drop everything and run to Germany. What would you have done there? You couldn't have practiced law. You'd have given up your career, everything you had studied for, and ended up as Mr. Mom, taking care of Charles and eventually resenting both him and me. I couldn't bear to do that.

"And I wasn't ready yet to leave the Army. Charlie, I'm accomplishing things I never dreamed I could accomplish. I'm working with soldiers who have seen and done horrific things, and I am actually able to make them feel better—to come to terms with things. Because of me, they will be able to go home and live normal lives instead of being plagued by nightmares and tortured by their actions like Vietnam Vets were. Charlie, I really make a difference in so many people's lives. How could I just say that doesn't matter and become a housewife just because I was having a baby? I couldn't do it.

"So I decided not to tell you for a while, until I got it all figured out. Then weeks turned into months, which turned into years. You married someone else. You moved on."

When Amy said that, Charlie visibly flinched. That marriage had been such a mistake. He had never truly loved Julia. He had enjoyed her company, could discuss work with her, and found in her someone to fill some of the emptiness Amy had left in his life. But he had never felt about her the way he felt about Amy. Now he began to think that if he had never married Julia, Amy might have told him about their child. As angry as he had been just moments before with Amy, he now was equally angry with himself. He couldn't admit that to Amy, though. He was not letting her off the hook that easily.

Loudly, he charged on, "Oh no you don't! Don't you dare blame me because you didn't have the guts to tell me you were pregnant. You stole years from me, and I can never get them back! You were pregnant when you left for Germany. You had Charles before I even married Julia. You can't blame me for that. You tore my heart out when you went to Germany. What was I supposed to do? Wait around forever for you? You made your decision, and I had to live with it. I never had a choice. You were the one in charge. You left for Germany. You had a baby. You chose not to tell me about him. You stopped talking with me. You even came back to visit your folks and probably wouldn't have told me about Charles if I hadn't found out on my own. I should send your neighbor flowers to thank her for spilling the beans."

Amy stared at Charlie. What had he just said?

"What did you say?" Amy asked incredulously. "What neighbor? How do you know my neighbors? Did you have someone spy on me? Have you known all along and pretended you didn't?" Amy was getting mad again.

"Uh, no. As a matter of fact," Charlie continued, "I realized when Julia and I split up that I had made a terrible mistake ever letting you go. I decided that I couldn't and didn't want to live without you and I flew to Germany to surprise you." At this, Charlie paused, giving Amy time to understand what he had just said.

"When I got to your house, your neighbor, a flirty little southern belle, told me that you and your son had gone to America to visit your folks. I thought you were married and couldn't believe you had a child with someone else. It broke my heart. Then she referred to your child as "Charles," which I thought was weird. You had named your son after an ex-husband. I asked her how old Charles was, and then it was just a matter of doing the math. I decided to charm your mother into telling me the truth. I invited her to lunch with me, playing on the fact that she always had a soft spot in her heart for me anyway. I called her from Germany before I headed back here, making her believe that I was just down the road a couple of miles. Then I hopped on the very first flight back to the States and met her at The Milepost for lunch. Imagine my surprise when you and Susan showed up at the same restaurant."

The two of them just sat in silence, each absorbing the ramifications of what Charlie had said. Amy had thought that she was doing what was best for Charlie but hadn't really looked at the situation through his eyes. She began to doubt her motives. Had she kept Charles a secret because telling Charlie would have complicated her life even more? Had she not told him because she feared he would insist that she give up the Army and come home? She thought about this for a few minutes as Charlie stared out into the bog. Finally, she decided that she hadn't been kidding herself. She really had thought it would be best for him but knew that she had hurt him in such a way that he could never forgive her. She certainly wouldn't forgive him if the tables were turned.

Quietly, Amy said, "I am so sorry, Charlie. I really am. I've made a mess of everything. Every day I work to help other people handle their emotions and their demons, but every night I struggle with my own. It has been torture to live without you. It has been so hard to be both mother and father to Charles and know how much you would love him if given a chance." Tears began sliding down Amy's cheeks as she quietly continued.

"Every time I looked at Charles's face when he was a baby, I saw you. It was so hard not to tell you. You called a couple of times when I was holding him, and I just stared at his face and talked to you. I wanted so badly to tell you about him and have you fly to my side and hold us in your arms and take away the pain. But I loved you so much I couldn't do that to you. I had to let you have your life."

Exhausted, Amy quieted and simply sat, staring out across the cranberry bushes.

After what seemed like an eternity, but probably wasn't more than a matter of minutes, Charlie's anger dissipated. He felt as though someone had punched him in the gut. Quietly, he said, "Wow. I hadn't thought of it from your perspective, Ames. Why has our life been so complicated? Why can't we just be two normal people who meet, fall in love, get married, live together, raise a family, grow old, and die together? I'm supposed to be your Noah, remember?"

Amy whispered, "You still are."

Charlie smiled a mournful smile and ran his fingers through Amy's hair. Then he brushed her cheek, turning her face up to his. They sat there for a long while, just looking at each other, trying to read each other's minds, each lost in thoughts of what was, what might have been, and what was to be. Charlie decided at that moment that somehow he would make this work. He was so tired of being in love with the idea of love. He wanted to be in love with a person who would walk through life with him by her side. He thought about the little boy who was his own and promised himself that he would be a good father. Suddenly his desire to be with Charles overpowered his desire to simply sit here with Amy. He jumped up.

"Let's go get the little guy and become a family," he said, pulling Amy up and heading back toward her folks' house.

As they walked, they talked about how they could make that happen. Charlie agreed to take it slowly, and Amy agreed to give them time together, thinking that they would have lots of time together when she left for Afghanistan. But, as she had been getting good at doing, she didn't tell him that she was leaving. She decided to save that for another day.

The Sail

George tried to steal Amy away when they returned from their walk, but Charlie put him off, saying that he really needed to have some alone time with Amy and Charles. George protested that he just needed a few minutes with Amy, but she too rebuffed his request, grabbed Charles by the hand, and skipped off toward Charlie's car.

George shrugged and muttered that he really needed to talk with Amy. He then resigned himself to waiting until morning. He wasn't too eager, after all, to endure her rage at his interference. He decided to let them have their private evening and only hoped that Amy wouldn't tell Charles that she was leaving for Afghanistan soon. Tomorrow morning he would tell her that she was not, in fact, going overseas, but staying right here in Massachusetts. He could only hope that she would love him for his concern and not hate him for his interference. After all, it was he who had repeatedly told her over the years how disgusted he was with generals who used their positions to provide special dispensations to their family members.

He would have to persuade her that this situation was different, that he was more tolerant and understanding of those who had kept their family members out of harm's way over the years. With a daughter about to head to an active war zone and a grandson who had just met his father, George felt quite differently about using his position to help them to have a safe and normal life.

Arriving at Charlie's house, Amy immediately realized that it was the very same one she had looked down upon longingly as she had flown out of his life seven years before—white house with green shutters, long dock with the sailboat tied up alongside, a bench perched at the end of the dock. She remembered the sole figure sitting at the end of that dock and knew now that it must have been Charlie. How ironic that it was Charlie she had seen as she left the United States and her happy life behind. A sad smile crept across her lips as she thought of how so many of the events in her life had been intertwined. Amy decided to wait for another time to tell Charlie of this realization. They had their hands quite full enough right now with trying to explain everything to Charles.

That night, in just a few short hours, the three of them become a family. Charlie's idea for dinner was to take a picnic out on the boat for a moonlight cruise. Since Charlie's Lightning was better suited to day sailing, he borrowed his parents' boat, *Grace*. It was bigger and safer for Charles's first experience on a sailboat. Thanks to Mary and Susan, they had their picnic. And he had the boat. He had just met his son and wanted to share his love for the sea with him. He wanted to show him what fun sailing could be. And he wanted Amy and Charles alone with no interruptions.

The three boarded the boat docked in front of Charlie's house. Amy felt misty-eyed over it being the same boat she and Charles had sailed on their ill-fated honeymoon but was happy to be aboard her again. After she secured a life vest on Charles, they motored out of the bay, the little boy on the adventure of his young life. The lights coming on along the shore and the big moon rising out of the ocean, the smell, sound, and feel of the ocean beneath the boat all mesmerized him. By the time Amy had set out the simple meal her mother and sister had prepared for them, Charles had the soul of a sailor. Charlie could tell that the little boy was in love and fostered that newfound passion by allowing him to take the wheel and steer the boat through the calm, dark water.

As naturally as his father had come upon the moniker for him, Charlie began calling his own son Skipper. "You are doing a great job there, Skipper," he said to Charles. "Did you know that the person who steers the boat is called the skipper?" Charles shook his head and asked, "So if I am the skipper, is that my name when we're sailing?"

Charlie and Amy laughed, looking at each other in silent agreement.

"Little man," Susan began, "How would you like your nickname to be Skipper? We could all start calling you that."

Charles's face broke into a broad grin. "Skipper," he said, trying the name out loud. "I like that. Wait until I tell my friends back home that I have a nickname. As the name settled in Charles's mind, he took his job more seriously, asking questions of Charles about how to know where to steer the boat. Charles stood next to his son and pointed out rock outcroppings and lighthouses, landmarks on shore, and the moon rising.

"We're not going to go too far out to sea this time, Skipper," he said. "You head for that buoy light for now, okay? and he pointed to a light bobbing in the distance. "I'll be your crew and keep the sails trimmed for you."

Charles looked confused. That was a new word. Never one to hear a word he didn't know and not question it, he asked, "What does 'trimmed' mean?" Charlie quickly explained that it meant keeping the sails from luffing in the breeze, quickly catching himself and going on to explain that luffing meant blowing around instead of staying taut and catching the wind, which led to him explaining that 'taut' meant flat and tight. Charles was mesmerized by this new language and asked if Charlie would teach him more. As they sailed, Charlie talked about sailing and taught his son as much as he could fit into their little sail.

After a while, they decided to set the sails and take a break for dinner, and as they ate their meal, they talked, Charlie asking his little skipper about his life in Germany, and Charles asking Charlie about his life in Massachootsetts (as he pronounced it). Charlie asked Amy very little about her life, gleaning everything he needed to know from his son's commentary. After they had been eating and talking for almost an hour, Charlie asked the little boy if he would be comfortable calling him Daddy. Charles looked like a deer caught in the headlights of an oncoming car. He just stared at this man he had just discovered was his father. He had really wanted a father, and now he had one. But he didn't really know him very well yet. He leaned over and whispered in his mother's ear, "Would it be okay if I called him Charlie like you do for a little while, Mom? He's not really my dad yet."

Amy hugged Charles and said cheerfully, "Charlie, how about if this guy just calls you Charlie for a while and we'll work our way up to Dad? Would that be okay?"

Charlie reached out his arms for Charles, who tentatively approached him and let his father hug him. As father held son, he said, "Charles, I don't care what you call me. I'm just so happy to know you, I don't care if you call me Daddy or Charlie. I'll answer to anything… you can call me Harry for all I care."

Even though Charlie was serious, Charles thought this was the funniest thing he'd heard in a long time. It appealed to his six-year-old sense of humor. As he wriggled out of Charlie's grasp, he said, "Okay, Harry."

And from that moment on, Charles called his father Harry!

After the new family finished eating, Charlie and Charles continued to sail, with Charlie explaining how to trim the sails and how to raise the jib, how to come about, and when to hard alee. He warned him about the boom as it would swing across the boat and showed him how to tell how far he could tack in one direction before changing his tack direction in order to keep heading toward their desired location. Meanwhile, Amy leaned back on a cushion and watched, listened, and surreptitiously took pictures of father and son at "work" on the boat. It was about time the photo album included pictures of them together.

Lost in thought, gazing up at the stars, Amy was surprised by fifty pounds of little boy landing on top of her, arms wrapped around her neck. He sleepily purred, "Mommy, I really like Harry. I think he's going to be my daddy real soon. This is the best night of my whoooooooooole life." And, with that pronouncement, he fell asleep right on top of Amy.

Amy carried Charles down into the cabin, tucked him into bed, and rejoined Charlie on deck. For the next three hours, Charles sleeping soundly, rocked by the gentle lapping of the waves against the hull and the moon glimmering on the water, Amy and Charlie made peace with the past seven years.

As they were heading back into the bay, Amy thought about how she had kept too many secrets for too long, and she told Charlie something she had not planned to tell him just yet—that she was shipping out to Afghanistan. Charlie fell back onto the banquette, looked up at her, and simply said, only half-jokingly, "Amy, I am never taking you sailing again for as long as I live. Just when I think that there is hope

for us and allow myself to be truly happy, you rip my heart out again."
He then realized how selfish that sounded when Amy had just told him
that she was going into harm's way and must be worried sick about
her—their—son.

He leaned forward and pulled her down next to him, wrapped
a protective arm around her, and soothed her worried brow with
butterfly kisses.

"Amy, tell me the whole story."

And she did. She told him how worried she was about Charles. He
didn't know yet that she was going away. He had just met his father.
He didn't really know her parents all that well and had never even met
Charlie's parents. She felt as though she was abandoning everyone and
she had no choice. She cried softly and Charlie brushed her tears away.
She leaned on his chest and took strength from his strength. She told
him that she planned to ask her parents the next day if Charles could
stay with them while she was away. At that comment, Charlie had to
speak up.

"Amy, he is my son. Please let him stay with me. We can get
acquainted. You know that no one in the world will protect him more
than I will."

And Amy realized that this was her heart's plan all along even
though she hadn't known it.

The Admission

The following day dawned bright and sunny. Even though Amy rose early, Charles beat her to the kitchen. As she bounced down the stairs more like a teenager than the woman she was, she could hear him chatting excitedly with her parents and his aunt in the kitchen. She stopped outside the door and listened for a few minutes.

"Harry is the best dad I could ever ask for. He knows everything about sailing and he can read the stars and he knows how to take mayonnaise off turkey sandwiches and he likes barbecue potato chips the best too and his boat has beds and a kitchen and everything and he let me steer it and he's been to China and he knows how to ski and he said he'd teach me how and...."

Amy whisked into the room laughing at her parents' raised eyebrows, and amid the laughter, Susan asked who Harry was. Amy looked at Charles who began laughing and said, "Why that is the man formerly known as Charlie, of course." This did nothing to alleviate the confusion, but Amy forged on.

"So, little man, it sounds like you had a good time last night. Did you tell Nana and Grampy what your new name is?"

At that, Charles's face broke into a huge smile and he announced, "My new name is Skipper. You know why? Because I was the skipper of the boat. You know what that means? It means that I was in charge and steered the boat." At that, he sat back proudly, enjoying the smiles he was receiving from his grandparents.

Amy loved seeing her mother and father sipping their coffee at the kitchen table, smiling and enjoying their grandson's enthusiasm. Her sister, meanwhile, was observing this little tableau, thinking how normal her life was by comparison to her sister's crazy one. She missed her little girls and her loving husband, even though she had only been

225

away from them overnight. She wondered how Amy could have spent so many years away from the guy who was obviously the love of her life. She decided that she was going to head home to her little family. She said, "Ames, I'm going to hit the road. You have a full day and don't need me around here. When the dust settles, either you guys can come to Maine for a visit or we'll all troop down here." With that, she hopped up off her chair, gave Amy a big hug, shared one with each of her parents, high-fived her nephew, and went out to her car to head back to Maine.

Susan left so suddenly that Amy didn't really have a chance to think much about it. She just nodded and called out, "Bye, Suze. We'll see you soon," knowing that Charles might see her soon, but she wouldn't.

Turning back to the kitchen, she heard the radio saying that it was going to be a beautiful, sunny, hot day. Amy had a thought. Charles loved the beach yesterday. Maybe they could all take a picnic to the beach today and she could take a long walk with him and tell him about her assignment to Afghanistan. She had to tell him sometime. It would be better to tell him while she still had some time to spend with him rather than tell him and then simply disappear from his life. Since it was Saturday, maybe Charlie's parents would like to join them and meet their grandson.

"I have one of my Mom's Magnificent Ideas!" she declared.

Charles knew that whenever she referred to an idea as one of her "Mom's Magnificent Ideas" it was going to be a big one. His eyes grew large as he waited to hear what it was.

"How about if we pack a picnic this morning and head to the beach for lunch—all of us? Are you tired of picnics yet, Charles?"

The little boy literally jumped up and down in the kitchen.

"Yay! That's a stuperific idea!" Stuperific was a word Amy had coined years ago and had taught Charles. It combined stupendous, super, and terrific and was reserved for the very best things.

"Mom," Charles added a little more seriously, "Could Harry come with us, too?"

"What's with this Harry business, Amy?" her mother asked, and Amy explained the conversation on the boat. With the explanation, her father chuckled.

"He's a clever little guy, Amy. Our lives are certainly happier with him around," her father commented. Amy smiled a sad smile, thinking that they had no idea how much he was going to be around in the near future.

She caught her expression quickly and continued, "Well, Charles, there is one more surprise." At the mention of his name, Charles frowned and reminded her that his new name was Skipper. "Well, okay, Skipper," Amy continued with a grin, "you know Nana and Grampy, but believe it or not, you have even more grandparents. Harry's parents are your grandparents too, and they live right by Harry. Should we ask them to go on our picnic today with us?"

Charles looked like he had won the lottery. He looked from his Nana to his Grampy and then back to his mother in disbelief. Then he remembered what his Grampy had told him about his name. What he didn't know, though, was that they lived right here in this same town.

"I have *more* grandparents who live here?" he asked. "Yeah! Let's ask them to come too. I can meet Charles Henry Donnelly One" And then, as though that issue were settled, he returned to his giant blueberry muffin.

Amy looked confused when her son referred to Charlie's father as "Charles Henry Donnelly One." Her father interjected, "He was a little confused yesterday, so I told him about his being "the third" and Charlie being "the second" and Charlie's father being the first one with the same name. He's a smart little guy, Amy. He remembered it and must have decided that made his grandfather One." George chuckled at his grandson's brilliance as Amy excused herself and went to call Charlie.

"Hey, Harry. How are you this morning?" she asked cheerfully when he answered the phone.

"You don't get to call me Harry, Ames. That's reserved for Charles." Charlie's tone was friendly, but she knew that he meant what he said. He needed to begin creating special memories with his son, and this was the first.

"Hey, listen. Ma and Dad and I are taking Charles out to the beach for a picnic at eleven thirty. We'd love to have you join us."

"Of course. I'd love to go! Should I meet you at your house or at the beach?"

"Well," drawled Amy. "You'd better come here because we can't drive out onto the beach like you can. Either Dad will drive and we'll just go to the bay side, or you can pile us all into that Jeep of yours and we can give my mother a treat bouncing across the dune road." As she said this, she glanced at her mother who pretended to be scared.

"I'll be there a little before eleven, then!" Charlie said and after talking a little about who would bring what, Amy broached the topic of his parents meeting Charles.

"Charlie, why don't you ask your parents to come along? It's about time they met Charles. I know they're going to hate me, but we have to do it sometime.

Charlie thought it was a wonderful idea and agreed to ask his parents to join them. Laughing, he said, "I can't remember the last time they actually stepped foot on the beach or had a picnic. This could be fun!" and he grinned on his end of the phone. "I'll call them right now. Do you think I should tell them why we're suddenly becoming 'those people who eat on blankets in the sand'?"

"Oh, that's up to you, Charlie," Amy replied with a chuckle. "What do you think?"

"Well," Charles began. "It's not the kind of thing I should tell them on the phone, but I have to give them some reason for this impromptu interruption of their Saturday plans. Don't worry about it. I'll think of something. If they're coming, though, I'll just ride with them and we can meet you in the parking lot, okay? That way, I'll make sure they show up."

Amy smiled nervously and agreed. She turned from her spot in the doorway to the back porch, watched her folks and Charles for a few seconds, then walked back into the kitchen, poured herself a cup of coffee and picked up a blueberry muffin—one of her mother's specialties. The muffins were still warm, and the blueberries melted apart, squirting the juice of contented moments of her childhood in her mouth as she bit the muffin.

"Mmmmmmmm, Mom. I've missed these. I'm going to gain ten pounds if I stay here much longer. Your cooking is soooooo good.

Charles, don't you think we should stay here forever so Nana could cook for us?" She winked at Charles, who couldn't answer because his little mouth was full of blueberry muffin, his little cheeks stuffed as though he were storing nuts for winter. He just nodded his little head up and down, eyes smiling all the while.

Amy giggled and said, "You little chipmunk! You don't have to eat the whole muffin in one bite. There are plenty of them."

Charles grinned which made his cheeks puff out even more.

"Well," her father interrupted, glancing conspiratorially at his wife. "I need to have some father–daughter time. Charles, how about you and Nana finish up breakfast, and your mom and I will take a little walk. Then when we get back, you can help me with some man stuff in the garage."

Not even bothering to ask his mother first, Charles nodded and managed to squeeze an "okay" through his chipmunk cheeks and blueberry lips.

Amy grabbed a muffin for her walk and took off after her father as he headed out the kitchen door.

Once father and daughter had reached the garden, around the corner from the kitchen windows, George pulled Amy down onto the garden bench next to him. He looked at her seriously, which scared her. What was he about to say?

"Amy," he began. "Amy, I have done something that is uncharacteristic for me but that I just had to do." Charging on without waiting for a question or response, he said bluntly, "You know that I have a few friends in the Army. When the decision was made for you to be restationed, I got a heads up." Amy began to open her mouth to protest, but he placed his finger softly on her lips. "When I found out that you were shipping out for Afghanistan, I said to myself, 'I'll be damned if a daughter of mine is going to go to a war zone and leave her little boy behind.' And I began to call in favors to get you reassigned."

As he spoke, Amy just stared at him, wondering where this was going.

"You know how the Army works. It took a while, but I just found out a few days ago that my request was granted and you are being reassigned to the Veterans Hospital in Bedford. "It's high time you came home," he added gruffly. Relieved that he had gotten it off his chest, he simply sat back and waited for the verbal explosion. He knew that Amy would be furious with him for interfering in her life.

Much to his surprise, her arms flew around his neck and her face nuzzled into his shoulder. "Oh, Daddy! How will I ever be able to thank you?" And father and daughter sat in an unexpected embrace for several minutes.

When he had processed that she was not angry with him, George smiled and moved her away from him so that he could look at her. Pushing his luck, he asked, "You're not angry with me?"

"Oh, Daddy, you just might have fixed my entire life!" she exclaimed gratefully. "Bedford is in Massachusetts, right?"

Grinning now, her father nodded and said, "It's exactly one hour and six minutes from here. Is that close enough?"

All the anxiety Amy had been feeling seemed to flow from her body. Her shoulders relaxed, her eyes opened, and the smile she radiated toward her father made his heart sing. This definitely was one of the best moments of his life. Her face then clouded.

"If you knew that I wasn't going to have to ask you to keep Charles here with you, why did you create such an amazing room for him in your house?"

"Well, Amy, I wasn't sure that the Army would change your orders, and I knew you would probably ask us to keep Charles if you had to go. We wanted him to be comfortable and happy while you were away. Now," he quickly added, "it's just a fun place for him to stay whenever you want your old mom and dad to babysit." With that, he winked at her, already a few steps ahead of her in his thinking of her future.

"Oh, my God!" she shouted. "If Bedford is only an hour away, we could stay here in Duxbury! Charles could grow up here! Charlie could spend time with him." She stopped short of saying the next thing she thought so as not to jinx it. "Oh, my God! I wish I hadn't told Charlie last night that I was shipping out. Well, I'll just have to fix that too."

George decided that there was no time like the present. To her he said, "Let's go back inside and get this day on its way, huh, Amy? It's going to be another big one." With that, her father took her hand in his as he had when she was a little girl, pulling her up off the bench and heading back toward the kitchen, each of their footsteps lighter than before.

The Book

As Amy and her father burst through the kitchen door, Amy noticed a grin and a wink pass between her mother and father. Her father then bellowed, "If you expect this old coot to go to the beach for lunch, I'd better get moving. I've got a lot to do this morning." He then turned to Charles and added, "You coming, Charles? I sure could use a helper. I'm not used to having another man around the house. It will be nice to have someone give me a hand."

Charles whipped his muffin-stuffed face toward Amy, his big green eyes asking if he could go with his grandfather.

"Get lost, you!" she said. "And take good care of Grampy, okay?"

Amy's mother called out from the other side of the kitchen, "You two be back here by eleven o'clock. If we're going to have lunch at the beach, we may as well escape the heat of the day around here and enjoy it by the water. Amy and I will have everything ready to go at eleven sharp."

"We'll be here, Nana, I promise," said a serious Charles, while his grandfather grunted his agreement in his wife's direction. He then winked at Charles, turned on his heel, saluted Mary, and said, "Ma'am, yes, ma'am." Charles took the cue and did the same, much to everyone's amusement. Then grandfather and grandson turned and headed for the door.

George said softly to Amy as he passed her on the threshold, "It will be a fun day with Charlie along. I've missed him around here, and I've missed the twinkle he brings to your eye, pumpkin." He kissed the top of Amy's head, much to her surprise, and followed the little tornado out into the yard.

Once her husband had closed the screen door behind a scampering Charles, and their voices receded as they walked away from the house, Amy's mother turned to Amy and said quietly, "Okay, Amy, now that they're gone, how about if you and I take a couple of these muffins and our tea out to the front porch and relax for a bit before we pack up the lunch?"

Amy knew her mother well enough to know that she had something on her mind. Actually, Amy had something pretty major to share with her mother, too. She quickly agreed, and the two placed their muffins and tea on a tray, which Amy carried, and they padded to the front porch where they settled into the big old white Adirondack chairs, the tray on the table between them.

Amy closed her eyes and let the ocean breezes wash over her as she listened to the rustling leaves and the sound of her little boy's laughter coming from the garage. How quickly he had fallen in love with his grandfather on this visit, she thought, with a sense of relief. And how eager Charlie was to get to know him. Now he has a family, she thought—a real family. He has a grandmother, a grandfather, and a father. He will soon have another grandmother and grandfather. He has an aunt and uncle and cousins not too far away. Amy thought her heart would burst with joy. It had been a long time since she had felt pure joy, and she was finding it exhilarating.

"Amy, dear, what's on that mind of yours? You suddenly look a million miles away," her mother said, concerned. And Amy noticed tiny wrinkles around her eyes that hadn't been there the last time Amy had seen her.

"Mom," she ventured, smiling. "I have something to tell you." Her mother just waited patiently for what was to follow.

"I guess I've been waiting for the right time to talk with you about this, but there really never was a right time, and then Daddy had that talk with me, and you probably know what's going on anyway." She paused and took a deep breath, looking up into the trees and then down at her toes, momentarily mesmerized by the single ray of light breaking its way through the thick leaves and shining a spotlight on her pale feet.

"Mom, I thought that I only had a few more days and then would have to report to duty again."

"I know, honey," her mother interjected. "Your father told me."

"Yeah, Mom. I figured he probably had. I have been dying since I came back, wondering how I was going to tell everyone that I had to go to Afghanistan. I guess it's a good thing that I tend to procrastinate when I don't want to tell someone something." With that comment, she laughed a little.

"We were having such a nice visit, I didn't want to spoil it and I wanted you and Dad to fall in love with Charles and not be upset when I asked if he could stay here while I'm away, and then Charlie came into the picture again, and I couldn't bear to tell him that I would be leaving again so soon, and he kept trying to plan a future, and he was so…Charlie…and I just couldn't tell him—but I did last night."

With that thought, Amy was aghast. "Oh, my God!" she exclaimed. "I told Charlie. I need to talk with him." She jumped up and ran for her cell phone. "Sorry, Mom. I'll be right back!" she cried over her shoulder as she burst through the screen door and into the house to call Charlie.

Charlie didn't answer his phone. It went straight to voicemail. She didn't care. She would tell him anyway. "Charlie!" she excitedly shouted into the phone. "I am not going away! I'm staying in Duxbury. Daddy fixed it all, and I don't have to leave you again. I'll tell you all the details when I see you. See you soon!" Grinning, she thought about how his face would look when he heard that message.

When Amy returned, her smile lit up the porch. She fell into the Adirondack chair next to her mother and apologized for leaving so abruptly.

"Sorry, Mom. I just had to tell Charlie. I couldn't keep another secret or wait to tell him the good news for a single minute. Thank goodness I hadn't told Charles that I was going. He's going to be a happy camper when he finds out that he gets to stay here with all of you. How did you ever stand being a mother in all of those places? It's so hard being away from family and trying to raise a child." The words tumbled out one after another and then she sat silently, looking down at her feet.

She didn't know what her mother must think of her right now. Would she be disappointed that Amy hadn't had enough faith in them to tell them sooner? Would she be scared that her baby girl almost headed into a war zone? Would she be angry that Amy didn't have more faith in her? Amy continued to look down for what seemed like an eternity. So intent was she on studying her toes and thinking that she didn't even notice her mother arise silently and move into the house, returning in seconds and lowering herself slowly to the chair next to Amy, a package in her hands.

Amy looked over at her and saw nothing but compassion in her mother's face.

"Amy, are you happy with this life you have chosen? When you lie in bed at night, do you miss Charlie and the life you might have had, or is your heart filled with pride for serving your country?"

This wasn't the response Amy was expecting since it had nothing to do with what she had just told her mother. Amy wasn't sure how to respond.

"Well, I guess it's a little bit of both," she answered. "Of course I wonder 'what if?' but I've always felt that I was destined to serve. You can't have it both ways. You ultimately have to choose, right?"

Her mother sat quietly for a long while, deep in thought. Then she told Amy her story. In her mind she was twenty-one again, remembering what it been like to be young and in love. She herself had sacrificed the life she had hoped to have in a town much like this one. Not that she had too many regrets. She had done a good job of maintaining a sense of family no matter where they went. Family was critical to her. It meant more than anything, and she would sacrifice anything for her family.

She had once dreamed of being a lawyer and had graduated near the top of her class at Vassar College, earning a BA in English Literature. During her junior year, though, a friend who was dating a West Point cadet had asked her to go along to a big dance, and she had figured, "Why not?" Her friend's boyfriend had a friend who needed a date and Mary was always up for an adventure. She and her friend Ellen drove to the town of Highlands, where Ellen's aunt and uncle lived. Mary's parents had agreed to let her go since the girls would be staying with Ellen's family, just south of West Point. On the ride there, Ellen gushed endlessly about the man she loved and promised Mary that she, too, was about to fall in love. Ellen's boyfriend had said that the friend he was bringing for Mary was quite the catch. Mary nodded and smiled but had absolutely no intention of falling in love. She had other plans for her life.

As Mary and her friend Ellen waited in Ellen's aunt's living room for the men to arrive, Mary was thinking about the LSATs she would be taking the following week. She was ready. She had talked with her advisor about what to expect and had been told that she should do quite well. Her analytical mind, evidenced by the clever essays she had written during her time at Vassar, should hold her in good stead as she sat for the exam. Lost in her daydreams of which law school she should attend, she didn't hear the doorbell ring and was startled to hear Ellen call out, "Mary! Are you coming or not?"

Mary turned and standing in front of her, hat in hand, was George. He was a fourth year at West Point and very handsome. As they say in the old movies, he took her breath away. She smiled at him, and as Ellen made the introductions, a little line formed between Mary's brows. *This boy could be trouble,* she thought. Mary was not one to believe in princes riding in on shining steeds or happily ever afters. She had not been raised to believe that a woman's place is in the home waiting on her man. No, her mother was a woman far ahead of her time, a professor at Smith College. Mary had been raised in a world of female empowerment well before the term had been coined. Hers was to be a life of using her mind, and she had determined that she would follow in her father's footsteps and that law would be her domain. Now here stood this gorgeous man looking at her in that interested way that foretold trouble.

Mary had heard foolish girls talk about men in uniform, and Ellen had spent many hours mooning over her Henry and how handsome he was in his West Point attire. Mary thought she was immune to all of that nonsense. Now, here she stood feeling like a silly schoolgirl, actually wondering if her hair was in place, if her makeup was right, if she was pretty enough for this man.

Stop it! she scolded herself mentally. *This is not who you are.* But her hormones were not listening. George was intriguing. He reached out and handed her a white orchid corsage and asked if she would like him to pin it on her dress. She agreed, and he deftly attached it. As he leaned in to pin the corsage, she could smell his cologne, masculine and sweet. She noted subconsciously that not too many young men wore cologne and thought it was very pleasant.

After the requisite photos that Ellen's uncle took of the two couples with his new Polaroid, it was time to go. George stepped forward and formally placed his hand on his waist, creating a crook for her arm to slip into, and asked, "Shall we, Miss O'Brien?" She actually blushed and heard herself meekly reply, "Certainly, Cadet Captain Sweetser." She placed her arm in his and swept out the door behind Ellen and Henry to the waiting car.

Having had a wonderful time at the dance, Mary returned to Vassar where she took the LSATs, but was conflicted when the results came back and she discovered that she did quite well. She and George dated long-distance for the rest of the school year. She attended his graduation from West Point, proud of her handsome George as he accepted his diploma and commission certificate. After graduation, he visited her in Northampton, Massachusetts.

Since she was spending her summer reading and swimming and hanging out with her friends who were home for the summer, George's visit was a chance for him to meet her family and friends. For two weeks they spent every waking moment together, and by the end of the two weeks, he had charmed her mother and impressed her father, who was not easy to impress.

As they said good-bye, they knew that he would be going back to assume his first commission and she would be returning for her last year at Vassar. They promised to write and to see each other whenever possible, and when he left, Mary admitted to her parents and to herself that she was head over heels in love with George. Of course, she was warned not to let love get in the way of her dreams for a legal career like her father's, but she wasn't so sure that her dream was still the same. All she could think about was George.

The two wrote every day and grew closer as they got to know more about each other. The other girls in her dorm were jealous of the handsome young officer Mary had snagged. They couldn't understand why she didn't drop out of school and marry him right away.

George and Mary began to talk about a future together and to plan how they could make that work. George didn't want to dissuade Mary from attending law school, but he also couldn't imagine spending another three years away from her. And if she did go to law school, what then? He would be stationed in various places around the world on his rise up the military ladder and would expect that she would want to be with him.

Mary's thoughts returned briefly to the present with this revelation. Her situation had been very similar to Amy's. Career or love? With that thought, Mary drifted back to 1979.

With law school applications due, Mary was becoming anxious. She completed applications to four schools and sent them off. She would see George during her Christmas break and was prepared to tell him that they would have to break off their long-distance relationship. As much as she loved him, she couldn't give up on her dreams of her career as a lawyer. She decided that when George arrived, she would tell him that it was over. The decision made, she sulked around her parents' house for days, rushing off to her bedroom frequently to cry over what might have been but knowing that she had made the right decision. While they were opening presents as the Northampton snow fell on Christmas morning, the doorbell rang and Mary jumped up to answer it. She blinked in disbelief when she found George, his uniform covered with snow, kneeling at her door and holding out a small box.

Hearing her gasp, her parents hurried into the foyer and witnessed the romantic scene. There, framed in their doorway, mistletoe overhead and snow falling softly on his shoulders, knelt George proposing to their only child. Of course, George had discussed the proposal with Mary's father and, although her father had misgivings and did not want his daughter to give up on her dream, he told George that it was her decision to make. He gave George his blessing to ask her but warned him that he might not like her answer.

Mary just stood in the doorway for several seconds looking down at George's hopeful face and loving him more than ever. As he said,

"Mary, would you do me the honor of becoming my wife?" she found herself exclaiming that yes, she would. He stood and she flung her arms around his neck in a crushing embrace....

"Ma!" Amy exclaimed. "I can't believe you never told me that story before."

Mary replied that she didn't want to influence her daughters as they made their own life decisions, thinking that if she shared her story, they would think that she expected them to make the same choices she had made.

She smiled and nodded to the object she had brought out of the house. She placed it in Amy's lap, and Amy's gaze turned to it. Sitting there was a navy-blue, leather-bound book. It was thick and heavy, but soft to the touch. On the front, embossed in gold, it said, simply, *Amy's Life*. Amy looked up questioningly, and her mother smiled ever so slightly.

"Amy, I have been keeping track of your adventures since you were born. Wherever we lived, my quiet moments were spent reflecting on my daughters' lives, on the children you were and the young women you would become. In this book you will find stories, anecdotes, reminiscences, and my hopes and dreams for you. You'll find an account of every birthday and Christmas, every broken bone and broken heart. And you'll find my story—the one we never talked about. You will discover who I was at your age and who I became. Amy, I hope as you read through it, you'll feel the love with which it was written. I hope you'll remember good times you may have forgotten. But mostly, I hope you'll understand how deep a mother's love is for her child.

Now that you have a child of your own, I thought you could appreciate this. I considered giving it to you on your eighteenth birthday, but you didn't need it then. You had Charlie. Then I considered giving it to you when you left for Germany, but that happened so fast that we were caught up in the details of your leaving and the time never seemed quite right. Now, though, I want you to read this book and let me know if it's okay for us to share its stories with Charles. I think the pictures of you as a young girl and the stories of your adventures and travels as you followed your father around the world may be of some comfort to your son. He will see that a career military parent sometimes has to make difficult decisions. Maybe as he gets older, he will understand the obstacles you and Charlie faced and how you chose to overcome them.

Amy said nothing. If she had spoken, she would have breached the floodgate to her soul. She just looked first at her mother and then at the tome in her lap. Then she picked it up and held it close, hugging the precious gift her mother had just given to her.

"Oh, Ma, this is amazing. When did you do this? I never saw you writing. Thank you so much for this book. I'll read it tonight. I think it's incredible that you did this for me. Did you make one for Susan, too?"

"Of course I did, silly. I wouldn't do it for just one of you, now, would I? Susan got hers when Rachael was born, under threat of death if she told you about it."

Amy simply said, "I always thought you were amazing, by the way. I don't know if I ever told you how much I appreciated how you made every move easier."

Mary wiped a tear of gratitude from her cheek. Once she had agreed to marry George, law school dreams became something of the past. All she could think of was starting a family with this man. She accepted completely that her job would be to be a good wife and mother. That often meant being the strong one who simply made everything easier for everyone else in the family. If her heart broke at leaving friends behind when George would receive a reassignment or seeing the pain in her daughters' eyes as they had to once again be the new kids in a new school, she never let it show. She smiled, did her research, excitedly talked about all of the wonderful new adventures in their new location, and hoped that her enthusiasm would be translated and absorbed by her children. Now, though, both her precious daughters had a chance at normal lives, putting down roots somewhere. She couldn't have been happier. In this moment, her life had meaning, and she knew that she had made the right decision all those years ago. She would have to remember to give George a big kiss when he came in.

Amy watched her mother's face transform before her eyes. All tension disappeared, and her mother suddenly looked years younger, as though a weight had been lifted. Amy opened the book and read the inscription:

To my darling daughter Amy: From the day you were born, you were independent and strong. I am proud of the child you are and know that I will be proud of the woman you will become. Someday, we will sit and talk as friends of the trials and joys of being a woman. Until that day, I will continue to record elements of your life that will help you to understand who you are. With all my love, Mom

Mary watched Amy read the words she had written to her daughter, smiling with pride at the woman she was now. Then she broke the silence. "Amy, what I really wanted to talk to you about was your reassignment to Bedford. We already knew about your overseas posting before you got here. Your father was trying to get you reassigned but wasn't sure if it would come through. Why do you think Charles's room is so wonderfully decorated and your father has gone out of his way to make the boy feel comfortable with us? We weren't sure if you would want him to stay with us or with Susan's family, but we hoped it would be with us. We thought you might have chosen Susan so that Charlie would have less of a chance to see him. But we figured that if we fixed him up a room and your dad made him his little buddy, he'd be happy here. Your father worked night and day talking with his old cronies and trying to get you out of that posting, but we wanted to make sure that Charles would be okay if none of that worked." More quietly, she added, "Thank goodness that now he can stay with you. But where will that be? You know you are both welcome to stay with us, but I'm guessing that once Charlie learns of your new post, he won't waste any time walking you down the aisle again." Her mother beamed.

Amy chewed on her lower lip, thinking about Charlie. If she were honest with herself, she would admit that part of the reason she had come to visit her parents was a hope that she would see Charlie again and introduce him to his son. She probably, on some subconscious level, wanted Charles to get to know his dad. She ventured, "Well, I guess Charlie and I need to figure that out."

She began to understand the disservice she had done to both father and son during the past six years. She really had been selfish. But she honestly had felt that she had taken the high moral ground. She had believed that she was saving Charlie the heartache of choosing between her and their son and his career and life in New England. She reasserted, "We'll work it out." Then she wailed, "Ma, I really have made a mess of my life, haven't I?"

Her mother replied, "Amy, all we can do in life is what we think is right at the time. Sometimes we're right and sometimes we're wrong. Sometimes we look back with regrets, and sometimes we look back and know that what we did in the past is what got us to where we are right now. Amy, you're in a pretty good place right now. And you're still so very young. You have your whole life ahead of you."

This teased a smile from Amy, and just as she was about to respond, Charles and his grandfather came around the corner from the direction of the garage, faces shimmering with perspiration from the heat of the day and dirty from head to toe. In fact, they looked happy and as though they knew they would be in trouble for being so dirty and not caring.

"Mom, we got a little dirty in Grampy's garage!" Charles exclaimed. "We were working on the carbonator in the car." He looked up at his grandfather, silently asking if he had that right.

"Close, little man," his grandfather replied with great seriousness. "It's called a carburetor."

Charlie repeated three times, "Carburetor, carburetor, carburetor" so he would remember it. They then glanced at each other conspiratorially and began laughing, throwing their heads back in the same way, displaying their family resemblance.

"You two get inside and wash up!" ordered Amy's mother with mock sternness, all the while trying not to smile. "And don't you get any of that grease on anything in my house."

In unison, as though rehearsed, grandfather and grandson clicked their heels, saluted, and replied, "Ma'am, yes, ma'am." They then broke into peals of laughter and disappeared into the house, the screen door slamming behind them.

Only after they were out of earshot and sight did Amy and her mother begin to laugh. Amy felt lighthearted as she had as a teenager sitting on this porch. She and her mother rose, hugged for a moment, and went into the house to pack up the picnic that would mean more than anyone knew.

At 10:45, as Mary was placing the red-and-white checked napkin over the top of the picnic basket, she and Amy heard Charlie's Jeep tossing up stones from the driveway as he careened off the road and up their long drive. It seemed like old times. Mary wondered how all of this was going to play out. Amy had given the requisite years to the Army for her West Point education and was technically free to leave. But would she leave completely, or would she continue to serve by working in Bedford? Would Charlie graciously accept that the future could be wonderful or would he resent the years lost? Only time would tell. And what was he doing here? They had agreed to meet at the beach.

The Reveal

"Ma!" brought Mary out of her reverie. "I think that napkin is suffi-
ciently tucked. Mary looked down and realized that as she had
been thinking she fiddled with the picnic basket.

"Well, I guess it is at that, isn't it?" she absent-mindedly replied. "I
hope we packed enough for all of us. I didn't hear you tell Charlie or his
folks to bring anything. I want to make sure we have enough." As she
finished her musing, she gave the basket a pat as she walked out of the
kitchen, leaving her daughter behind.

Mary reached the front door just as Charlie was opening the screen.
Surprising him, she wrapped her arms around his neck, put her face
close to his ear and whispered fervently, "You keep hold of that girl,
you hear me? Don't let her slip through your fingers again." With that,
she pecked him on the cheek and sidestepped past him out onto the
porch, leaving him to wonder what had brought that on.

Before he had a chance to think too much about it, and was searching the room for Amy, George and Charles came bounding down the
stairs, seemingly in a race that Charles was bound to win. As Charles
jumped the last two stairs and landed at Charlie's feet, George huffed
and puffed his way down the remaining steps. He raised Charles's arms
into the air in victory and loudly pronounced him the winner of the
stair race.

"You men stop fooling around in there and get going," Mary called
from the porch. "I'm stifling out here and could use the sea breezes at
the beach to cool off. Go grab that picnic basket and get out here!"

"Ma'am, yes, ma'am," replied three male voices, and then laughter
erupted from all three as they hurried into the kitchen to get the picnic
basket from Amy.

"Well, it certainly is louder around here than it ever has been before," Amy commented with a phony scowl. As she said it, she noticed her son's grin. He obviously loved the male companionship of his grandfather and father. He really was going to be fine. These wonderful people would see to that.

"So did you listen to your voicemail?" she asked Charlie.

"Voicemail? No," he replied. "I was persuading my folks to go to the beach and then they finally agreed but wanted to take their car—'as a novelty' I think Mother said. So I ran home, showered and changed, and hurried over here. Why? Did you leave me a voicemail? Have plans changed?"

Amy smiled back at him. "I'm not saying a word, not a single word," she said. "But saying that the plans have changed is a major understatement." And, as she was leaving the kitchen, she said over her shoulder, "Listen to the voicemail from me."

Thirty seconds later, as Amy, Charles, George, and Mary were piling into Charlie's old, tattered Jeep, he came bounding down the stairs of the porch without touching a single one. Flying to the car, he whisked Amy up into his arms, spun her in the air, and yelled, "Really? Really? Really?" She simply nodded her head as it was spinning around. "Sorry, George. Sorry, Mary. I couldn't help myself. I just got some good news."

As he spoke, they both burst into laughter, her father saying, "Yeah, we thought so."

At this point, everyone seemed to notice at the same time that Charles was confused. Used to living a quiet life with Amy, all of this noise and commotion, emotions, and throwing people around in the air was new to him, and a little frightening. Amy got to him first and grabbed him in her arms.

"Charles, darling, we got some very good news from your Grampy today. You and I are going to get to stay here in Duxbury. We'll be able to live here in a real house and you can go to a real school and learn to sail and play tennis with Harry and go to the beach whenever we want. We can have picnics and go for long walks on the beach. Oh, Charles, everything is going to be wonderful."

When she said that, he surprised all of them by simply saying, "Just like Grampy said it would be." And he climbed into the middle of the backseat of the car and put on his seat belt.

The adults around him began laughing and climbing into the car, Amy and her mom flanking Charles in back and her dad riding shotgun.

The Beach Adventure

On the way to the beach, Charlie shouted over the wind, grinning as he began, "So I talked to my mom this morning. She really gave me a hard time about going for a picnic on the beach. She said it was Saturday and she had an appointment to get her hair done and then she had to shop for something to wear to the Make-A-Wish Gala next weekend. She was quite adamant that it was impossible."

"Oh, I'm guessing you worked your charms on her, Charlie," cooed Mary. "There isn't a woman on the South Shore who can refuse you," she added, looking pointedly at Amy.

"Were you able to persuade her?" asked Amy, ignoring her mother's looks.

"But of course, ma'am," Charlie formally replied, with a very proper Old Boston accent. "Haven't you heard? I have it on good authority that there isn't a woman on the South Shore who can refuse me." With that, George actually guffawed, nearly choking on the muffin he had snuck into the car.

"What's more, I told her that they *both* had to come. You should have heard her exclamations and protestations. She informed me that it was one thing for her to upset her day, but that it would be simply impossible for my father to do so." Charlie paused and then continued. "I told her that I had some earth-shattering, life-altering, game-changing, stuperific news, and that if they didn't come out to the beach they would regret it for the rest of their lives." By now, everyone in the car except Charles was laughing as they pictured Charlie's mother hearing that pronouncement.

"After a great deal of harrumphing and questioning—none of which I would answer—she reluctantly agreed and called to my father as he was just leaving to play golf that if he knew what was good for him he would stop in his tracks. I don't think I have ever heard my mother say 'stop in your tracks' before." Charlie smiled. "They're meeting us at the east end of the parking lot. I was very James Bond about the whole thing. I told them to bring folding beach chairs and leave the rest to the Sweetsers." Looking at Mary in the rearview mirror, he added, "I know you, Mary. You always have enough food for half of the town. I didn't mean to impose, but my folks are confused enough right now without asking them to pack a lunch."

By this time, the Jeep had ambled across the little wooden bridge, and Charlie was turning left into the sandy parking lot. Amy noticed absently that it was high tide and the water was beginning its journey back to the sea. While in Germany, she found that she had missed the way the weather reports always included commentary on the tides here on the East Coast. It was one of the things she had found had quaint about this town when they'd first moved here. Midwesterners might find it odd, but after living in Duxbury for a while, she totally understood. If you were taking a boat out, for example, you wanted to go with the ebb of the tide and return with the flow. It just made coming and going in the bay easier. And, if you were going to have a party, you always wanted to time it for high tide because the bay was so pretty when filled with water but kind of muddy and smelly at low tide. Some people's boats, in fact, floated prettily when moored at high tide, but at low tide actually sat in the mud.

After Charlie slammed on the brakes and pulled in next to his parents' black Lexus, he and the Sweetsers piled out of the Jeep. His parents emerged from their air-conditioned car dressed for a yachting party—he in khakis and baby-blue polo shirt, the soles of his docksiders gleaming white in the sun, and she in crisp white capris and a sleeveless navy blouse she had bought just this week at Talbot's. Even with the heat, a navy-and-white cotton sweater was flung around her neck, competing with the shell necklace she was wearing. Her navy espadrilles were already sandy, but as she hugged Charlie and was about to ask him what this command performance was all about, she saw Amy.

With a gasp, Grace exclaimed, "Amy! Is that really you? What are you doing here?" Turning to Charlie, she asked, "Why couldn't we have had a nice afternoon tea party or luncheon for Amy's return? Why did we have to come to the beach?" Then catching herself, she turned to Amy's parents. "Oh, where are my manners? Hello, George. Hello, Mary." But it was Amy who had piqued her curiosity. She hurried to Amy's side as Amy came around the Jeep to meet her. They embraced as Amy uttered a quiet but enthusiastic, "Hello, Grace." Mid-embrace, the taller Grace espied a young boy coming from behind the Jeep.

"And who might this be?" she asked, smiling first at Amy and then at Charles. Were it not for a recent Botox injection, her brow would have furrowed in confusion.

Charlie hurried over to where they were standing, interrupting the big introduction. "Dad, come over here!" The elder Donnelly strode over to his wife's side, pecking Amy on the cheek as he approached. He, too, noticed the small boy, and a knowing look borne of thirty-five years of marriage passed between him and Grace.

"Mom, Dad, I think that you are going to be happy you decided to come out here today." He motioned to Amy and Charles to come stand by his side and he wrapped a protective arm around each of them. Taking a deep breath, and squeezing each of them just a little tighter, he said, "Mom, Dad, I would like you to meet your grandson Charles Henry Donnelly, the Third." And to little Charles he said, "I would like you to meet my parents, your grandparents."

Totally taken by surprise, for even though he had hoped, he couldn't be sure, it was the elder Charles who regained his composure first. Falling to a knee in front of Charles, he said, his eyes glistening behind his dark glasses, "It is very nice to meet you, young man." He offered his hand to shake hands with his newly found grandson and visibly jumped at the electric shock of warmth that coursed through him as a small hand returned the grasp.

By this time, Charlie's mother had quickly assessed the situation and, after a somewhat icy glare at Amy, softened her eyes. She too knelt on the sand, putting her arms out for a hug from the little boy. When he hesitated, shyly looking up to his mother for guidance, Grace immediately said, "Don't you worry, Charles. I won't rush you," and she stood again, brushing the sand from her knee.

Then the questions poured forth with everyone talking at once.

Putting an end to the spectacle in the parking lot, Charlie asked everyone to please be patient and he would explain everything. Looking down at Charles, silently letting everyone know that this was about a little boy, not about them, he said cheerfully, "Let's go have a picnic. I think this guy would really like to hit the water. Right, Skipper?" and the little face smiled and nodded. The elder Charles smiled when he heard the nickname applied to his own grandson.

As the men grabbed the chairs and cooler and picnic basket from the cars, the women picked up the blankets and towels. The newly formed family then paraded up over the path through the dune and down the other side to the beach, finding a spot to themselves close to the receding water's edge. Everyone pitched in and in short order, the little group was sitting in a circle, food and beverages in the center where all could reach whatever they desired.

George, realizing that Charlie and his folks might want a few minutes to talk about what they had just learned, was the first to speak. He called out to Charles, "Hey, little man! I'm hot. Wanna go take a dip with me?" An appreciative Charles nodded and hopped up to join his grandfather, who was already walking toward the water.

Once they were out of earshot, Grace began. "Charles Henry Donnelly the Second, what is going on?"

Charlie took a deep breath and, holding Amy's hand, brought his parents up to date on the events of the past few days.

The Questions

The next couple of days flew by in a whirlwind of picnics, barbecues, sailing, swimming, and hanging out at Charlie's house. He was trying to pack the six years he had lost into a few days.

"Mom," Charles tentatively began as he and Amy and Charlie sat in Adirondack chairs on Charlie's sloping front lawn, watching the sailboats dance in the bay. "What's gonna happen with Harry and you and me? Can't we just stay here? I like it here."

"Yeah, Mom," Charlie chimed in. "What's gonna happen? Can't you just stay here?"

Their four eyes were on her, waiting expectantly for her to respond.

"Well, I like it here too, Charles," she stammered. "It's a pretty wonderful place, isn't it?" Both of the men in her life nodded in agreement first to her and then to each other. "Would you really truly like to stay here, Charles?" she asked.

"Absotutely!" he enthusiastically replied using another of their secret made-up words. He grinned at her and then at Charlie. Then a cloud floated over his little face. "But where would we live? Would we live with Nana and Grampy or with Harry?"

"Yeah, Mom," Charlie prodded, grinning at Amy. "Would you live with Nana and Grampy or with Harry?"

Exasperated, Amy shot Charlie a daggers look. "You are not making this any easier, thank you very much," she said under her breath.

"I'm not trying to," he said in all seriousness. "I really want to know too. Ames, it's been seven years, and when I saw you at the Milepost all of those years melted away, and it was as though we were together yesterday."

"But, Harry, we *were* together yesterday," Charles said, confused.

Both parents smiled at their son, and Amy realized that she had to just come out and tell Charles what was happening. She had just found out for sure herself a couple of hours earlier.

"Okay, here's the scoop," she began, facing Charles. "Our time in Germany is over."

Charles was conflicted by the news. On the one hand, he would miss his friends and his teacher and his home, but on the other hand he might be able to spend more time with Nana and Grampy and Harry. And his new Grandma and Grandpa. And he could get to know his cousins. They were girls, but that might be okay because they were family. His attention returned to his mother's words.

Amy continued. "Our time in Germany is over, but my time in the Army is not over. I received papers that I need to report to a new assignment soon. Charles's face clouded, and he asked, "Are we going to be dandelions?" Charlie was confused by Charles's question, but his frown was one of concern for what Amy would say next, not about the meaning of dandelions. This was a new twist. Could it possibly be that the Army had played a terrible trick on them yet again?

"Grampy and Nana were not too happy with me, and Grampy and I had a long talk yesterday. Grampy had some papers to give me from the Army." Charlie looked guardedly hopeful. "Grampy helped me to understand that I have served my country for seven years when all I really absolutely had to serve was five on active duty and three in the reserves. He reminded me that I have actually been serving my country since the day I was born, since we were a military family, and when one member serves, the whole family serves. After a lot of talking and telephone calls, and Nana throwing her two cents worth in, I will be reporting to Bedford, Massachusetts, to the Veterans Hospital in two weeks. I will be working only an hour from here, which means we can keep living in Duxbury.

Charles's little face erupted in smiles.

"But that's not all," Amy continued. After talking with Grampy for a long time when you were asleep last night, Charles, I have decided not to reup but to put my papers in for an honorable discharge at the end of this two-year stint. By the time you are nine years old, your old mom will be a civilian. Charles, I have decided to leave the Army. I want to stay here in Duxbury and get a job at a hospital or maybe even hang out my shingle and go into private practice."

She looked up to see Charlie's eyes glisten, but Charles was confused.

"What that all means, Charles, is that we will stay here in Duxbury with Nana and Grampy and Harry for good."

Having learned the victory sign from his grandfather, both Charles and Charlie jumped up and raised their arms in the air, shouting "*Yes! Yes! Yes!*" as they jumped around on the lawn.

When they were all jumped out, they dropped to the ground in front of Amy, asking questions, Charlie mimicking his son's.

"So where will we live?" asked Charles.

"So where will you live?" asked Charlie.

"Does that mean we're a family?" asked Charles.

"Does that mean we're a family?" asked Charlie.

"What about my friends in Germany?" asked Charles.

"How did this all happen so fast?" asked Charlie.

"Can I get a puppy?" asked Charles.

"Will you marry me?" asked Charlie.

"Whoa, you two," Amy admonished. "How about we take those questions one at a time? I'm not sure I even heard all of them right," and she looked quizzically at Charlie.

"Oh, you heard them right, all right," he replied. "I'll be right back!" he called over his shoulder as he ran off toward the house. "Answer Charles's questions first and then mine," he added, disappearing behind the hedge.

"Okay, so what are your questions?" she asked Charles. "One at a time."

"Can I have a puppy?"

"Well," she smiled, "I think that could probably be arranged. I've always wanted a dog named Spinnaker. Do you like that name? Charles grinned and nodded approval. That was one of the new sailing words Harry had taught him. He thought the spinnaker was the best part of a sailboat. It was a great name for a puppy. Soon, though, his grin faded back into confusion.

"Where will we live?"

"Well, I guess we'll stay with Nana and Grampy for a little while, and then we'll have to see."

Charles then quietly asked, "Can I live with Harry while you're working—sometimes?"

"You can live wherever you are happy, little man," she said, pulling him up into her lap. "You know that everyone wants you to live with them. You're quite a popular guy."

"Oh, Mom!" he wriggled. "I'm too big for this mushy stuff."

"Well," Charlie's voice rang out from behind her as Charles looked up and Charlie winked at him. "I'm not too big for mushy stuff." He scooted around her chair, got down on one knee and, looking hopeful, opened a little blue box to reveal her original Tiffany's engagement ring. Amy had sent it back to him when she signed the divorce papers. It had been expensive, and she didn't feel right keeping it. But Charles had kept it all these years, hopeful that one day he might once again be able to place it on Amy's finger. Even when he was married to Julia, he somehow could not part with Amy's ring. He hid it in his parents' safe. When Amy returned, Charlie had retrieved it, hoping that he could make good use of it again.

Charles, would you please sit with your mother? Charles jumped up onto her lap.

Amy looked at the ring and then at Charlie and then at Charles beaming in her lap.

Amy Sweetser Donnelly and Charles Henry Donnelly, the Third, will you please marry me and come to live with me in this big, beautiful house that I bought seven years ago for us to live in someday?"

"Are you sure?" she asked.

"Ames, this is your ring. It always was and it always will be." He looked from her to the house at attention behind her. Motioning to the house and the grounds, he continued, "This is your home. It was bought for you with love and has never felt right until now." He then turned his gaze to Charles, reached up and roughly brushed the little boy's hair, which elicited a groan and his hand being pushed away. "This is our amazing, stupendous, terrifical little boy sitting here who needs a mommy and a daddy and a home—and a puppy," he whispered to Charles.

The little boy's eyes gleamed. He turned to his mother and said, "Mommy, is Harry really asking us to live with him?"

Amy just nodded. She was afraid that if she said anything at all she would cry.

"Now I need to be clear here," said Charlie. "Did you just say, 'Yes I am asking you two to live here or yes you will marry me—again?"

Amy reached out her right hand and took the ring from the box. Still holding Charles, she slipped it on the ring finger of her left hand that was resting on Charles's shoulder. Charlie leaned forward and kissed her, then tousled Charles's hair again. "Well, little man, what would you think of living with me? Of course, you could stay with your Nana and Grampy any time you wanted to, too. Since I go to work every day—usually," he added, "and your mom will be going to work pretty far away too, maybe you could stay with Nana and Grampy during the days and with us at night and on the weekends. Do you think that would work?" As he asked this last question, he looked first at Charles and then at Amy.

Charles looked to his mother for guidance in how to answer the question.

"I think that would work just fine," she replied. "Of course, Grandma and Grandpa will want to claim some of your time too, I would suppose."

"Oh, my god," Charlie exclaimed. "I forgot all about them. They live right next door, though, so that shouldn't be a problem."

Amy got up, unceremoniously dumping Charles onto the grass next to Charlie. "Well, troops, we have a lot to do tonight. We need to share our good news with the parents. Let's get going," she added as she rose.

Wearing the same grin, Charles and Charlie jumped to attention, saluted her, and cried out, "Ma'am, yes, ma'am!"

"Hey, Skipper, if you and your mom are going to come live with me in our house here and we're all going to get a puppy, is there any chance you could call me Daddy?"

Charles thought hard for a minute. He looked at Charlie and then at his mother and then at Charlie again. He looked at the house and at his mother's ring. A tiny voice then said, "Okay, Daddy." Charlie and Amy couldn't contain their emotions. While Charlie whipped Charles up into his arms and swung him around in circles on the lawn, tears trickled down Amy's cheeks, stopping only when they reached her smile.

The Rest of the Story

In case you're wondering what happened after Amy agreed to marry Charles again and create the family she'd always wanted....

George retired from the Army, joking that the country was in trouble now with no Sweetsers to defend it. He spent his days enjoying his grandson whenever possible, teaching him to fish and to work on cars and other "manly" pursuits. He often was called upon for speaking engagements on issues of Homeland Security and national defense and began sitting on his front porch on nice days with a laptop perched on his lap writing a novel of military intrigue.

Mary decided that you are never too old to pursue your dreams, and at age sixty-one earned her JD from Harvard Law School. With Charles Donnelly's help, she secured a position in a South Shore firm, not too far from home. One rainy evening, visiting Charlie and Amy at their house, she sat on the three-season porch with Amy and shared how fulfilling her life had been so far. She felt that she had lived an entire lifetime and was now beginning her second. Amy was proud of her mother's accomplishments and grateful for the years of dedication to family that Mary had given. Mary reminded both of them that one never really knows where life is going, something they knew quite well.

Charles Donnelly discovered that he had been right about how wonderful it would be to have a grandson. He slowed down at work and actually took days off to teach Charles III to play golf and tennis, go sailing, head in to Boston for Red Sox games, and just sit and play board games. The usually impatient man found boundless reserves of patience when it came to his grandson. Not one to retire completely, though, he and Grace joined forces with George and Amy and started a foundation for families of veterans suffering from PTSD. Ongoing therapy could be expensive, and it was the foundation's mission to help families to be able to afford it so that their lives could return to normal. The elder Donnelly chaired the foundation's board.

Grace Donnelly eventually forgave Amy for keeping Charles from them for so long and welcomed them both into the family wholeheartedly. She even coerced Amy into joining the Junior League of Boston with her and enjoyed referring to her when speaking with her friends as her "favorite daughter-in-law." She and Amy had quite an influence on the League, introducing them to a new cause—veterans' support. With the new foundation the grandparents had formed, Grace had a new cause as well, and chaired many successful fundraisers for veterans. Grace enrolled her grandson in cotillion, much to his chagrin, and loved shopping for him whenever she went on a spree.

Susan and John moved into a new house on the ocean in Falmouth, Maine, where Rachael and Jennifer began learning to sail. Susan continued to enjoy being a stay-at-home mom who volunteered at the library and at her girls' school. She belonged to the garden club and happily met Amy frequently in Boston. They became close again, shopping, going to lunch, visiting museums, and just walking around the city. Their families often attended Red Sox games together. Having a passion for sailing in common, the cousins became close, confirming Charles's belief that girl cousins were okay because they were family.

Charlie, meanwhile, happy with his life turning out the way it was always meant to be, flourished at his job. He earned a reputation as a fair and honest defense attorney and was called upon to represent high-profile clients, always making sure that he handled a number of pro bono cases each year. His father told him that those cases should be handled by the junior partners and senior associates, but Charlie felt blessed in his own life and wanted to help those who hadn't been given the privileges he had enjoyed. He also reminded his father that he had a son to raise and he wanted to set a positive example as someone who was compassionate and fair.

One day, on their way home from the golf course in Duxbury, Charlie thanked his father for the underhanded way he had dealt with Julia. Charlie acknowledged that if the elder Donnelly had made Julia a partner, Amy would not have come back into their lives and he might have lost even more time with his son. His father resisted the urge to take credit and merely said, "I'm glad it worked out the way it was always meant to be, Son."

Amy, true to her word, retired from the Army. She had put in twelve years and was proud of her contributions. With so many years of experience dealing with veterans with PTSD, she was an expert on treating the disorder and possessed a strong empathy that helped guide her patients through the darkness. She opened up a private practice in Boston, working with civilians who suffered from PTSD after automobile accidents, fires, and other catastrophes, eventually specializing in children who had endured traumatic events. After her first year in private practice, Ben and Jerry became her best friends again. This time she told Charlie right away.

The Discussion Questions

1. Charlie and Amy found themselves repeatedly facing challenges of place and time. Have you ever found yourself torn between a relationship and a career?

2. Do you think that Charlie and Amy handled their transitions well? College? Law School? Posting in Maryland? Posting in Germany?

3. Both Charlie and Amy knew when they first met each other that they were destined to be together forever. Do you believe in love at first sight?

4. Amy and Charlie seemed to know that somehow at some time they would find their happily ever after. Do you believe in happily ever after or do you find the idea cliché?

5. What was your feeling toward Amy when she made the decision to keep her son's existence a secret from his father? Did you have sympathy for her, or did you think she was making a big mistake? How would you have handled it?

6. When Charles discovered that he had a father, do you think that Amy and Charlie handled the situation well, following him as he ran to the beach? Would you have handled the situation differently?

7. What were your feelings toward Charles Donnelly when he decided not to grant partnership to Julia? Did you think that he was meddling, or would you have done the same thing? Do you think he should have said something as soon as he discovered her past?

8. Did you think that Amy's father, George, should have called in favors when Amy was sent to Germany so that Amy and Charles could stay together? Did you understand why he chose not to?

9. What did you think of Amy's mom, Mary, deciding to give up her dream of being a lawyer to become a wife and mother? What did you think of her decision to go to law school in her sixties?

10. Have you ever experienced a faraway love?

Acknowledgments

It takes a village to raise a book from initial idea to paper on the shelf. I am happy to have many wonderful people in my village.

The original idea for this book came to me years ago when my younger son, Andy, wanted to attend West Point. I thought about how it would be difficult for him to have a relationship with someone not in the military. At that time, I wrote about twenty pages of ideas and set it aside. Jump ahead a few years and my older son, Robbie, asked me if I remembered always telling him and his brother that they should always finish what they start. I knew it was a trap, but I answered that I did remember that. He then grinned and told me that it was time for me to finish my novel. This book is that story.

I also need to thank my friends and family who served as beta readers and gave me excellent feedback. Raylene Matheny, Sally Lyon, and my sister Diane Gurney agreed to be brutal when I handed them the manuscript. They weren't brutal but they were incredibly helpful in letting me know where I had overused a word or written something confusing.

Lastly, I'd like to thank Jennifer Caven for her detailed editing and the folks at Maine Authors Publishing for shepherding this project through to publication.